SILVER STAKED

BOOK ONE OF THE BLOOD BORNE SERIES

SILVER STAKED

NY Times and *USA Today* Bestselling Authors

SHANNON MAYER

DENISE GROVER SWANK

Silver Staked (The Blood Borne Series, Book 1)
Copyright © Shannon Mayer 2015
Copyright © Denise Grover Swank 2015
Copyright © HiJinks Ink Publishing, Ltd. 2015

All rights reserved Published by HiJinks Ink LTD.
www.shannonmayer.com

    All rights reserved. Without limiting the rights under copyright reserved above, no part of this publication may be reproduced, stored in or introduced into a database and retrieval system or transmitted in any form or any means (electronic, mechanical, photocopying or otherwise)without the prior written permission of both the owner of the copyright and the above publishers. Please do not participate in or encourage the piracy of copyrighted materials in violation of the author's rights. Purchase only authorized editions.
    This is a work of fiction. Names, characters, places and incidents are either the product of the author's imagination or are used fictitiously, and any resemblance to actual persons living or dead, business establishments, events or locales is entirely coincidental. Or deliberately on purpose, depending on whether or not you have been nice to the author.

Original illustrations by Damonza.com
Mayer, Shannon

Chapter 1

LEA

"Lea, the mark is outside of Victoria's Secret, drooling over the displays and scaring the ladies." Calvin's voice came through with a lot of static in my earpiece. I adjusted it, clearing the white noise. "Cal, what is it with this vamp? He's a fucking perv, isn't he?"

The sound of Calvin's soft laugh brought a smile to my lips. His laugh was one of the few joys I had left. "Aren't they all pervs?"

The words drove a slice of pain through the place where my heart used to beat, and just like that, the smile on my face was gone. "I'm going to see if I can draw him over to the service hallway now."

"Remember your perfume, Lea. He'll smell you a mile off."

I ran my hands through my hair, loosening it up so it hung nicely over my bare shoulders. The steel door I stood behind provided a slight reflection. More makeup than I ever willingly wore clung to my skin, highlighting my nearly black eyes and giving my lips the perfect bee-stung look the humans so loved. My raven-black hair fell in waves down my back. Not my usual braid, but that was the thing about hunting. You had to be flexible and use the tools at hand. "What a bunch of nincompoops these young vamps are, so easy to kill."

Calvin laughed again and my lips turned up as I opened the door. "You like that word, don't you?"

"Word of the week," I said softly, my boot heels clicking on the concrete floor as I headed away from the steel door. My hand fished into my pocket and pulled out a bottle of perfume. The bottle was marked "Guess," and not for the first time, I wondered what the answer was. I spritzed it over my shoulders, neck, and hair, the scent sticking to me nicely.

We were hunting in the Montreal Underground City. The shops inside were decorated to look like full-scale buildings, rooftops and all. This was not our first time here, though. The young vamps had started flocking to the mall over the last few years. They loved it, and I could see why. The mall was open 24/7, so it provided them with the opportunity to avoid the sunlight and pretend they were still human. Which made it an excellent hunting ground for Calvin and me.

I pushed past a door that led into the main section of the mall. I didn't need the sign pointing to Victoria's Secret to lead me to my mark. His scent flooded the air, a combination of fresh blood and chocolate that made my mouth fill with saliva and my fangs extend. I swallowed hard, fighting the desire to open my mouth and let the scent curl over my taste buds.

"Hold it together," Cal whispered in my ear. I forcibly slowed my breathing, blocking out the smell of the vampire up ahead.

"Sorry," I whispered. "Caught me off guard; haven't eaten yet today."

Calvin grunted and I strode forward, letting my hips sway. Two thin stakes with silver tips rested inside the top of each of my almost thigh-high boots well within reach. But I knew I wouldn't have to use them out here.

Nope, my mark was far too hungry to be smart. He was shorter than me by a good bit, his shaved head barely coming to my chin. Tattoos wrapped around his neck and disappeared under a grungy wife-beater tank top that hadn't seen a wash in years. As I so often did, I wondered what he'd been like before he was turned. This one had the look of a petty thief; he had the marks of it. Probably sold steroids on the side, which would explain the oversized muscles.

I let my hip bump him as I walked by, lightly, with just enough force to put him off balance. Sufficient to get his attention.

He spun, and if any human had been watching, it

would have looked like he was never standing the other way. Dumb ass; it was a wonder we hadn't found him sooner. A wonder he was out here at all without his master guiding him.

His eyes widened as he took me in. I knew what he saw and I helped him along with a little mental projection. A girl with a rack that hovered with gravity-defying perkiness, long black hair perfect for grabbing and wrenching aside as he buried his fangs into the side of her neck, long legs that would wrap around his waist, holding him tightly to her. His mouth dropped open as I sent the detailed thoughts to him. That didn't work on everyone, but on those without a spine it was a charm I used liberally.

Like a puppy dog, he fell in behind me, trailing me as I glanced now and again over my shoulder, smiling at him. Carefully, though. It wouldn't do to show him my fangs just yet.

Calvin was quiet. He knew if he spoke with the vampire this close, my mark would hear him, and we'd have a fight on our hands.

Not that I minded. But in the middle of the Underground I wasn't so keen on dealing with the fallout of so many humans watching two vampires battle it out.

"Hey, beautiful girl." The vamp made a grab for me, but I spun lightly away from him, laughing.

"Oh, I won't be that easy to catch." I winked at him, the weight of my false lashes making it a slow, sultry move.

He licked his lips and I fought not to curl up my nose. Pervs. Calvin was right, they were all pervs.

I strode forward, seeing the skylight up ahead. The sun was high in the sky outside, and I fought not to cringe away from the pattern the bright beams made on the floor.

I forced myself to walk through the patch of sun. For a moment, it was warm, a caress of a lover long gone but still desired. That caress quickly turned into a sharp slap, but I stepped out of the light before it could burn me. I raised an eyebrow at the vamp, who lingered just on the other side of the sun falling on the floor. "You coming, big boy?"

He flashed me a grin that showed a fair amount of fang. Idiot. "I've got a place close by..." His eyes narrowed and he lifted his nose, sniffing lightly. Shit, did I not use enough perfume?

An older man, stooped with age, his long gray hair tied back in a ponytail, shuffled toward us, his cane thumping. "Hey, you two get out of here. It says no loitering." He smacked his cane against a sign saying just that, then looked at us and let out an exasperated sigh. "*Pas flânage!*" As if French would help the creature in front of me understand what was about to happen to him.

But the vamp didn't even look at him. Nope, he stared at me, his eyes slowly going wide. "You...you're her, aren't you? The Cazador." The Hunter. Yup, that was me. Rather than answer, I leapt across the space, yanking one of the thin stakes from the top of my boot at the same time. But he was as fast as I was and possessed the same super speed I did, and in that split second, he spun and ran.

"Go get him," Calvin said in my ear, and I bolted after the vamp. He shot straight through a group of humans, sending them flying like bowling pins. As I streaked past, I heard bones break and cries ring out in the air.

This guy really was an idiot. Who the hell had made him and sent him out so unprepared?

Peter. Is this one of yours? I pushed the thought away as soon as it rolled into my head. This was not the time or place to be thinking about the vampire who would have me call him master.

My mark took three quick corners, and then the sound of his footsteps disappeared. I froze at the third corner. He'd either quit running or fled to higher ground. "Calvin, have you got any cameras up and running?" I asked softly, starting to creep forward. No matter how stupid I thought this vamp was, I wasn't about to get myself staked because I was overconfident.

I slid around the corner of the closest shop in a low crouch, ignoring the stares and titters of a group of teenagers. They laughed and pointed at me, but that was all peripheral.

"He's climbing the rafters," Calvin said. I looked up. "The kids are going to see you leap."

"And who's going to believe a bunch of pot-smoking teens?" I muttered. Muscles bunched, I jumped straight into the air, landing lightly on the roof of the shop. I glanced at the teens. Their mouths hung open like a school of fish waiting to be fed. I shook my head and jogged along the edge of the roof until I found a place where I could pull myself into the rafters.

The vamp's scent curled around my senses, and I

followed it like a bloodhound, blocking out everything except the hunt. The chase. And finally the kill that would come.

Rafters and steel girders flew underneath me as I scrambled through them, picking up speed the closer I got to the vamp. He glanced back, saw me, and let out a scream that turned into a hissing growl.

I grinned at him, letting him see my fangs this time. "You're going to die, but not yet, little man."

His bravado slipped and he let out a whimper. "Please don't hurt me." Definitely a petty thief.

"He could be bluffing," Calvin said.

"I know."

But the vamp didn't come at me. He'd backed himself into a corner and pinned himself down. Young, he was so young and fresh; these were rookie mistakes. Which meant someone was still making vamps despite my warnings.

"Nincompoops," I snarled and crawled through the rafters until I was on top of him. He shivered and whimpered, and I knew it was no act. The scent of frightened vampire was its own flavor. Ammonia and shit seemed to pour from his skin, a kickback of the human blood left in him.

I grabbed his neck and jumped, dropping to the floor with him. Keeping a hand on him, I pushed him ahead of me toward a service hallway door. Using his head as a battering ram, I opened it.

The old man we'd seen near the skylight hobbled toward us. "Calvin," I said, "how did you get here so fast?"

He smiled at me, a whisper of the man he'd been when I'd met him almost fifty years past. "Floor escalators."

"Cheater."

"Why haven't you killed him yet?"

The vamp let out a soft cry, his skin so oily with fear it was hard to hold him. I didn't want him to touch my clothes; I'd never get the stink out.

"He's fresh."

Calvin looked him over. "When were you made, boy?"

The vamp shook his head. "I can't tell you. They said you would question me."

I spun him around to face me and slammed him against the wall. The light above us stuttered. "Who is 'they'?"

He shook his head. "No, I can't tell you. I can't. I'm not a snitch."

I shrugged. "Listen. You are going to tell me everything I want to know. Who made you. What they told you about me. Where your little vamp rookery is. Only then will I stop the pain. Do you understand?"

His pale blue eyes watered. Almost as if he was going to cry, but that wasn't possible, unless he was so new that...shit. Tears slipped down his cheeks. Tears dried up about a week after a vamp was made. He had been unleashed on the humans after only a week?

How bloody stupid were the vamps who'd made him?

"My flechettes, Calvin," I said, not taking my eyes off the vamp. The creak of a box, the sound of metal grating against wood. The vamp shivered under my grasp.

I took one hand from him and held it out to Calvin.

He settled the handle of my smallest fletch into my palm. Its razor-sharp blade was so thin, it took a moment for the pain of one of its slices to register. But that changed quickly as the depth of the cuts increased. I glanced back, and it was all the time the vamp needed to make his move.

"Lea!" Calvin cried out as I was shoved away from the vamp and slammed into the opposite wall. My head bounced against the concrete, but it wasn't me I was worried about. I wouldn't break.

Calvin would.

He was on the floor, but when I rushed to his side to check on him, he shook me off. "Get him!"

I didn't want to leave Cal, but he was right. The vamp was our mark and I couldn't lose him.

I didn't have to go far. He cowered at the end of the hallway. "I know you're going to kill me, but I'm not betraying my rook." He slid his hand into his front pocket and pulled out a tiny red pill. I frowned. What the hell was this?

He popped the pill into his mouth and swallowed. I lifted my eyebrows and walked toward him. "That won't dull your pain, and it won't stop me from torturing you. You're not my first kill, and you won't be my last. I will wipe you all out. I will cleanse this world of the vampire virus once and for all."

He convulsed and then screamed as he fell to his knees. I wasn't sure if it was an act, but I decided to see how it played out.

Good thing I did. He flopped onto his back, body

arching on the tips of his heels and the back of his head as the skin on his face *melted.*

"Holy shit," Calvin whispered from behind me.

"*Dios mío,*" I whispered as I crossed myself, falling back onto my roots. The vampire's skin lit up like a torch, burning until there was nothing left but ash and a pair of scuffed-up shoes. The smoke triggered the sprinkler system and alarms went off, clanging through the hallways.

"He's dead. Let's get our asses out of here." Calvin tapped me with his cane. I knew he was right, but I found myself standing over the vamp's ashes, water dripping down my hair and face. I crouched and touched his shoes. Without another thought as to why my instincts were telling me to do something so weird, I scooped up the boots.

"I have a bad feeling about this," I said as we strode down the hallway, the sprinklers soaking us through.

"Why? He's dead."

"But that kind of technology...you and I both know vamps don't do technology well, not without help. The older they are, the more stuck in their ways they are, unable to adapt." I glanced at him. Calvin was my helper, the one who kept *me* up to date on everything.

"They always have help."

I shook my head and looked at the brand-name, well-worn boots in my hands. Stitched into the tongue were words that meant more than the simple letters that spelled them out.

Property of Rikers Island.

I tipped the boot and showed it to Calvin. "What do you think? Wanna go to New York?"

Calvin laughed and nodded. "New York it is."

CHAPTER 2

RACHEL

I hated New York City. I'd moved to the city about a year ago, and on nights like this one, I would rather be back in Iraq.

Flashing lights bounced off the brick buildings around me, exacerbating the dull pounding in my head. I stood on the city sidewalk with a small group of journalists—a familiar enough situation given that these were my people, but something about this scene made the hair on the back of my neck stand on end.

I wasn't even sure why I was there. Lately I had been up to my eyeballs researching my next big story—why the inmate population in several New York prisons was declining despite an increased incarceration rate. That's what I was doing this evening when I heard the police scanner go off about a homicide at an Upper East Side apartment building.

It didn't fit the profile of the other major story I was currently working on—a series of murders—but some instinct steered me to the subway station to check it out. If nothing else, I could get a scoop and make some extra money. If there was any scoop to get. Homicide was literally an everyday occurrence in a city with eight million people as residents and even more as tourists. And despite the fancy address, most were run of the mill murders. Anger, greed, jealousy, lust. Sometimes a switch just flipped in someone and they killed the person closest to them. Or sometimes promises of money or power were enough to sway a person to do the unthinkable. Either way, murder was ugly and brutal. Unfortunately, I was no stranger to death.

But this one—and several others lately—had just felt *different*.

"I hear it's grisly, Rachel," the man next to me said. He leaned into my ear, his arm brushing my shoulder longer than was necessary.

I fought the instinct to cringe. "Oh, yeah?" I knew him, but mostly by reputation. Phil Mahoney wrote for the tabloids. He was scum, both in terms of his irresponsible reporting and his attitude toward women. Still,

I could use information. It wasn't worth ditching him yet. "What'd you hear?"

A sleazy grin spread across his face.

What a waste of a good-looking man. My eyebrows rose as my gaze pierced his. "About the crime scene."

His grin didn't even falter. "A guy said he found his neighbor's door open. When he investigated, he found the neighbor pushing up daisies on his living room floor. Tons of cuts all over his body."

"Again," I murmured to myself. So my gut had been right yet again.

"Speaking of daisies, Rachel," Phil said, "how about I get you a bunch and take you out to dinner when we're done here?"

My mouth parted with disgust. "Does that ever work for you?" I wasn't surprised he was hitting on me. I was used to it. My long blonde hair and blue eyes had always garnered unwanted attention. Even my characteristic lack of makeup did little to dissuade jerks like this guy.

"*What?*" he asked in confusion.

Before I could give him a snappy retort, a cop emerged from the entrance to the apartment building and the reporters around me pushed forward, yelling out questions.

I rolled my eyes and moved away from the crowd, wondering when they would ever learn. Hell would freeze over before an NYPD cop would offer information to shouting reporters, yet it never stopped them from trying.

Sticking close to the scene, I made my way to a small

group of residents huddled together about twenty feet away. I slid in behind them and eavesdropped.

"Martin's really shook up," a woman said. "He said Eli was naked and lying on his back, slash marks all over his chest and holes in his neck. Blood everywhere."

"Holes?" another woman asked.

"Like snake bites. The pet store half a block down lost one of its giant boa constrictors."

The other people in the group groaned and shot down her idea, but my interest was piqued. The wounds fit my serial case; there were slashes and bite marks at the last six crime scenes. But two things about this murder bucked the profile. One, the neighborhood was ten times nicer than the previous crime scenes; and two, there had been a curiously distinct lack of blood at the other scenes. The victims had been drained, although the police would never acknowledge the fact. A coroner's assistant had told me, on the condition that I not report it.

Why would the murderer leave blood this time?

I gasped as it hit me—he'd been interrupted.

After a quick glance to make sure no one was watching—particularly the other journalists and the cops—I walked around the corner, looking for the alley behind the building. A serial murderer wasn't likely to get caught in the act and run out the front door. He'd head out the back.

The alley was dark, and common sense told me I was an idiot for checking it out, especially if my suspicions were correct. But the fact that the murderer had used some sort of blade instead of a gun was reassuring. I could most likely handle a knife-wielding assailant. It was bullets I couldn't dodge. I opened the flap on my messenger bag and pulled out a small LED flashlight. Flipped it on, kept the beam pointed at my feet.

I stopped and listened before I stepped into the dark, my ears trying to separate the sounds of the city from that of any threatening presence. When I was satisfied, I eased my way into the narrow space and made a shallow sweep with the flashlight beam, stopping when I heard a bang by a Dumpster twenty feet away. I picked up my pace and swung the light behind the Dumpster. The smell of burned flesh and sulfur hung heavy in the air, making my heart race. Then I caught sight of the man squatting in the beam of my flashlight, and it was as if my racing heart stopped in an instant. I would have recognized him anywhere.

"Derrick?"

As soon as I uttered his name, guilt and shame flooded through me. I'd deeply hurt this man the last time we saw each other, and I'd regretted it ever since.

His eyes squinted from the light shining in his face. He stood as I lowered the beam, looking just as shocked as I felt. Even so, he still looked just as good as the last time I'd seen him. His dark, almost black hair had grown longer and framed his face. Derrick had always been a good-looking man, and when you added in the fact that he was thoughtful and easy-going, it wasn't difficult to understand why plenty of women fell all over themselves to meet him.

"I thought you were still in the Middle East," I said.

"What in God's name are you doing in a New York City alley?"

His gaze traveled up and down my body, but not in the predatory way I was used to. "From the looks of you, I'm guessing we're both doing the same thing: working."

I'd first met Derrick Forrester seven years ago in Iraq. I was a green field journalist at the time, and he helped show me the ropes. Our paths crossed often during my years in the Mideast, but we lost touch about two years ago. All of that aside, Derrick had always been more interested in military operations than civilian crime. I couldn't think of a single reason why he would be here.

"I'm checking out the murder scene. It seems a little out of your field."

"Don't be so sure about that." His gaze lowered to the asphalt and mine followed.

The flashlight revealed a pile of ashes, still smoldering. *That explains the smell.* I inched closer, shocked to see the ashes were laid out in the shape of a body. "What the hell is *that*?"

He looked into my eyes. "Let this one go, Rach. You don't want to get involved."

I shook my head, my mind racing with questions along with a list of possible explanations, every single one of them absurd. "Too late for that."

"Afraid I'll scoop you?"

"Don't insult me." I snorted. "You're the only person I've ever trusted, no matter what I said before you left. Two years without contact hasn't changed that. Now tell me what's going on here."

Moving toward me, Derrick grabbed my arm and

pulled me away from the ashes. "Rachel, I'm not screwing with you. This is dangerous."

I let him pull me, keeping my eyes on his face as I tried to puzzle out what he could be working on that he would consider too dangerous for me. He knew dangerous situations didn't scare me away. There could only be one reason he'd warn me off.

"The government," I said as it hit me. "What the hell are you chasing?"

An engine whined at the opposite end of the alley, and a pair of headlights hit the pavement. My back stiffened. I'd recognize the sound of a military Jeep in my sleep. "Derrick."

He looked down the alley, then back at me. "I've got to go."

I grabbed his arm, panicked at the thought of losing him again. "But I just found you."

"I'll meet you at your apartment later."

"But I didn't give you my address."

A smile softened his face. "Rach, I've known where you lived practically since you moved in."

If any other man had just confessed that, I would have kneed him in the balls for stalking me, but Derrick's intentions had always been honorable. If anything, I was shocked because I'd been searching for him since the day he'd walked away from me. If he had watched me that closely, he had to have been worried about my safety.

"I'll come to you, but you *have* to pretend you don't know anything, and for God's sake, don't tell them you saw me." He spun around and sprinted for the street as the military Jeep's headlights landed on me.

It screeched to a sudden halt, and men in fatigues raced around the sides, pointing machine guns at my chest.

I lifted my hands into the air, my heart racing. "Slow down there, boys. I'm no threat."

"Down on your knees," one of the soldiers shouted. "Hands on your head."

If they expected me to argue, they were sorely disappointed. I knelt down on the pavement, rocks digging into my knees through my jeans, and placed my palms on my head. I knew the drill.

The passenger door opened and another man in fatigues rounded the front of the vehicle, blocking the beam of the headlights and casting me in shadow.

"Rachel?" a familiar voice asked.

A wave of nostalgia washed over me, followed closely by anger. *What the hell?* Was this some sick sort of impromptu reunion?

"Put down your weapons," he said in disgust, then leaned over and helped me to my feet.

The soldiers stood down and retreated to the sides of the vehicle.

My heartbeat pounded in my head as I stared into the face of the one man I'd allowed close enough to break my heart. Same sandy blond hair. Same dark brown eyes. Same irritating as hell smirk. Yeah, it was Sean Price, U.S. Army. Now *Lieutenant* Price, according to the insignia on his shirt.

His face searched mine. "What are you doing here?"

"Working a lead on a serial murder." I nodded toward the pile. "But I could ask the same of you. Last time I checked, New York wasn't a militarized zone." Sarcasm drenched the last sentence.

He glanced at the ashes, his brow furrowed, and then returned his gaze to me. "Has Derrick snagged you into his madness?"

"Madness?" Derrick was the one who'd introduced me to Sean while the three of us were in Iraq, a fact I had chosen not to hold against Derrick given the way my relationship with Sean had ended. It was such a surreal feeling to see both of them in a matter of minutes after years of being out of touch. I was struggling to keep up, a feeling I hated. Now Sean had added another piece to the puzzle—he was questioning the character of his friend. Maybe *former* friend. "What the hell are you talking about?"

He shot a wary look at the soldiers, then ushered me over to the other side of the Dumpster. I followed, more confused than ever.

When I reached the corner of the huge bin, he pulled me out of the others' view.

"Rachel, you have to listen to me." His eyes were wild and desperate. "Derrick's had a mental break, and he's on some conspiracy theory quest."

"*What*? That doesn't sound like Derrick at all."

"When was the last time you talked to him?"

I brushed back several stray hairs. "I don't know. Two years ago? He told me he was working on something in Syria, but didn't tell me what."

"And tonight?"

Holding his gaze, I pretended surprise. "He's here, in New York?" When he didn't answer, I continued. "I haven't seen him." Something weird was going on—Sean's presence alone proved that. I had to trust one of these two men, and there was no hesitation as to which one I would pick.

He studied me, but I kept my cool. I was an accomplished liar, a helpful trait for a journalist. Too bad he was well aware of that fact. I saw a hint of disappointment wash over his face. "If he contacts you, please let me know."

I narrowed my eyes. He'd said Derrick was obsessed with a conspiracy theory. If Sean, a military man through and through, was hot on his trail, that meant Derrick was really on to something. "What are you going to do to him?"

He released a groan of frustration and grabbed my arm, pulling me closer until our chests touched. "Nothing. I'm trying to protect him."

The sincerity in his voice was convincing, but firsthand experience had taught me that he was an accomplished liar, too.

His hold loosened and his voice turned husky. "You look good, Rach."

I wanted to be angry—and only angry—but I couldn't ignore the heat washing through me. There was no denying that while we'd had multiple issues, chemistry had never been one of them. "You don't have the right to say that any more, Sean."

"I know it's two years too late, but I'm sorry. I was shitty to you. You didn't deserve that."

I jerked out of his reach, pissed that one touch from

him could almost make me forget the way he'd betrayed me. Almost. "You're damn right I didn't."

"There's nothing I can say that can make up for what I did."

"You mean *who* you did?"

Regret filled his eyes. "I never deserved you."

"Too bad you didn't figure that out before you screwed me, Sean." Anger billowed in my chest. "And I mean the literal first time and not the figurative last."

He reached into his pocket and pulled out a business card. "I deserve that and more. But right now we need to think about Derrick. If you see him, please convince him to call me. I don't want him to get hurt." His voice lowered. "He's in danger, Rachel. Help me save him."

I had to admit Derrick had been acting paranoid, which was completely out of character for him. I might have considered that Sean was telling the truth—if it weren't for the Jeep full of military personnel behind him. I snatched the card and stuffed it into my jeans pocket. "I have no idea if I'll ever see him. But if I do, I'll pass along the message."

Sean's shoulders sank with relief. "Thank you. That's all I can ask."

I turned and started toward the end of the alley, but Sean jogged after me and blocked my path. "Be careful, Rach," he said, handing me my flashlight. "Don't buy into Derrick's madness."

I grabbed the flashlight and hurried for the street, irritated over Sean's wasted words. Another military Jeep had barricaded the end of the street. Did he really expect me to believe Derrick was crazy? He should have warned me not to get sucked into his own madness.

CHAPTER 3

LEA

The blacked-out windows of the sleek Mustang made it easy for us to travel during the day, but it wasn't the sunlight I was worried about. It was the U.S. border. We'd chosen a small, backwater crossing that should be quiet. Easy to get through. But I was getting a premonition that things weren't going to go as smoothly as planned. I tapped my fingers on the back of Calvin's headrest. "Old man, how are we getting over the border this time?"

His eyes flicked to the rearview mirror. "What, you didn't like sneaking through under the cover of darkness?"

I snorted. "That was at least thirty years ago. Things have changed." The vamps had kept us north of the border for a long time. No, that wasn't entirely true. We'd done some international work in that time, but the vamps in the United States had been flying under the radar for years.

"How about you bat your eyes and give the customs guy something sweet to dream about later?"

I rolled my head back. "And if they pull me out of the car and my skin blisters up like I've been dipped in boiling water?"

"Don't let them pull you out of the car," he said. Like it was going to be that easy. That was the only problem with Cal. Even though he was supposed to be the one helping me keep up with all the rapid-fire technological changes in the "outside" world, more and more, I was the one who had to point out the issues we faced. I knew it was time for a new helper, but I just couldn't bear to let him go.

I closed my eyes. "Let me know when we get close. I'll think of something."

He grunted and flicked the radio on to a news station. The reporter was very excited, her voice giving off her emotions loud and clear.

"This is the seventh death in what the press has begun to call the 'Vampire Murders.'"

I jerked forward, any thoughts of rest gone. "Turn it

up, Cal." I didn't need it louder, but I knew his hearing was not as good as it once was.

"Already done."

The reporter continued, now at full blast. "The chief of police will only say they have leads, but he has asked people in the Manhattan east and south sides to stay home after dark unless absolutely necessary. He will not confirm that the bodies were drained of blood, but several anonymous tips have come in from those who were at the scenes. The deaths have been described as 'ritualistic, nausea inducing, and straight out of a horror movie.'"

Apparently that was the only real information she had, because she went on to interview a psychic named "Madame Dupree" about the crimes. Calvin turned the radio down. "Guess if there was any doubt that New York was our place, that wiped it out."

I leaned back in my seat. "Seems rather like a calling card, don't you think?"

"Like someone is throwing down a challenge?"

I flicked my tongue over one fang, a habit that wasn't really my own. It was a tic of the vampire who'd made me, and whenever I thought of him, I couldn't help but repeat it.

As if he could hear my thoughts, Cal said, "Could it be Peter? Or that asshole Stravinsky?"

"*Madre de Dios*, I hope not."

Memories of Peter and Stravinsky washed over me the moment I closed my eyes again.

Sleep had been a matter of enjoyment when I was human. No longer. Each time I rested, my mind peeled through my memories, watching the past as if it were a movie rolling in front of my eyes.

Cazador. Vampire Hunter.

I stared at the image in the mirror reflection of my silver stake. My hair cropped short to my head like a boy's, my body laced tightly in leather and light chain mail. Thin silver stakes strapped across my chest from shoulder to hip. I lifted my chin to look at the priest who was to be my guide.

"Father, let us find the demons." I mounted my horse, settling into the saddle. The priest, a young man who looked to be in his early twenties, mounted his own steed.

"Cazador." He nodded to me, but I caught the curl of his lip. The priests didn't like women becoming Cazadors, but that hadn't stopped me. I leaned toward him. "Do not let my gender fool you, Father. I am the best this group has because there is nothing left for the demons to take from me."

His dark eyes flicked over me. "Except your soul."

I snorted. "I will die before I let them turn me."

"Easily said now. But none of the others fell on their blades when they were turned to the darkness." We trotted our horses down a dirt road that wound through the hutches and hovels of a small outlying village.

My jaw tightened. "You are new to our group, and for that I will forgive you. A Cazador loses their mind when they are turned. It is torture for a hunter to become one of the demons they are sworn to destroy."

"Then you'd best keep your eyes open." He lifted a vial of holy water so I could see it. The water bubbled and slowly turned red.

I slipped from the horse's back and pulled two of the silver stakes. "They come, Father."

"Hey, we're within a mile," Calvin said, breaking my memories apart.

Shaking off the memory, I sat up and peered ahead. The line was short. Damn, I'd hoped there would be more time to prepare. There were two guards waiting in the tiny booth, and when it was our turn, Calvin drove up and handed them our passports. Fake, of course, but that had never been an issue before.

"Sir, can you get out of the car please?"

I gritted my teeth, the pressure making my fangs drop. Calvin slid out of the car, exaggerating his limping gait. "Hang on, boys. I get stiff from sitting so long." They didn't touch him, didn't offer him any help.

Not a good sign. I leaned back and slid on my arm wraps and the shrouded cowl that covered my head and lower face. Sunglasses last. The guard opened my door and I slipped out behind him before he even saw me.

Ignoring the heat of the sun on the few patches of exposed skin, I grabbed the guard around the neck and spun him. His body flew fifteen feet before crashing into a cement barrier.

Guards came running, far more of them than such a small border crossing warranted. Almost like they were waiting for something.

Or someone.

Hesitation kills in a battle. I'd learned that the hard way. "Cal, get back into the car. Now."

He kicked the guard beside him in the knee, breaking it cleanly, then punched him in the throat for good measure. "You sure you don't want help?" For an old man, he still had some good piss and vinegar. But I couldn't lose him, and these guards would kill him without a thought.

"Get the car started."

The guards lined up in front of me, forming a human blockade. "Either we're going to play Red Rover, Red Rover, or you all want to shoot me."

They lifted their guns as a single unit. All right then, message received.

Just as their trigger fingers started to twitch, I leapt straight up and forward, landing behind them. A full roundhouse kick took down three of the ten. The rest spun with me, guns going off. I dodged most of the bullets, but one caught me in the stomach.

Everyone froze, and I went to my knees. Holding a hand over the wound, I slowly raised my eyes to the remaining guards. "You didn't really think a bullet would stop me, did you?"

Adam's apples bobbed in chorus, and sweat beaded along their foreheads. I took a breath and flexed my stomach muscles, pushing the bullet out. It popped into my hand, slick with blood. "Who wants a souvenir?" I tossed it into the air and the idiots watched the trajectory.

I used their distraction to dart toward them. Before the bullet fell to the ground, I had smashed two skulls together and broken three arms and five noses. There was silence except for the groaning of the guards who lay splayed out on the asphalt.

"You done playing?" Calvin called from the car.

I walked over the downed men, scooping one of them up as I went. "Yes. But I want a souvenir, too." I hadn't eaten in too long and it was making me irritable. Or at least more irritable than usual.

Stuffing the guard into the back of the car, I watched him try to breathe through his crushed nose. A slow gurgle was all he managed as his face swelled at a rapid rate. He didn't even register he'd been taken until we were driving down the road.

"We're going to have to ditch the car." Calvin's eyes caught mine before looking away.

"I'm not going to make a mess, Cal. I just want to know what he knows."

"The quickest way to do that is to *feed* on him, and making a mess is what you do." Disgust laced his words.

I tightened my grip on the guard. "True." The smell of blood beckoned. My teeth extended as I jerked the guard's head back, exposing his jugular. It would be a death bite. That was the only way to access a person's recent memories.

The guard squirmed and his eyes widened, but I didn't feel bad. My job was to wipe out what was left of the vampires in this world. When I was done, Calvin would stake me. Another life lost in the process was no big deal in my eyes.

I tapped the guard's neck, making the vein bulge more. "This is going to hurt."

He screamed as I latched onto his neck. I could have made it pleasurable for him, but I didn't want to give him any ideas. His blood rushed into my veins, lighting me up like a Christmas tree on crack. Images flickered and danced in front of my eyes, and I struggled to put the pieces together.

The guard whimpered and cried out as I drained him of the last of his blood.

"Calvin, pull over."

The car jerked to the side and I pushed the guard out, his body landing with a squish, as if all his bones had been extracted and replaced with those gummy worms Calvin loved.

I slammed the door, but not before a splash of late fall sunlight blistered my cheek. I rubbed at it, smoothing out the burn as it healed.

Calvin rapped his knuckles on the dashboard as he sped down the road. "What did you see?"

I settled into my seat and rolled my head back, peeling through the guard's memories. "They were told to watch for our car. They were supposed to detain you and kill me."

"How the hell could they know what we were driving and where we were crossing? There is no way..."

But there was a way, despite his protest to the contrary. "The humans are developing all sorts of technology. You know that, so do I." I reached forward and grabbed my cell phone. "They could have traced us."

I crushed the phone in my hand, shattering it completely. A tiny, red flashing dot was attached to the middle of the SIM card. I showed it to Calvin. "Someone's tracking us."

"Hellfire." He grabbed the pieces from me and chucked them out the window. "Who gave you the phone?"

"Victor."

"I knew that asshole would be a problem. His father,

now he was a good patron for you. He had just as much money, but he knew to stay the hell out of your business."

"Victor wants something from me." I leaned forward and put my chin on the back of the headrest, breathing in Calvin's smell. A mixture of leather and Old Spice cologne. His wife had bought him a bottle right before she was killed. He still wore it every day. I swallowed the spurt of jealousy. Not my place, not at all. I was one of the demons. I had no right to anything other than the life in front of me.

"He wants you to change him, doesn't he?"

I nodded. "Fucking twinkling vampire movie has made everyone think being a vampire is romantic. None of them think about what you have to give up to be a bloodsucker. *Estupido!*"

Calvin was silent for a moment. "You never chose this."

Not going there.

"We need to change vehicles. Now." I pointed at a small dealership, "Daddy's Deals." Calvin pulled in and turned off the engine. "What do you want this time?"

"Pick anything that will work." I slumped into the backseat of the car, throwing my arm across my eyes to get some rest.

The vampires were waiting for us in a clearing surrounded by tall, flowering jacaranda trees.

"We hear you are the chosen one." They circled us. Six of them. Six. Since when did they hunt in packs?

I shifted my stance. I would go down fighting with honor. "Father, if you get the chance to slip away, go."

"I will not leave you now." His voice was resigned. *We both knew what we faced.*

The first vampire hit me from behind, and I rolled with him, slashing his throat with my silver blade. The gurgle of air and blood seemed to echo in the night.

Everything became a blur. Blood and silver, the screams of the dying. The priest calling out last rites for the two of us as we fought, knowing we would die.

Neither of us stayed dead, though. I woke to the priest's high-pitched scream. My hand flew to my neck as I sat up. The wounds were gone, but I knew what that meant. My mind raced. How long would I have until I went mad?

How long until I lost myself?

Above me stood a vampire, his light green eyes watching me closely. "Well, well, the beauty awakes."

"Who are you?" I whispered as horror flickered through me.

He crouched, brushing a hand over my head in a gesture that was...kind. "Hush, I am your master. But you may call me Peter."

Standing up, he beckoned to me. "Come, leave the priest to his death. You have much to learn."

Peter slid into the night as if I would follow, and my body inclined to do as he commanded. I pushed away the desire to do as Peter wished. I would not be ruled by a monster. A demon that had no soul.

Every move I made away from Peter burned, but I gritted my teeth and forced my body to obey me. I was in charge.

Not that damn vampire.

I rose and went to the priest, pulling my hood up to protect me from the morning light. They'd nailed him to a cross and stuck it into the ground. As the sun rose, it crept down the cross, inch by inch, blistering his skin. Though a vampire could stand some light, the younger they were, the weaker their blood, the faster they burned. His eyes, blinded from the sun, still turned my way.

"Kill me, Cazador. Do your duty until your soul is called to rest."

I slipped a silver stake out of its sheath, the handle blistering my skin, and threw it, pinning him to the cross. His body burst into flame, burning bright like a star that had fallen from the sky. Sliding my last stake from the top of my boot, I turned, lifted my head, and scented what vampires were left.

Peter was there, somewhere in the darkness.

"This was a mistake you will not live to regret," I said softly, following their trail into the shadowed forest.

"We got a car. It ain't pretty, but it will do." Calvin knocked on the roof of the Mustang. I slipped up my shrouded cowl and put on my sunglasses. Even though I was mostly covered, the sun could slip through, and it hurt like a son of a bitch.

I was in the back of the new car, an older Camaro with a giant eagle on the hood, in three heartbeats. "Classy."

Calvin peered through the window as he moved our gear from one vehicle to the other. "Don't complain. He didn't ask any questions since I was willing to give up the Mustang for this piece of shit."

A few minutes later, Calvin settled into the driver's seat, and I slumped lower into the back. He shoved the blackout blanket back at me. "Cover up. We've got a few hours of sunlight left."

I pulled the blanket over my head and tried not to

think any more about the memories that haunted me, that ate at my soul. If I had one left.

A few hours later, the sound of heavy traffic pulled me out from under the blanket. Vehicles flowed around us on one side, and a large green space beckoned to me on the other. Central Park. "We close?"

Calvin held up the vial of holy water, the silver backing facing me so it would block out my vampire essence. I could hear the water as it boiled and frothed, and knew without seeing it that it would be bleeding from clear, to pink, to blood red. His eyes met mine, a glitter in them. "What do you think?"

Chapter 4

RACHEL

After my encounter with Sean, I hailed a taxi to my East Harlem apartment. Call it a hunch, but I wanted to get off the streets as soon as possible.

I tossed and turned all night, trying to figure out which man to believe, but in the end, there was no question. While I'd tried to keep in touch with Derrick, I had never expected—nor wanted—to see Sean again. I'd listen to what Derrick had to say.

If he ever showed up.

He'd told me he would come by my apartment, but so far I hadn't heard from him. The fact that Sean was actively looking for him had me freaked out.

I spent the next morning calling a few sources, trying to get information for my story about the prisoner population decline. I felt hopeful when I got in touch with a former prison guard who agreed to meet with me the day after the following afternoon with a piece of evidence.

"I saw the men get on that bus for the transfer, but my buddy at the work farm they were going to said they never showed up."

"And you said you have a copy of the transfer order with the list of inmates?"

"Yeah."

We set up the time and place for our meeting. Later, in early afternoon, I called Tom, my contact in the coroner's department. He confirmed that last night's murder victim had been mostly similar to the other victims.

"There was blood loss," he said, "but not like the others."

"You mean he wasn't drained like the others."

"Yeah. It's like the job was half done."

That fit with my theory that the murderer had been interrupted. But by whom? I chewed on the end of my pen as I looked out the window of my sixth-floor walk-up apartment. "Do the cops think the guy is some kind of psycho?"

"You can't use this, Rachel. You can't use my name."

My pulse increased when I heard the hitch in his voice. He knew something. "You know I'll keep this confidential, Tom. I'm not about to jeopardize what we have. The other news outlets are calling these 'Vampire Murders' and suggesting it's a cult, but I *know* this is just a single psycho."

He was quiet for a moment. "You're right. They've determined it's the work of one person, probably a man. And the marks on their chests…they look like they're occult symbols."

"You're kidding."

"Nope. I'll let you know if I hear anything else. But listen, Rachel. Be careful. This guy is dangerous."

I hung up and looked at the map of New York City pinned to my wall, push pins marking the locations where the bodies had been found. If the markings were really occult symbols, the locations of the bodies could have a deeper meaning. I should have asked Tom if he could sneak me photos of the symbols.

A knock on the door made me jump, jarring me out of my thoughts. I walked over and peeked out the peephole, relieved to see Derrick.

But when I opened the door, I tried to hide my shock. His hair stood on end and his coat and pants were stained. Dark circles underscored his eyes. He had a large duffel bag slung over his back. Even in his state of dishevelment, the sight of him pulled at the loose strings of my heart. I'd made a terrible mistake two years ago. Could I shelve my pride enough to admit it to him?

I was silent long enough to prompt Derrick to ask, "Can I come in?"

I blinked and stumbled backward, still amazed he was there. "Yeah, of course. Sorry. You look like shit."

A sly grin lit up his face as he walked past me. "Still call it like you see it, huh?"

I clutched my shaking hands, telling myself to get it together. He was here, so that was a start.

I lead him to the kitchen area of my loft apartment. "I'm an old dog, D. Too late to learn new tricks."

He snorted. "Thirty-one is hardly old, Rachel."

"Ha! You're just saying that because you're two years older."

His grin spread.

I pulled two bottles of water out of the fridge and handed him one. "What are you doing in the States?" It seemed like a safe place to start, although I had a million and one questions begging for attention.

He took a long drag and lowered the bottle. His gaze drifted to the map on my wall and he moved closer, studying the pins. "This doesn't seem like your kind of story."

I knew what he meant. On the surface, it seemed undeniable that this was a serial murderer story. Even though I didn't get to pick and choose all my assignments, I rarely took stories about crime. What I liked to do most was ferret out the truth about abuses of power. But I couldn't deny something about this story had sunk its hooks deep. I followed and stood next to him, watching his face. "You know what's going on here?"

His brow wrinkled as he looked down at me. "You're like a dog with a bone, but you need to let this one go."

"But *you're* not letting it go."

He groaned.

"Let me cook you dinner," I said, formulating a plan

to get him to spill what he knew. "You haven't lived until you've had my spaghetti."

A ghost of a smile lifted the corners of his lips. "I've had your spaghetti. Closer to the grave seems more likely."

I laughed. "I've got a new recipe. It involves liberal amounts of red wine."

He turned his back on the map and wandered over to my sofa. "In the sauce or in a glass?"

"Both."

"Count me in." He looked around and his smile fell. "So if you're inviting me to dinner, you must have forgiven me for what happened."

I rested my hands on the back of an overstuffed chair and looked down at the worn seat. "That night still haunts me."

"Rachel."

"I'm so sorry." I glanced at him. "You have no idea how much I've missed you. You were my best friend. I haven't been the same since you left."

Sighing, he crossed the room in a couple of steps and pulled me into a hug. "You didn't do anything wrong. I had terrible timing, so much so I'm shocked to be standing here in your apartment."

"Just because I'm not *in love* with you doesn't mean I don't care about you, Derrick."

He dropped his hold on me and stepped back. "It was too damn hard." He shook his head. "I said some stupid things I wish I could take back."

"So did I," I interrupted. "There's plenty of blame to go around."

He gave me a half-hearted smile. "You were right, though. Instead of being there for you as a friend—which is what you needed—I was too busy gloating over the fact I'd been right about Sean turning into a first-class asshole."

I grinned. "You didn't gloat, but there may have been an *I-told-you-so* in there." Then I turned more serious. "But I told you all this in the dozens of voice mails, texts, and emails I sent you. Why didn't you ever call me back? Did you change your number?"

"My number is the same." He pointed to the map. "This is why." He moved closer to it, studying the pins. "This is a dangerous story and there's no sense in both of us being in danger."

"Why don't you tell me what you know about all this—" I pointed toward the map "—and I'll decide for myself if it's too dangerous for me."

A lazy smile lit up his face, giving him a boyish look. "Good try. I need a shower. Do you mind if I take one here?"

I decided to let him change the topic for now. Besides, he was right. "Of course, but you look like you could use a nap to go along with it."

He shook his head. "I've got a meeting tonight at nine."

I glanced at the clock on my stove, then turned back to look at him. "It's barely two. Take a shower, then a nap. I'll wake you at seven and we can eat before you go."

He looked torn.

"Come on, Derrick. Stop being stubborn. If this case is as dangerous as you say, you need to be rested so you'll be on your toes."

He grinned. "Okay, but make sure I'm up by six."

"You'll find clean towels in the bathroom, and feel free to crash on my bed."

"Thanks."

He started down the hall and I called after him, "I've missed you, Derrick."

"Me, too." His voice was gruff as he headed to the bathroom. I watched him, wondering what had brought him to New York City, wondering what he was hiding. It looked like we were both working on stories that weren't our usual gig.

I finished a puff piece for the online site I did freelance work for. Derrick emerged from my makeshift bedroom, a small area separated by two folding screens, rubbing his eyes as he sat on a barstool at my counter. He looked worse than he had before his nap.

"How long has it been since you got more than four hours sleep?" I asked, pouring each of us a glass of wine.

"Too long."

I handed him his drink. "How long have you been in New York?"

"Two weeks."

That was exactly when the murders started. Even if he'd heard about the first one immediately after it happened, it would have taken him a couple of days to fly over from the Middle East, presuming that's where he had been. Which made me question whether he'd followed the murderer himself. Not the crime.

"Where are you staying?" I asked.

"Rach. It's too dangerous. I shouldn't even be here *now*."

I'd seen his bag. His non-answer confirmed what I suspected. "You're staying here tonight."

He shook his head. "I have that meeting."

"Then go and come back." I tasted the sauce, then handed the spoon to him.

He licked it and whistled. "When did you learn to cook?"

"When I got back to the States. A few months ago I got tired of takeout."

"Why'd you come back?"

That was a complicated question. One we didn't have time to delve into, so I kept it short. "No one learned anything over there. The sins of the fathers kept repeating themselves—on all sides. It became too depressing, so…I came back."

I fixed two plates and set one in front of him.

We sat at the island counter and made small talk while he downed his first glass of wine. I poured him another and decided it was time to put on some pressure.

"You know who's committing these murders."

He took a bite of his garlic bread, then sat back in his chair. "This is *my* story, Rachel. Stay out."

I leaned forward. "I have sources that can help. We can work together."

"Why does this intrigue you?" he asked.

"I can guess why it intrigues *you*," I said. "You're all about cover-ups and conspiracies, and Sean's involved, so this must have something to do with the U.S. government."

"*He's* involved now, huh? I suspected." He set his

fork on his plate. "I've suspected for some time, but it's good to have confirmation."

"Why? What's he doing now?"

"National security."

"Terrorists?" I asked.

His mouth twisted. "In a way." He studied my face, then sighed. "Bioterrorism."

"Shit." I pushed my plate way, suddenly losing my appetite. "Creating it or stopping it?"

"You know the fact you had to ask is damning in and of itself."

I didn't deny it.

He picked up his wine. "I'm close to breaking this. I know it. The guy I'm meeting tonight has answers. He could be my Deep Throat."

"And this started in the Middle East?"

He just stared at me and took a sip of wine.

"Sean thinks you've lost it."

He forced a smile. "It's easier to dismiss me that way." He stood. "I need to head into the city. Can I leave my bag here?"

My head was still reeling. Bioterrorism scared the hell out of me. A few weeks before Sean had cheated on me Derrick had told me that he'd heard whispers of it. Experiments in an Iraqi prisoner camp. But when I'd asked him about it a week later, he'd given me a tight smile and told me it had turned out to be nothing. Something in his eyes had told me he was lying. Now I was certain of it. "Derrick, let me help."

He moved around the table and placed his hands on my shoulders. "You'll help me more by staying here and watching my bag. All of my research is on my laptop. You can't let Sean get it."

I nodded. "I won't. I promise."

He headed for the door.

Did he really think I'd give up that easily? "Derrick."

He tuned to look at me.

"Please be careful."

He grinned. "I'm always careful. See you in a few hours."

I locked the door behind him, placing my back to the wood. I could wait for Derrick to come back and tell me what this was all about, or I could look for answers myself.

Like that was even a question.

I hurried into my room, grabbed his bag off the floor, and rushed back to the kitchen. After putting the dinner plates in the sink, I set the bag on a bar stool and began riffling through his belongings. When I pulled out his laptop, I found several folded maps in the bag. I spread them across the island's surface. They were terrain maps of the Middle East, Iraq in particular, and several places were circled. One I recognized as a U.S. military base rumored to conduct medical experimentation even earlier than the prisoner camp Derrick had mentioned. Of course, few people had believed it at the time, but Derrick had been certain there was a kernel of truth to the tall tales.

I opened his laptop and felt a small amount of guilt as I tried to figure out what his password could be. But I was doing this for his own good. He needed my help, whether he would admit it or not.

The password only took three tries. The winner turned out to be the name of his favorite childhood cat, something I had learned while we hung out with the troops in the heat of the desert.

His iPhone messages popped up first, and I offered a silent prayer of thanks that his texts were in his cloud. The most recent was from "CV," and it had an address on the Lower East Side, the words Asclepius Project, and the time 9:00. I tapped my chin, battling with my conscience, but who was I kidding? Wild horses couldn't keep me away. Too bad I'd spent most of my transportation money on a taxi the day before. But the subway would take too long. I'd have to cab it again.

Just after I restored the maps and laptop to the bag, making some attempt to put them back the way I'd found them, a knock came on the door.

I bolted upright. I rarely had visitors, and I knew this wasn't Derrick. I hurried to the door and peered into the peephole. Two men in dark suits. Shit.

The taller man pounded again, glaring at the door as if he could see me. "Open up! FBI!"

FBI? I hadn't been doing anything to warrant their attention, which meant they'd followed Derrick here. What if they'd also followed him to his source? I needed to act *now*. Grabbing his bag, I sprinted to my closet as I called the last number I had for him. After five rings it went to voice mail. "I need to talk to you ASAP. *Call me.*"

The pounding continued, becoming more insistent as I threw dirty clothes out of the way and found the trap door I'd made after my apartment was broken into a couple of months before. The space wasn't big, and

I prayed the bag would fit inside. When it did, I started praying they wouldn't notice the cracks in the wood slats. I couldn't let the Feds find Derrick's research. I couldn't. After shoving the laundry back into the closet, I ran into the bathroom and flushed the toilet before heading into the living area. Just as I reached the middle of the room, the door burst open—as in swinging, not crashing— which meant they'd picked the lock.

Not something the FBI was likely to do.

The two men walked in, their eyes wide with shock when they saw me. In a matter of seconds, they trained their handguns on me.

I had a feeling things were about to get a lot more complicated.

Chapter 5

LEA

With the holy water bubbling in the front seat, we both knew we were close. "Calvin, find a place already. You take any longer and the sun is going to come up before we're parked."

I was itching to get out and move. The sun had set and I wanted nothing more than to slam my silver stakes into a vampire's heart. Maybe that would help me erase the memories that had haunted me as we drove.

"You think it's easy to park in the heart of New York City? What am I, an overpaid chauffeur?" he grumbled at me.

I drummed my fingers on the back of his seat. Patience was something I had developed over the last several hundred years, but at moments like this one, I felt it slipping away.

"Calvin, forget about it. I'll find you later." With that, I pulled on my elbow-length leather gloves and jumped out of the car the next time he slowed at an intersection.

"Damn it, Lea! Get back here!"

Ignoring him, I ghosted through traffic, dodging cars with ease. I still wore my shrouded cowl, black jeans, and boots, plus the molded leather chest armor that had softened to fit around me over the years. The long gloves would allow me to handle the silver weapons that were the only effective tools against a vamp.

Silver stakes and my silver netting was all I had with me, but I likely wouldn't need more than that. A single vamp out in the open was generally an easy catch, and there was no indication this serial killer vamp wasn't working alone. But what the hell was the connection to Rikers Island then? The only thing that made sense was that the thief had broken out, and then been turned. And maybe if it were any other jail than Rikers Island I could have been able to convince myself of that.

That only left one option. Someone pulled the thief out, turned him, and then set him loose somewhere I would find him.

But again, why? And who?

I stalked deep into the park, honing in on the

vampire's scent within a few hundred feet. Following the vampire's winding path, I frowned. There was no pattern to the movement, which was strange. Like whoever it was wandered instead of hunted.

"What the hell are you up to, bloodsucker?" I searched through a clump of half-dead bushes for footprints. They were there in the rain-softened ground. A good-sized foot. Unless there was an Amazonian female vamp I didn't know about, I was looking for a male vampire.

Central Park was the perfect hunting ground for a vampire. Lots of cover, and contrary to popular belief, the more people who were around, the easier it was to cut one from the herd. But tonight, there were only a few people out. A slight drizzle might have been keeping the humans away. But I doubted it.

A vampire on the prowl would notch up the humans' natural survival instincts. They might not realize they were avoiding the park, but they would still follow their hindbrain's instructions to hunker down somewhere safe until the storm had passed.

And those who didn't?

A man strode in front of me, head down and shoulders hunched. "Dinner," I whispered at him from my hiding place in the shadows.

He stopped and looked around. "Hello?"

Damn, his hearing was good. I didn't move, just waited for him to continue on his way.

Except he didn't. He took a step toward me, shocking the shit out of me. There was the slight bulge of a weapon under his jacket. So he thought he was safe? Humans and their guns…they thought a bullet would solve every problem to come their way. I wasn't sure if I agreed with them or not.

Slowly he backed away from me, his eyes tight with concern and a healthy dose of fear. I could almost see his skin prickling with gooseflesh.

"Get a hold of yourself, Derrick. You're acting like a little girl," he whispered.

I couldn't resist playing with him. Hell, he was making it too damn easy. I whispered his name, throwing my voice so it bounced around him, summoning him from several directions at once.

He stumbled back, his eyes wide. "Shit." His hand shook on the butt of his gun, but he didn't grab it. Guts. This one had guts. I almost felt bad about teasing him.

Almost.

Grinning to myself, I was about to give him something else to think about when I caught the scent of the other vampire again. The wind came toward me, and brought the flavor as if I'd dipped my mouth into an ice cream sundae. Though I didn't feed from other vamps as a general rule, I'd drank a few down when I had to. It was fucking delicious.

This vampire was no young pup. He approached Derrick from behind, without making the slightest crunch or creak.

Long flowing trench coat, dark clothes, no hat to protect his head from the rain. His auburn hair was slicked back into a ponytail. Blue-green eyes peered out from the deep crevices of his eye sockets. I did a mental search through my vampire database. I didn't know who this was, and that made me nervous. The old vampires were notoriously egotistical. They liked me knowing who they were.

It looked like one of them had finally gotten smart and kept his info from me.

But not for long.

I tensed and pulled the thin netting of silver filament loose from the pouch on my belt. Wrapping a vamp in the filament would keep him incapacitated, and I would be able to ask all the questions I wanted.

Of course, he'd probably be screaming because the filament would burn the shit out of his skin, but that wasn't really a concern of mine. That's what gags were for.

"I believe you are looking for me," the vamp said, his voice cultured and smooth.

Derrick spun around, pulling his gun as he did. "I know what you are. Don't come any closer."

Damn, he was quick for a human. But how the hell did he know what the vamp was? We had some pretty strict rules when it came to being outed.

As in, don't tell the humans unless they were a) dinner or b) going to be turned into a vampire.

The vampire lifted his hands. "I believe we can find a mutually beneficial understanding, Derrick. I am not going to hurt you. Please, put the gun away. This sort of thing is below two gentlemen, don't you think?"

I wanted to snort. There was no way the vamp was going to talk. Which meant Derrick was in for a wicked surprise.

"I think I'll keep it out, if it's all the same to you."

Hmm. I was liking this Derrick more and more. He

wasn't falling under the vampire's sway. I itched to jump out and ask the vampire what the hell he was talking about, but there was no need. The idiot spilled the beans right there.

There was a soft click, the depression of a button, if I was hearing right. Derrick lifted a voice recorder with his free hand. "For posterity. Tell me your name, age, and what you do for a living."

The vampire smiled, his fangs glittering for a split second. "My name is Caine, I am three hundred years old, give or take a few years. I eat people for a living."

Derrick backed up a couple of steps. "What do you think this is? Interview with a fucking vampire? I've done everything you asked. Now it's time for you to give me information. No more games."

I had to bite my tongue. Oh man, if he only knew the truth.

Caine held his hands up again as he slowly shifted to the side, trying to get closer to Derrick again. Definitely here to take care of the nosy reporter, then. "Yes, this is an interview with a vampire, though why you should be surprised is beyond me. I told you when we spoke that you would have a hard time believing me. Information is power. It is the most reliable currency in the world now."

Derrick stepped sideways, giving me a good look at his face. He frowned, but his gun hand was still steady. Probably the only thing that was keeping his neck from getting chewed on. The old vamps were smart enough to know a bullet might not kill them, but it would slow them down in a big way if it hit them in the head or heart.

"Derrick, vampires are very, very real. We're just well

hidden, and at the moment, rather endangered." Caine tucked his hands into his pockets and shrugged, looking like nothing more than a good old boy. "Here is the truth. We are being killed off at a rate we won't long survive, and because of this, we went to your human government for protection. They are helping us repopulate at a pre-determined rate in exchange for our help."

Derrick's gun slowly lowered to his side. His thumb flicked the safety on. Not smart, my friend, not smart.

"What kind of help?"

"Bioengineering."

Mother in heaven, he had to be shitting Derrick. Had to be. Because if that were true...

But I didn't get a chance to see what else he would have said. The wind shifted and Caine's eyes swung toward my hiding place. The vampire leapt on Derrick, and rose with the human's back pinned against his chest, using him as a shield.

"Cazador, I smell you. Come out now, and let us have a chat."

I moved slowly, keeping my speed in check. "Caine, I don't believe we've met. I have to ask, how do you know what I smell like?" I stepped out of the shadows, my hand holding the silver filament at my side.

"Honey and blood, those are your scents. We all know. We have been warned." His eyes flicked over me. "Not that many have escaped you, but enough that we know what to look for."

Derrick struggled in his arms, but Caine had an arm across his throat, effectively controlling his breathing. A little more pressure and Derrick went still. "You should let the human go," I said. "He isn't saving you from me."

"Really?" Caine's eyebrows rose. "You would let him live after what I told him?"

"Information is the currency we deal in, yes?" I parroted his words back to him. "He has information, and I want it. Just as I want what you know." I flicked the silver netting out, letting it catch the light. Watched Caine's eyes tighten as they followed the movement.

"Torture?"

"Of course." I laughed softly as I stepped toward him and he stepped away. "This dance is going to end the same way regardless of how we start it, Caine."

"Then I think perhaps—" He reached down and sliced Derrick's leg open across the thigh with his razor-sharp fingernails, then threw him at me, as if that would keep me off him. Caine was treating me like I was a young vamp who would be distracted by the blood.

What a nincompoop.

I dodged the flying body, letting Derrick fall, and sprinted after Caine. He was slow—he shouldn't have been. This was almost too easy. I tackled him to the ground. His fangs caught me in my upper arm and he bit to the bone.

"Son of a bitch!" I dug my fingers into the side of his mouth and pried him off as if he were a feral dog.

A gunshot went off and a tuft of dirt exploded beside us. I ignored it, but Caine shifted me toward Derrick, angling my body so my back was to him. Which could only mean one thing.

Silver bullets.

I twisted, yanking Caine around as the gun went off a second time. Caine's body jerked, and his grip on me slipped. "Good shot, man." I grabbed the edge of Caine's shirt and ripped it off. The bullet was buried an inch below his heart. Good shot, indeed—any higher and Caine wouldn't be answering any questions. I flipped out the filament and wrapped it around the other vampire in a matter of seconds. The sizzle of flesh under the silver was immediate. Caine shook under the netting, his eyes glazing over as he passed out.

On to the human. I turned to see the disappearing figure of Derrick as he ran from the scene. He was limping, the scent of a wound fresh on the air. The trail would last for a few hours at least. It would be easy enough to find him later, after I'd dealt with Caine. And I would find him. He was obviously onto something big, something that had brought him this far into my world. Not a good sign.

I booted Caine, which made the filament slide down and rest against his cheek. He jerked back to consciousness, but he didn't scream. "You think you're tough enough to face this, but you aren't."

"You will end up in a cage, Cazador. They want your blood more than anyone else's. You've never shared it with anyone. Like a fine wine, never sipped." He spat at me—a hunk of saliva and what may have been a piece of my upper arm.

I grinned down at him, letting my fangs fully extend. "Come on, big boy. We have some talking to do." I bent and picked up the coiled section of the filament, dragging Caine behind me.

Of course, I called it talking, but we both knew what I really meant. Having been trained during the Spanish

Inquisition, I knew how to make someone share—or, more accurately, *scream*—their secrets. Taking the life's blood of a human allowed me to have their memories, but the effect wouldn't work with a vampire as old as Caine. He knew how to block me from taking those memories, so it would have to be old school.

Not that I minded one bit.

I dragged him to the edge of the park and crouched beside him. "Caine, you are going to wish your maker had never lusted for your blood before this is done."

He groaned, but said nothing.

I knew how to bring men to their knees, how to make them beg for mercy as they condemned even their own mother as a child of the devil. Anything to make the pain stop. The trick was to take them right to the edge before they started to tell you what you wanted to hear. A fine line, and one I'd perfected walking over the years. By the time I was done with him, I would know everything he did.

And he would be grateful when I cut his heart out and ended his pain.

Chapter 6

RACHEL

I stood in the middle of my small living area with my hands up as the *agents* rushed toward me.

"Oh, my God! Can a person not go to the bathroom without having her door busted in? Ever heard of patience?"

The men stood still and silent as the sound of my toilet running filled the space.

"You can't just bust in here!" I added for good measure.

It took them a moment to shake their stupor, and then the shorter man moved around me while the taller one spoke. "Where's Derrick Forrester?"

I shook my head, my hands still up. "I don't know."

"We know he was with you."

"If you were watching him, then you know he's not here."

"Where'd he go?" the taller guy asked.

"Why didn't you ask him when he left?"

The taller man tilted his head toward my room. "Search the place."

His partner headed to the back and my anger soared. "Hey! Where's your search warrant!"

He grinned. "We don't need one."

What that hell was Derrick onto? Oily anxiety coated my nerves.

When I heard a banging in my sleeping area, followed by a crash, I took a step in that direction. "Hey!"

The agent watching me waved his gun. "I don't think so."

"You think I'm going to stand here while he tears up my apartment when you don't even have a warrant? I don't think so."

His finger tightened on the trigger.

There was another crash in my room and I clenched my hands into fists. "Dammit!"

The one-man wrecking ball emerged five minutes later. To my relief, he didn't have the bag.

"Are you boys done yet?" I asked. "If you looked under the bed, then I think you've checked all the places he could be hiding."

The agent with the gun walked over to my end table and batted my lamp onto the floor. The light bulb shattered on the wood floor, so the only light came from the light over my kitchen sink, but I could still see the evil grin spread across his face. "Oops."

I gave him a smartass smirk. "Oh. Big man. You can break a lamp. I'm impressed."

His eyes darkened, but his buddy stopped him with his hand.

"Enough. There's nothing here."

"I could have told you that," I said. "If you'd *asked*."

The taller *agent* pulled a card out of his pocket and tossed it onto my kitchen counter. "You seem like a smart girl. You managed yourself pretty well in that skirmish in that little Iraqi town a few years back. So you should be smart enough to know to call that number when he shows up again." He paused. "Or this will look like nothing compared to what happens next."

What the…

I knew what he meant, of course. Sean had been in full-scale seduction mode at the time, and he'd secured me a place on that raid. Most women wouldn't have found that sort of thing sexy—and I didn't—but the fact that he'd made it happen had impressed me. Now it was just another reminder that he'd always known how to manipulate me.

His asshole friend had just made a fatal error.

The taller agent and his buddy turned and walked toward the still-open door. I was half tempted to pick up a drinking glass at the table and hurl it at the back of the asshole's head, but ten-to-one he'd turn and shoot me.

If they could do this without a warrant, killing a nosy journalist who had a well-known tendency to meet with unscrupulous sources would be easy.

But one thing was certain. Those guys might be government, but they sure as shit weren't FBI.

After they walked through the threshold, I shut my door and locked it. That didn't seem like enough, so I wedged a chair under the door handle to barricade the entrance. I had to laugh. My jerry-rigged extra security wouldn't keep a five-year-old out, but it was better than nothing. It was at times like these I wished I had a German shepherd.

I snatched the card off the counter and looked at the hand-scratched number on an otherwise blank space. While tons of people loved to believe the world was full of conspiracies, I'd always found that most turned out to be nothing even close. But I couldn't ignore that weird pile of ashes or the swiftness with which Sean and his goons had appeared in that alley.

And I couldn't ignore that word Derrick had tossed out—bioterrorism, for God's sake—or the fact that one of his maps featured a military facility in Iraq rumored to be used for medical experiments. Even so, there had to be some logical explanation for all of it, but damned if I could come up with one.

I stuffed the card into my jeans pocket and found my canvas jacket buried in the pile of clothes scattered across my floor. Slipping it on, I made my way through the rubble to my secret hole. For all I knew, the *agent* had bugged or put a video device in my room, so I blocked the entrance to the closet, pretending to dig through the scattered clothing as I lifted the lid to the hole and dug out my Glock from underneath Derrick's bag. While I knew how to use it, I didn't carry it often. It wasn't worth the risk, particularly when I knew other moves that could get me out of most sticky situations—the one good thing about growing up with four brothers and a father who was a cop—but I had a feeling it might come in handy tonight. I stuffed it into an inner pocket of my jacket, along with additional ammo. Then I grabbed my bag and looped it over my shoulder and opened my bedroom window.

I had no doubt I was being watched. I just had to make sure they didn't see me leave. I slipped onto the fire escape and climbed to the top of the building. Anyone watching my apartment would be looking at street level.

After living in a hot zone for several years, it was safe to say I was on the paranoid side in wanting an escape plan. Even from my own home. So the beautiful part of my apartment was the proximity of its roof to the top of the building next door. Someone afraid of heights would be terrified of the three-foot gap, and I had to admit I was skittish, but this was all about survival. I'd do damn near anything to survive.

It was easy after the leap. I found the stairwell and descended eight flights, then pulled a stocking cap out of my bag and put it on, cramming my hair underneath. Sure enough, there was a black car parked down the street from the entrance to my apartment, but no one bothered me as I walked in the opposite direction and hailed a cab. When I gave him the address in Derrick's text, he punched it into his GPS system and turned around, giving me a questioning look. "Fifth Avenue and 66th Street. That's the lower end of Central Park."

Shit. Of course, the park. "Yeah. I need to get there in ten minutes."

He shook his head. "We'll never make it in ten. There's roadwork."

"I'll pay you double, if you do."

That was all the incentive he needed to jerk around, throw the car into drive, and take off like a bat out of hell.

I turned to make sure we weren't followed, then pulled out my phone to see if I'd missed a call or text from Derrick. Nothing.

I sent him one instead. *My place is compromised. I'm coming to you. Stay on the island.*

By the time the cab driver pulled up to the park with nine minutes on the meter, I handed him double the fare. When he looked surprised, I said, "A deal's a deal."

He pulled away from the curb and I tugged down the cap I was still wearing in an attempt to keep dry in the cold drizzle. I tried to get my bearings. A city park at night was a safe place to meet—there was darkness for anonymity, but this side of midnight was busy enough for plenty of witnesses.

I stayed close to the hedges and eased my way to the entrance. Of course, it would have been too easy if they were having a powwow on the park bench to my right. My best option would be to make my way through the park like I was on a stroll. I really could have used that German shepherd about now. Central Park was huge, but at least I knew the general area they'd agreed upon.

After walking for a few more minutes, I found a path leading to a more private area, in the direction of the park's famous Shakespeare statue. Shaking my head, I walked down it, wondering if I was heading into a trap. But a few moments later I heard voices—one of them was Derrick's. I crouched behind several bushes to try and overhear their conversation, but I couldn't make anything out.

Suddenly the man grabbed Derrick—so inhumanly fast it was a blur—and held him to his chest, one arm around his neck, as he stared into the darkness.

A shrouded figure emerged, moving with a slow stealth I had only seen big cats use to catch their prey. And currently Derrick was the literal middleman between the hunted and the prey. I pulled out my gun and turned off the safety.

The shrouded person continued to advance, and Derrick seemed to stop fighting as much. The hunter and the hunted man spoke low, too low to hear. I debated trying to get closer or waiting for a good shot at the man currently holding Derrick hostage.

But then the man decided for me by slashing Derrick's thigh and hurling him toward the hunter. The hunter leapt for the man and pinned him to the ground. Then, to my surprise, the man leaned forward and bit the hunter's arm. I had no clue who was friend or foe, but I knew I had to get them to scatter so I could get Derrick out of there.

Derrick had other plans. He was already on his feet, his own gun in hand, and he didn't hesitate to fire at his attackers. The pair stopped their struggling and shifted their stances as Derrick fired again. Was he out of his mind?

He took off then, rounding a corner, and I had every intention of going after him. But then the hunter wrapped something around the guy who'd held Derrick captive—metal filament? What the hell? Whatever Derrick had been after was still going down. I'd catch up to him later. His wounds didn't look fatal, and if this was what had brought those agents to my door, I wanted to know as much about it as possible.

The hunter stood and kicked the man, who let out a low sound, and then the hunter dragged the guy along the ground.

I followed, keeping a good distance. If I was right about the hooded figure being a hunter, he'd notice me following. At one point the figure stopped and slowly moved his head around as if sniffing me out. Which was impossible. My finger tightened on the trigger of my gun, but he must have decided it was nothing. Then the hood slipped a little, revealing part of the hunter's face.

The hunter was a woman.

I stifled a gasp as she took off again, and I was nearly paralyzed with questions. Who was she? How was she so strong? Why was I the only person in this park who had noticed her dragging him?

I considered calling 911. I was obviously witnessing a kidnapping. But then I'd never get answers, and I desperately wanted answers. I pulled out my phone and texted Derrick.

I'm in here in the park. I saw everything. I'm following them now.

He shot back instantly with three words. *Are you crazy?*

I swallowed my laugh. He knew I was crazy.

They're heading toward the entrance, I sent back. *Meet you there.*

The hunter stopped at the entrance. I hid about thirty feet back, wanting to see where she was going, but afraid to get too close.

I'm across the street from the entrance.

Derrick texted back, *I see them.*

Seconds later she rounded the corner, dragging the man with her. As soon as she was out of sight, I raced to the entrance and hid around the corner. A car pulled up and the trunk popped open. She shoved the man into the back, slammed the trunk shut, and climbed into the backseat. The car took off, the taillights lighting up the drizzle that had turned to rain.

Movement across the street caught my eye and I saw Derrick limping toward a sedan. Dodging an oncoming car whose driver lauded me with horn blasts and shouted expletives, I intercepted him. He stood on the sidewalk next to the dark gray sedan and I stood in the street.

"What are you doing here, Rachel?" He sounded angry, but his face was pale even in this bad light.

"Yell at me later. Is this your car?" I pointed to the sedan as I jerked the damp cap off my head.

"Yeah."

I jerked on the driver's side door. "Unlock it. Let's go."

He shook his head. "I can't get you—"

"Involved? I'm already involved!" I jerked the handle again. "Dammit, Derrick! They're getting away!"

I heard the lock unclick and hopped into the car; he climbed into the passenger seat and tossed me the keys.

I tore away from the curb, ready to do what it took

to catch up with them, and shot Derrick my best bitch glare. "I think it's time you told me everything."

He swallowed and his face became even paler as he shrugged off his coat. "You're never going to believe me."

"Try me."

I turned the corner, trying to catch sight of the hunter's car when I saw a familiar face in my rearview mirror. Sitting in the dark sedan directly behind me was the agent who'd trashed my apartment.

Shit.

"And in case you're not convinced I'm involved, those *agents* behind us just cemented that I am. Start talking."

But before he could say anything, a gunshot rang out. I punched the gas and took off, wondering how in the hell I was going to outrun imposter Feds in New York City.

"You can't let them catch me."

The uncharacteristic fear in Derrick's voice scared me. But I'd never admit that to him.

"Hang on. This is about to get bumpy."

Chapter 7

LEA

I threw Caine into the trunk of the car. The silver filament would hold him. Every twitch he made would drive the net deeper into his muscles and flesh. I rubbed my hand over my right bicep. Through the material of the shirt, I could feel the ridged scars from my own encounter with the mesh.

"Calvin, drive."

"Where to?"

"East side. Now."

He grunted and gunned the engine, sliding out and through the traffic like it wasn't jamming up around us. Headlights and billboards lit up the dark of the night, making it feel like it wasn't really night at all. But that wasn't where my head was. Bioengineering with vampires. A shiver slid through me. The humans were going to get us all killed, if that was true.

And then there was Caine. I didn't know him, but the more I thought about him, the more certain I was I'd heard of him. The auburn hair was what had twigged my memory. We'd caught rumors of a red-headed vampire, one who liked to feast on little boys as he sodomized them. Rage lit my senses, urging me to pull him from the trunk and ram a telephone pole up his ass while he begged for mercy I would never give. Calvin tensed.

"Lea, easy, I feel your energy from here, and it's wigging me out."

"Sorry," I gritted the word out.

Somewhere behind us, a sound of a gunshot caught my ears. Calvin didn't twitch. I wasn't surprised he hadn't heard it. Did the gunshot have anything to do with us? The chances were slim, yet I knew better. On a night like tonight, I had no doubt the shot was somehow tied to us.

I ripped off the seat cushion and punched a hole through to the trunk. Calvin didn't even yell at me. He knew me well enough to trust that I had my reasons.

After tearing through the layers of material and metal, I stared down at Caine, who was trying to work around the filament to grab at one of my guns. The silver netting had cut through to the bone, and the smell of burning flesh was starting to fill the small space. "Caine, you'd think at your age you'd know better than to fight the inevitable." I reached past him, fingers twitching to bury themselves into his eye sockets, and pulled out my rifle.

My 30-06 Winchester. The old school hunting rifle's wood stock was worn from use—she was one of my first guns and she still shot straight and true. I knelt on the back seat, tucked the gun against my shoulder, and looked through the scope. Another gunshot echoed, this one closer than before.

"Lea, who's after us?"

"Keep steady, Cal. I don't think those shots are meant for us." But the two vehicles weaving in and out of traffic—the obvious source of the firefight—were drawing closer. I didn't recognize the driver of the one in the lead. Long blond hair and a death grip on the wheel was all I really saw as she jerked the car over the curb to avoid smashing into the jam in front of her. "Good driver."

I shifted to get a look at her passenger.

The journalist.

I wanted to talk to him. Which meant keeping them alive was a good idea. The second vehicle was the classic black sedan used by most government officials.

I punched the back window, wanting as clear a shot as possible. The glass spider-cracked rather than shattered. With a snarl, I ripped out what remained of it. The woman driving the journalist barely dodged the hunk of window.

Settling the gun stock tight into my shoulder, I sighted down the scope. My crosshairs settled on the forehead of the driver in the black sedan. "Easy as pie," I whispered, breathing out and squeezing the trigger.

The gun bucked, the shot muffled by the roar of traffic and honking of pissed off drivers. The driver of the black sedan slumped forward, a spray of blood hitting the windshield, and a second set of hands reached forward to try and steer. They weren't successful, of course—the sedan veered off the road and slammed into a row of oncoming traffic. Less than ten seconds later, sirens and lights were coming in from all directions. The cavalry was arriving.

"We still have a tail," Calvin pointed out. "Or are we leading them on a chase?"

"I still want to speak to the journalist." I leaned into the trunk, grabbed Caine by the hair and dragged him toward me. "Unless you want to talk?"

He spit a gob of blood and bile on me, hitting me in the chest. I wiped it off. "You're lucky that didn't go any higher."

"Or what, you'd torture me?" he sneered.

I leaned close enough that our noses touched. "There are worse things than torture, Caine. I could make you my pet, make you love me even as you wish me dead. I could take your greatest fears and make you want them so much you beg for them on your hands and knees. That is a gift of mine." I slid my fingers around his cheek and dug them into his thick hair. I gripped him hard. "I could make you my bitch."

Horror flickered through his eyes, followed fast by lust. That was the problem with this particular threat. It either worked like a charm or it turned the assholes on.

"Do it then."

I shoved him back into the trunk, kicking him for good measure. I didn't care that he was still wrapped in the mesh. Being 'fair' was not my game when it came to vampires.

"Lea, we're here." Calvin's voice held more than a hint of displeasure. He didn't like to be reminded of how bad I could be. Neither did I, if I were being honest. But this was the calling I had. I was a Cazador, the last of the hunters, and I would wipe out the vampire blood lines even if it cost me my soul and what was left of my humanity.

If there was even any left inside me.

I looked out the window to see just where we'd stopped. We were parked on the curb in front of an abandoned building in the south end of Harlem.

I stepped out of the car, strode to the trunk and popped it open. Caine grinned up at me. "You aren't so tough. You want to make me love you. You're lonely, just like the rest of us."

Tipping my head to one side, I listened for the sound of tires, ignoring Caine and the words that were too close to the truth for my comfort. "Damn, you lost our tail, Calvin."

He grunted. "I can only go so slow. Get your bloodsucker and let's get this done." Calvin hefted a bag that held my fletchettes and an array of other unpleasant things. Silver pins, holy water, wooden splinters...the perfect tools for torturing a vampire.

Calvin had taken us to a building that was run-down and very obviously empty. Gang tags littered the exterior and the doors were missing; even the stairs leading to the entrance were partially destroyed. A chain link fence surrounded the property, warning signs hanging off it.

"Condemned. They're demolishing it soon." Calvin pointed at the sign on the chain link fence that said exactly that. The date was only a week away. Which meant it was perfect for our uses. We pushed our way through the fence, me dragging the groaning vampire behind us.

Up the broken stairs and into the main hall we went. I wondered briefly what the place had once been. Huge double-wide stairs with ornate railings led up and down, but there was really no question as to which direction we were going.

I jogged ahead of Calvin, letting Caine's body bounce down the stairs. This would just be the warmup.

The basement was dank and smelled like shit and piss. I curled my nose. "Good place for you to die, Caine?"

"Fuck you."

I crouched beside him. "In your dreams." I twisted a gloved hand into the filament and turned it, twisting it deeper into the flesh of his chest. He screamed, finally giving way to the pain.

"It's bad, isn't it? Is this how the little boys scream when you rape them?" I whispered as my guts churned with acid. As good as I was at this, I hated it. Hated the crying, the pleading. Hated feeling like I'd finally become the type of monster I'd sworn to wipe off the face of the earth.

And yet, this asshole deserved this and so, so much more.

His blue-green eyes flew to mine, and I saw the truth

there. "You don't know anything about me." But the lie trembled on his lips.

I leaned in and put my lips to his neck, fighting the urge to cringe. "It can be over in an instant. You and I both know I need your permission to access your memories. Give it, and I will show you mercy." Damn, I didn't really want permission, I didn't need more horrors to fill my mind.

He head-butted me, breaking my nose. I rolled back, holding a hand to my face as I choked and gagged on the heavy blood flow. Spitting a gob of it out, I nodded. "Fine. Then we do this the hard way."

Calvin reached the bottom step and shoved my bag across the floor to me. Neither of us liked this part, but this time I was going to make an exception. This sodomizing bastard deserved everything I could think up.

From my bag, I pulled a twenty-foot length of rope. Feeling Caine's eyes on me, I flipped the rope up over an exposed beam in the ceiling. A few quick knots and I had a noose settled over Caine's neck.

"Now, we all know you don't really need to breathe; that's not what this is for." I played with the rope a bit, loosening and tightening it until I had Caine on his tiptoes, dangling in the air in front of me. "Don't worry, that's just a plain old rope. No silver in it. Wouldn't want you to end yourself before I'm done with you." I smiled at him, baring my fangs. With one quick jerk, I yanked the net off. The movement spun him around and I was able to grab his hands and tie them behind his back with a section of the netting.

Long ago, I had realized a hard truth about myself. I hated this torture.

But the vampire in me—the monster—loved it.

After a few more minutes, I had his arms and legs tied so he was spread-eagled in front of me. Behind me, Calvin set up the folded-down dog crate I'd had made specifically for vampires. The wires were thick, hardened steel wrapped in silver. I pointed at it, barely two feet by three feet by three feet. "That's for you when you don't want to give up the answers I like. That's your home, dog."

Caine shivered and I stripped his pants off him. He was naked in front of me, but he didn't look away; there was no shame. His muscles rippled as I put a hand over his belly button, avoiding the welts and wounds that the netting had caused. For now, anyway.

"Tell me about the bioengineering."

"Fuck off and die."

"Not quite the answer I wanted." I pressed a finger into the hollow of his belly button, feeling the hard knot that had been his tie to a mother who'd been dead for hundreds of years. A shiver ran through his body. I lifted an eyebrow. "You tell me when you want me to stop and chat."

I pressed, slowly pushing him until the ropes restraining him stopped his body. Yet I kept pressing. My finger popped through the belly button and he grunted. I didn't look at him. I hooked my finger and dragged him back with me, the wound somewhat superficial at that point. "Calvin, hand me—"

"This is stupid, I don't need my stomach any more than you do. I don't need any of my organs," Caine snapped, fear making his voice waver.

"Oh, I know. But it hurts the same as if you did need them. The one thing," I held up a pair of pinchers with my free hand as I fished around in his gut for a line of intestine, "no one tells vampires is that along with their increased sensitivity to hearing, smelling, touching, and fucking, they also are blessed with an increased sensitivity to pain. But you already know that, being as old as you are."

I tugged a loop of his guts out through his belly button. I hooked it with the pinchers and rolled the tool 360 degrees. Caine's jaw dropped open and his eyes stared at his innards as they dripped fluid onto the floor. I didn't flinch. All I had to do was think about all the children he'd hurt, how many of them had suffered so terribly, their last minutes filled with horror and pain.

Yes, this time I was going to enjoy getting my answers.

I twisted the pincher again and tugged at the same time, spooling the guts as if they were pasta. "I think even when you're ready to talk, Caine, I might not be."

He looked at me, and I smiled up at him. "For your sins, Caine. Though I doubt this will help your soul go anywhere but hell."

CHAPTER 8

RACHEL

Self-defense wasn't the only thing I'd learned from my dad and my brothers. They'd helped me develop all kinds of skills my other friends had never dreamed of acquiring.

How to track just about anything.

How to use firearms.

How to drive like a NASCAR pro. That third one was coming in handy at the moment, although the streets of

Ohio were a hell of a lot easier to maneuver than midtown Manhattan.

"How'd you know where to find me?" Derrick rested a hand on the dash as he juggled his attention between the black government-issue car behind us and the older sedan ahead.

"Please," I groaned, swerving around a stopped taxi. An oncoming car jerked away from us and laid on the horn, its tires squealing. "We've moved *long* past that shit, Derrick. Who the hell am I chasing and why is the government on us like white on rice?"

He let out a low moan as I veered around another taxi and into oncoming traffic, barely missing a Volvo before swinging back into the appropriate lane. I snuck a glance at Derrick, about to chastise him for his stubbornness, but I saw blood seeping through the shirt he'd taken off and wrapped around his thigh.

"Shit. That's bad."

He untied the shirt, moved it around to a dry spot, then retied it, trying to hide his cringe from pain. "Flesh wound. Don't lose that car."

I looked into the rearview mirror. "I'm more worried about losing them." I motioned my head toward the black vehicle still chasing us.

Derrick paled even more when he saw how close they were. "My bag. My research…is it…"

"Hidden. They sacked my place trying to find it, but they didn't. It's safe."

"Thank you." He paused. "If they catch us…" His words came out breathy. "If they do, you have to leave me behind, Rachel." He grabbed my arm. "Promise me."

"Absolutely not." I shrugged him off with more force than intended, but I wanted the message to come across loud and clear.

"Rachel."

I shifted a quick glance his way before looking back at the road. "No. This is like the desert, you dickhead. No man left behind."

"This *isn't* like the desert, Rach. This is bigger than the both of us. What I've uncovered... One of us has to get out of this and get this information to someone who can do something about it."

"And who is that?"

He was quiet for several seconds. "I haven't figured that out yet. This stretches into the higher levels of government."

I remembered the circled area on the Iraqi map. "The Pentagon?"

He remained silent.

My anger surged. "I know you're trying to pull some macho save-the-chick bullshit right now, but the car riding my fucking ass proves that I'm *in this*. They know where I live, Derrick."

He let out a deep sigh. "Yes, I think someone in the Pentagon is involved."

"Then go to the CIA or the FBI. Those guys hate each other."

"They're in it, too."

"*What?*"

The government car smashed into my back bumper, slamming us forward. I whipped the wheel and skidded around the car in front of us, barely missing an oncoming vehicle. The driver screamed at us with his horn while jamming his middle finger into the air.

Gunshots rang out behind us and Derrick and I both ducked.

My heart skipped a beat, then kicked into overdrive. "Those fuckers aren't playing around."

"They want this quiet. They'll blow off this car chase by calling us terrorists." He groaned. "This is exactly why I stayed away from you the past two years. I knew you'd catch wind of it and end up in the thick of it. But when I saw you in the alley…" He turned to look at me, fear in his eyes. "I never should have come to your apartment."

"What you should or should not have done is a moot point. I *am* in this now, so deal with it. I take it they want your information. Is it backed up anywhere?"

"Like on the cloud?" he asked in disbelief, but his voice was weaker than before. "I'm not a fucking idiot."

"So the stuff in your bag is all we've got?"

"No. There's a backup in a safety deposit box in New Jersey. Under an alias."

The back window of the car I was chasing burst out and landed on the road. I swerved to miss the debris as I saw a rifle tip extend out the open window. The woman from the park was holding it up.

"Derrick! Duck!"

Derrick and I both hunched down in our seats. A gunshot rang out and the government car accelerated and shot into oncoming traffic.

The car in front of us sped up and darted around a taxi. I pressed the accelerator, about to swerve to clear a motorcycle, but the oncoming traffic began screeching to a halt, the cars swerving into the lane in front of me.

"Shit!"

I managed to avoid hitting any moving vehicles, but could only watch as the taillights of the car we were chasing careened around a corner.

"Did she take out his tire?" I glanced over my shoulder.

"No," he said, looking behind us. "She took out the driver."

I shook my head in disbelief. "How? There's no way she could have made that shot with such accuracy at that distance."

Sirens sounded in the distance, and it hit me that during our several-minute chase we hadn't encountered a single law enforcement officer.

The passenger door of the government car pushed open and one of the men who had been in my apartment stumbled out, blood trickling down the side of his face. My pulse kicked into overdrive when I saw the gun in his hand.

"We have to *go*, Rachel." Anxiety thickened Derrick's voice.

"No shit." But that was easier said than done. The traffic in front of us had no intention of moving anytime soon, that much was obvious. I backed up several feet, then headed for the sidewalk.

"And we have to follow that car. We can't let them get away."

"I'm working on it." I needed to get out of here before the cops showed up. A gunshot rang out, shattering the back glass. The fact that they were being so blatant in their pursuit only proved that they would do anything to catch us. I was pretty sure we wouldn't walk away from this alive.

"Rachel."

I gunned it, sending pedestrians scattering left and right as I pulled around a parked sedan and into an open lane.

"They turned that way." He pointed to where they'd disappeared.

"I know!" I hadn't meant to be short, but it wasn't an everyday affair for me to take part in a car chase and shootout. I breathed a sigh of relief as I turned the corner, heading away from the parking lot of cars. The police were behind us, thank God, along with our trigger-happy tails, but the car was a good minute ahead of us. I had no idea how we were going to find it.

Derrick must have been thinking the same thing. "You live here. What's in that direction?"

"Correction. I live in *East Harlem*. But lucky for you, I know this area. There's nothing much over here. Just a few abandoned buildings a couple of blocks ahead." He was on to something. "So who's the guy?"

He remained silent.

Dammit. "Do you think she wants the same information you're after?"

He hesitated long enough to draw my attention.

"Derrick! I'm not some fucking idiot, so stop treating me like one. We need that information, all right?"

"I don't know why she wants him, but I need the information Caine has. He's the key to everything."

"Since she didn't kill him, she must want to know what he knows, too. Which means we need to find him before he spills it all and she kills him. An abandoned warehouse would be the perfect place for her to get information."

"I think we have time. He's probably somewhat resistant to torture and not easy to kill."

"What is he, military? CIA?"

He laughed, but it sounded ragged. "No. Definitely not."

"Then who is he?"

"Like I said, you'd never believe me. Hell, I'm not sure I even believe it. But I do know I need to find him."

We drove around for fifteen minutes before I stomped on the brakes. "There!" Parked halfway down an alley was the older model sedan, the back window conspicuously missing. "There's no one in the car. They must have taken him inside that building."

His brow lowered as he studied the car. "Yeah, you're probably right."

There was no doubt it was a good place to take a kidnap victim. A fifteen-foot chain link fence surrounded the property. Not that it had deterred the taggers from spray painting designs on the dilapidated building. Stairs led up to a slightly ajar door.

"I bet you ten dollars they've gone up there." I pointed to the door. "How do we want to do this?"

"*We* aren't doing anything," he grunted, pulling out his revolver. "*You* are staying in the car."

"*What?* You really expect me to wait in the car? Have you lost your fucking mind?"

His eyes burned with intensity when they met mine. "This isn't a game, Rachel!"

"No fucking shit it's not. I just outran government goons while getting shot at. That was my second clue. The first was when those same goons sacked my apartment." I opened the car door and grabbed my messenger bag. "Let's go."

The passenger door opened as I walked around the front of the car. He stumbled out, grabbing the top of the door for support.

"Derrick?" I hurried over to him, surprised to see he'd bled through the shirt-bandage again. I tried to grab his arm to help him up, but he pushed me aside.

"Just give me a moment."

"You shouldn't walk on that leg."

"I'm fine." Anger drenched his words. "Just give me a minute."

Movement on the stairs caught my eye. "Get down." I pushed him back into the car. "They're leaving."

I squatted and quietly pushed the door closed, then moved around to the front of the car, keeping an eye on the two figures making their way down the front steps, about a hundred feet away. One was unmistakably the woman from the park even though a hood covered her head. The other figure, a man, confused me. While the woman moved with stealth and grace, he hobbled down the stairs, taking his time as he maneuvered a broken step. When he reached the bottom, his face was illuminated by the moonlight and I blinked in surprise.

He was old.

That didn't make sense. I'd caught a glimpse of the

woman, she couldn't be much older than twenty-five, but this man had to be close to eighty. Was he her co-worker? Her grandfather?

They walked soundlessly across the lot from the old building to the chain link fence. She was in the lead, so she grabbed a portion of the metal and lifted it, letting the older man duck through before following him to the car.

He opened the car door, but she stopped, standing perfectly still, and slowly pivoted around, lifting her face to the air. Then she turned toward the car and got inside before the old man drove away.

Where was the guy she'd thrown into her trunk? He could still be back there, but I stood by my assertion that the abandoned building was the perfect spot to interrogate him. Had she gotten her information already? Was the informant already dead? Only one way to find out.

Once I was sure they were gone I hurried to open the passenger door. "I'm going inside."

"What?" He pushed the door wider and swung out his legs. "I'm going with you."

"Not a chance," I said. "You'll only slow me down."

His face twisted with anger. I knew it was a low blow, but I had to get through to him.

"This isn't your fight, Rachel." But his words lacked the bite they needed. His body was tense with pain.

"If this involves bioterrorism, it *does* involve me. It involves all of us."

Derrick cursed under his breath, then reached into his jacket and pulled out a voice recorder. "His name is

Caine. He has red hair, pulled back into a ponytail. He is *dangerous*, so if he's restrained, do *not* release him."

I held up my Glock. "I can take care of myself."

He shook his head. "No. If what he says is true, you'll need this." He reached into his coat again and pulled out a handgun.

I snorted. "My gun works just fine."

"No," he insisted. "This one has silver bullets."

"What?"

He pushed the gun into my hand. "If you're going in there, you have to be prepared. This gun has silver bullets."

I laughed. "Do you think there's a werewolf down there?"

His serious eyes met mine. "I don't know."

My jaw dropped. "Oh, my God. You really think there might be one."

He rubbed his head. "No. I don't know. I'm not sure if they exist. But he's something else."

"Did you suffer some brain injury I don't know about?"

"No," he groaned. "Be alert. They move silently, so be on your guard."

"So now they're ninjas."

"This isn't funny, Rachel. This is serious. You need to be ready. Find Caine. Ask him where the facility is. Who's running it. Ask him if they are close. Get it all on the recorder. And hurry. I suspect his kidnappers won't be gone long."

I took the gun and tucked it into my messenger bag.

"Don't worry about me," I called back as I made my way to the fence. "I've got this covered."

As I crawled through the chain link fence and then strode across the overgrown parking lot, I wondered what I had gotten myself into.

Chapter 9

LEA

Caine writhed at my feet, the pinchers wrapped in four feet of his guts now. Not a lot, really, when you consider how many feet of intestine are in a human body. I knew I was running the facts to keep myself calm. As much as he deserved what I was doing to him, that didn't keep me from feeling like a monster.

"I have to tell you, I thought you would have spilled

your guts by now," I said, then covered my mouth. "Sorry, bad pun."

He grimaced. "You won't get me to speak."

I looked up to see Calvin staring at us, completely dispassionate. In some ways, he was better at this than I was. "Did you bring the blood?"

He gave a tight nod and carefully went through our bag of tools. I crouched beside Caine and drew in a deep breath. "We don't have time for games, my friend. So that means we're going to do this the even harder way."

He spit a gob of blood at me, hitting me in the throat. "Fuck you."

I wiped the blood off, flicking it to the floor. "No, Caine. This most definitely will not fuck me. You, on the other hand..."

Calvin handed me a silver flask. My gloves kept the metal from burning me. I unstopped it with my teeth, spitting the cork across the room. I took a long sniff of the contents and wrinkled my nose. "Blood of an alcoholic priest. Do you know what that means, Caine?"

His eyes widened and he tried to scoot away, but I pinned him to the floor with ease. "It's a myth."

"No," I leaned over him, knees on his arms and one hand on his mouth to hold it open, "it's not."

I poured the blood into his mouth, and while he fought to spit it out, we both knew his efforts were in vain. Our bodies absorbed blood the instant it touched our mouths. Like leeches, we took it in; that was what we were designed to do. A vampire expelling blood would be like a human trying to reject air. It just wasn't possible. I handed the empty flask to Calvin.

Caine swallowed the last of the blood, gagging. I sat on his chest, drumming my fingers lightly on his bare skin. "You know, for years I wanted to find a way to make you assholes speak the truth. To say things you were bound by vows to your master not to say. But the blood of a priest is a cleansing thing, and even better, an alcoholic...well, you can imagine the combination. Do you feel it now, Caine?"

I peered into his eyes, which were going misty as the blood coursed through his veins. I should know; Calvin had used the blood on me in a trial. He never spoke of what I'd said while...well, under the influence...but according to him, it had worked. I chose not to think about the questions he'd asked me or what he might know of my past.

Caine gave a low groan under me.

"Why were you talking to the reporter?" I eased up a bit, sitting further down to give him the illusion I trusted him.

"The government," he mumbled. "The government is helping us."

I kept my face straight. A part of me had seriously doubted his earlier words to Derrick. "The human government?"

Caine tried to nod but only managed a shift of his head. "They're protecting us from you, actually."

Calvin sucked in a breath. "Explains why you elders have gotten so hard to find lately."

Snickering, Caine rolled his hips under me. "I'd really, really like to fuck you. Seriously, that should be taken for the compliment it is. Because we all know I'm not into full-fledged women. You, though, I'd do you in a heartbeat. Especially if I could tie you up and take you from behind. I'd lay money down that your ass is still virginal, isn't it?"

I slapped him hard, the crack of his vertebrae making me more than happy. "What else do you know about the government helping the vampires?"

His eyes rolled. "They keep us in a safe place. Safe from you."

Calvin leaned over Caine's head. "Where?"

"Close by, with all the other monsters," he snickered. This was a bad side effect of the blood. It made vampires fucking goofy, and while they still spoke the truth, the longer it was in their system, the harder it was to get that truth to make any sense.

"Give me a name. Someone who's helping you."

He grinned at me, his teeth still pink from the blood. "Oh, I have a name, and it's a good one. A perfect name just for you. Are you ready for it?"

I grabbed him by the shoulders and pulled him up so we were face to face. "Tell me."

He licked his lips. "Victor."

I reeled back, anger lighting me up as I let out a scream. "That fucking bastard. I'm going to rip out his throat and watch him bleed at my feet."

Calvin grabbed my hand, a dangerous thing to do when a vamp was worked up, but he knew I would sooner cut off my own arm than hurt him. "Easy, Lea. Victor is your patron. Maybe he has information for us. We don't know what kind of 'truth' this is from Caine."

Hearing his name, Caine rolled on the floor snickering.

I kicked him in the back for good measure. "Get the net, Cal. We're going to speak to Victor and we can't have Caine leaving before we're done with him."

Call it a hunch, but if something *was* going down with the vamps, then Victor would be here in New York as well.

"Oh, not the net," the vamp whimpered, holding a hand up to me.

I grabbed the pincers still wound around his guts, using them to lift him into the air. A silent scream opened his mouth as he bounced on the end of his intestines like a fish on a hook. "You're lucky I don't shoot you full of liquid silver."

Calvin handed me the net and I wrapped Caine in it, and then hung him from the ceiling. His hands were bound behind his back, his guts pressed against the net. Everywhere the filament touched, his skin sizzled and the scent of cooking meat slowly filling the air. Calvin stuffed a rag into the vamp's mouth and slapped a piece of duct tape over it.

I pointed at Caine. "Don't you fucking move. I'll be back."

His eyes rolled back into his head. By the time we got back, the priest's blood would be completely out of his system. Hell, it was probably almost gone now. That was the problem; such a small amount burned out so fast.

I strode out of the building, tugging my cowl around my head. Calvin was much slower, but he would never allow me to help him. A long time ago, he used to lead the way. But now...now he had no choice but to follow. To sit back and let me do the lion's share of the work.

We both knew what was coming, though neither of us talked about it. I needed a new helper and he was going to have to train them.

I paused as I opened the car door and tipped my head to scent the air. There was no sign of any other vamps; no one was coming to rescue Caine. My diversion also gave Calvin time to catch up with me again without creating the impression I was waiting for him. I slid into the backseat of the car; Calvin took his place in the driver's seat. I said nothing, but then, we both knew.

"Say it," he grumped at me.

"No. Not yet. Let me believe you will be with me forever," I said softly. "You are my one friend, Calvin. Let me pretend for a little while longer."

He pulled away from the curb. For a split second, I thought I saw headlights across the way, but nothing moved in the darkness and there were no other flickers of light. Seeing things was not a good sign in my world. When vamps went crazy, people died. A lot of people.

"Do you know where we're going?"

I nodded. "If Victor really is a part of whatever's unfolding, he'll be in town. And if he's in town, he'll be at his restaurant."

Calvin jerked in his seat as if I'd goosed him. "Love of Blood?"

My jaw twitched. "He named it for me. Thought I'd appreciate it."

A laugh bubbled out of him. "Did he think you'd suddenly spread your legs for him?"

My mouth twisted. "Apparently."

I gave him directions, and before long we had

reached *Amore Sangre*. Calvin waved at me. "You go in, I'll follow."

The thing was, the restaurant was at the top of a twenty-story building and exclusive in that hoity-toity way Manhattan restaurants had down to an art. I took the stairs. Bolting up them, I was faster than any elevator. Once I reached the top, I pushed the door open and approached the bouncer at the front of the restaurant.

"Reservations?"

"I'm here to see Victor."

"The boss is eating with a companion tonight, and he's not to be disturbed."

Like that was going to stop me. I strode forward and the bouncer blocked me.

Or tried to. The moment he stepped in my path, I grabbed his arm and flung him into a wall across the hall. The restaurant hummed with low voices that came to a grinding halt the moment I stepped into view.

I had to admit, swathed in my black cowl, weapons at my side, I probably looked like a hitman. I scanned the crowd, finding Victor with ease. Mid-thirties, the body of a young Adonis, blond hair, and bright green eyes that saw far too much. Victor wasn't just a billionaire, he was an intellect, and that was what made him dangerous. His father had been my patron—basically funding my hunts because he believed wholeheartedly in killing the 'demons'—before him.

Victor Senior had always stayed out of my way. His son, on the other hand, was a complete pain in my ass who need to be put in his place once and for all. He could dabble with the government all he wanted, but the second he put his toe into vamp-infested waters, that was my territory. And if what Caine told me was true, then Junior was playing both sides of the fence. Paying me to kill the vamps, while he funded a government program to keep them safe like endangered animals.

The person sitting with Victor confirmed Caine's accusation.

I strode across the room, heading straight for them.

Their conversation came to a stuttering stop as I slammed my hands onto their table. She had the smarts to try and back away, but I snaked a hand out, circling her throat. She bared her fangs at me and hissed, which seemed to shock the hell out of my patron, if his widening eyes were any indication. I tightened my fist, but my eyes were on him.

"Victor, how many times have I told you not to play with vampires?"

His jaw dropped and I had the satisfaction of watching him squirm. "I didn't know."

She glared at him and hissed out, "Bullshit."

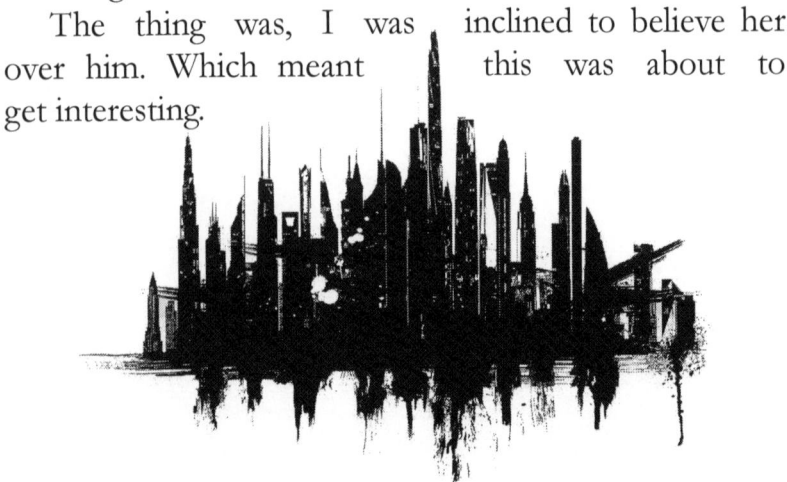

The thing was, I was inclined to believe her over him. Which meant this was about to get interesting.

Chapter 10

RACHEL

As I made my way up the rickety steps, I asked myself once again: What the hell was I doing? Derrick was right. This wasn't my story…or at least it wasn't the story I had thought I was pursuing. I barely knew anything about it. The responsible thing to do would be to call 911 and let the police handle the whole mess. But I hadn't ever been known for taking the safe road. Maybe it was all that influence from my older brothers.

Even in the Middle East, I'd been known as Risky Rachel, willing to rush into danger to get a good story. If I were completely honest, I was an adrenaline junkie. I loved the rush of danger. Still, contrary to what people thought when they first met me, I didn't embark on fool's errands. I always had some idea of what to expect. I had multiple scenarios and escape routes sketched out in my head. There was always a plan.

This time I had none.

At the top of the stairs, I slowly nudged the door open, my gun drawn in my right hand and a flashlight in my left, my senses alert. I let my eyes adjust to the light and crept into a trashed room. It looked like a grand hall with wide stairs going up and down. The ornate railings hinted that this place had once been something grand. Now it looked like the perfect setup for a haunted house.

The question was, which way to go? Then I silently groaned. I'd seen enough horror movies to know the answer.

The basement it was.

My pulse kicked into overdrive, a dull beat in my temple. My body was primed for fight or flight, and the hyper awareness that came with it was such a rush. God, I'd missed this.

But I pushed the horror of that realization to the back of my mind. I'd psychoanalyze myself later. Right now, I had to find a man named Caine.

I crept silently down the stairs. A soft light fanned out from a door at the bottom of the stairs. When I pushed it open, the smell hit me first—a combination of urine and feces and another distinctive scent, one that I knew all too well.

Blood. A lot of it.

My throat tightened and I forced myself to take a deep breath and confront the very real possibility that Caine was dead. Either that or I was entering the torture chamber I had suspected from the outset. As I crept closer, the smell of blood grew stronger, and I decided it was probably both. Then I heard a muffled moan of pain that confirmed he was probably still alive…in some form.

For all I knew it was a trap, but nothing could have prepared me for what I saw as I rounded a stack of shelves.

A naked man, covered in blood, hung from the ceiling, suspended in a silver net. His hands were tied behind his back and duct tape covered his mouth, but it was the sight of the intestines spilling from his abdomen that made me almost lose my lunch. Huge puddles of blood covered the floor.

His eyes were wide with fear and panic when he saw me. His body flinched and a sizzling sound filled the air, joined by the smell of burnt flesh. How could he even still be alive?

I backed against a wall, holding my gun as I looked around the room to see if we were alone.

"Is anyone else here?"

He shook his head wildly.

"Is your name Caine?"

Surprise filled his eyes. He didn't respond, but that was answer enough. Derrick had warned me that Caine was dangerous, but he looked pretty incapacitated at the moment. What the hell was I going to do? I couldn't leave him like that.

I pulled out my cell phone to call 911, then cursed. No service. "I'm going to go call for help." I made a move to exit, but he panicked, thrashing enough to make his body sway and touch the net, which burnt his flesh with a loud crackle.

What the hell was that? An electric filament? I didn't see any cords attached to it. The net dangled from what looked like a meat hook.

I crept closer to him and carefully reached through the loops in the material to rip the tape off his face and pull out his gag.

"Help me," he pleaded, his voice a whisper.

"I need to call for help."

"No! Don't leave me!" He shook his head, panic in his voice. "Just get me down."

There was no way I could lift the net off the hook with him inside it, so I glanced around to find something I could use to cut him down.

A utility knife lay on a table next to a bottle of red water that looked like it was boiling. "What the fuck..." I whispered.

"Please!" he pleaded again, regaining my attention. "They'll be back soon. Save me!"

I stuffed the gun in the back of my pants. I'd suspected the net was electrified, but I saw no evidence of any cords, so I grabbed the knife and hurried over to him, holding the blade up to cut the net. Then I lowered it. "I want answers first."

"What answers?" he squealed. "What are you talking about?"

"I know your name is Caine."

"No! My name is Matt. Please!"

"Cut the shit. I saw you in the park. I saw her take you, and I know you were with Derrick." The real question was how he was still alive, holding a coherent conversation?

"She's going to kill you." His voice changed. The panic was gone, replaced with authority. "She's going to kill us both. Cut me down."

I found myself reaching up to slash the net, but I pulled back again, shaking my head to clear out the desire to please him.

Please him? What the fuck?

I took a step back. "Where's the facility?"

He groaned, then asked, with a hint of humor, "Where's *Derrick*?"

"He was injured, which you should know since you're the one who hurt him. He sent *me*."

He laughed. "*You?* Do you even know what the facility *is*?"

"I know enough."

"You're dabbling into things that don't concern you, little girl. Dark, ugly things. Your worst nightmares come to life."

I released a harsh laugh. "You obviously don't know me very well."

"I'd like to get to know you better." His words were husky and held the sultry promise of pleasure. "I'd like to fuck you until you beg me for more."

A wave of heat and lust gushed through my body. I shook it off, horrified that this literally gutted man could do this to me. "What is that? Hypnosis?"

"You really don't know what I am." He laughed, but the movement jarred him against the filament, searing his flesh. "Cut me down!"

His voice pushed into my head and every fiber of my being wanted to obey. I started to saw through the net before the fog cleared from my head. What the hell was he doing to me?

I took several steps back this time. "What type of bioterrorism is the facility trying to create?"

"How are you resisting me?" he roared, thrashing his body in his frustration. But I must have sawed through enough to weaken the remaining fibers. His body dropped into the bloody pool beneath him.

I scrambled backward as he flailed with the net, pulling the gun from the back of my jeans. I didn't get to it in time. Without warning, I was slammed to the concrete floor. Pain shot through my head, but I was too stunned to assess my injuries because I was looking into Caine's face.

A slow, predatory smile lit up his face. "You have no idea how much I need you right now." Then his lips widened, exposing his teeth, and two long canines extended past his other teeth.

I tried to thrash away from him, but he didn't even budge.

His right hand grabbed my head and turned it roughly, exposing my neck.

"What kind of sick pervert are you?" I bucked again, my panic escalating.

He released a low chuckle as he slowly lowered his mouth to my neck, murmuring in my ear, "The very worst kind."

Chapter 11

LEA

I squeezed the female vamp's neck slowly, breaking the bones through sheer pressure. I kept an eye on her, and one on Victor. Her eyes bugged out as she scrabbled at my hands. The patrons around us ran screaming as they realized someone was being killed in the middle of their entree course.

Not all that appetizing for the humans, apparently.

Victor, though, he was anything but bothered. The cold bastard cracked open one of the oysters on his plate and sucked down the slippery juices. If he thought I was impressed, he had another thing coming. I grabbed his steak knife and jammed it into his companion's chest, breaking the blade off against her ribs as she bucked and writhed.

Victor coughed into his hand. "Would you kill her already?"

I held her where she was. Young, she was very young, like the vampire in Montreal. I pulled her across the table so her feet kicked him for me. One heel caught him in the cheek, cutting him open.

The scent of his blood caught me off guard and I breathed through my mouth, taking in the flavor as if it were a wine, tasting it all the way in the back of my throat. "Victor, you smell different than you did the last time we spoke." I suspected he was dabbling in vampire blood. But just from this pretty girl? Or someone else? He paled and I bared my teeth at him. "Who are you working for, *Vic*? No games. I know the government is in on something with my marks."

With a snort, he leaned back in his chair. His momentary lack of composure was gone in a flash, covered by his usual arrogance. If I didn't know he was such a slimy bastard, his looks and confidence would have drawn me to him.

In some ways, he reminded me of Calvin when he was younger. Except Calvin had never been anything but painfully honest with me.

You're a fucking vampire. We work together; there will never be anything else between us.

I shook off the past and glared at Victor as the female

vamp slowed her flailing. "Victor, tell me what you know or you will join your cheap whore here on the table."

"You wouldn't dare."

I threw the vamp across the room with enough force that her body shattered through the plate glass. She hung suspended for a moment and then fell from the sky. Victor scrambled backward as three of his thugs came out of nowhere, rushing me.

The first one I caught with the heel of my boot, right over his Adam's apple, his throat bursting open from the blow. Number two pulled a gun and nabbed me with one of the bullets. I thought nothing of it until the burn of silver arched my back. *"Pinche cerdo!"* I screeched in my mother tongue, stumbling to my hands and knees with the pain.

The report of a second gun going off, and the thug's head bobbed once, a bloom of red right between his eyes.

I caught Calvin's scent as I struggled to control the pain long enough to take out the third bodyguard. I jerked as a hand touched my shoulder. "They're gone."

"Victor, too?"

"Yes."

I bit my bottom lip as the pain cascaded down and then back up my entire body, a wave of mind-numbing heat. "Dig it out, it's sitting at the top of my shoulder blade." I couldn't push silver bullets out of my body. And these wounds would heal far slower. Damn Victor and his games. I should have turned his father into a vamp so I wouldn't have to deal with his idiot son.

I wobbled to my feet and splayed across the table

where Victor had been dining moments before, wanting to make it easier for Calvin. Sirens were approaching from a distance, drawing closer with a speed we would be hard pressed to outmaneuver. He put one hand on my back, his body pressing against mine as he leaned into his task.

"You know better. Victor doesn't react well when he's cornered."

I kept my eyes closed as the knife sliced through my skin and dug into the muscle. Having a body that was sensitized not only to pain but pleasure, I was having a hard time not thinking about this particular position. Calvin would not appreciate it if he knew I was wondering whether he still held to his rules about cross-species hanky-panky. A giggle escaped me and he let out a sigh as he popped the bullet out.

"Endorphins kicking in already?"

Laughing softly, I nodded, my face rubbing against the high-grade linen tablecloth. "Sorry."

"Yeah, yeah, I know. Pain and pleasure. You vamps are fucking sick."

And just like that, the endorphins were gone. I pushed myself to my feet and looked away from Calvin. I still saw him as the young man I knew fifty years ago. And he still saw me as the vampire he only helped because I was killing my own kind. "Time to go."

I jogged to the open door. The elevator pinged softly, no doubt bringing a riot squad right to us. I glanced at Calvin. "Think you can play the feeble old man who couldn't get away with the others?"

He glared at me as he slowly went to his knees and

stuffed himself under a table. "Fine. Go deal with Caine. And don't play with him this time, just get the information and finish him off." He handed me the car keys and I stuffed them down the front of my top.

I gave him a mock salute and ran for the window I'd thrown the vamp through. Reaching out, I hooked my fingers into the tiny grooves of the building and quickly worked my way down the side. There wasn't so much as a peep from the cops. A sharp blast of air curled around me as I paused and stared up at the restaurant. There should have been police crawling all over the scene. But the sirens had stopped and there were no lights. No flashing bulbs indicating evidence being collected on camera.

My mouth went dry. What if it wasn't the police who'd shown up?

I scrambled back up the side of the building, driven along by fear for Calvin's safety. I'd left him there, and we'd just assumed he'd be safe in the hands of the authorities. But the closer I got, the more certain I was that we had been wrong. "Fucking Victor, when I find you I'm going to cut you into pieces."

I pulled myself into the restaurant as slowly as I could. The room was undisturbed, but the table Calvin had been under was empty. Lifting my head, I scented the air.

Two vampires and a human I didn't recognize.

"THIS IS THE POLICE, PUT DOWN YOUR WEAPONS." I clapped my hands over my ears as the voice boomed into the room. I had no choice. I had to go even though it tore me up to essentially walk away from my...from Calvin.

As I worked my way down the side of the building once more, the activity going on above sounded just like it should for an in-progress investigation. But Calvin was gone, and a small part of me thought—hoped—maybe he would be waiting for me at the car.

It was empty. I dropped into the driver's side and slammed the car into gear, my foot hard on the gas. Nothing was going to stop me from getting the information I needed from Caine. I'd gone easy on him before.

It seemed like it only took seconds to return to the broken-down old building. I hit the brakes hard next to a parked car a half block away and stared into the passenger seat, the smell of blood hitting me in the face.

The reporter stared back at me, his eyes dulling as death curled around him. I got out and opened his door. "What in God's name is going on here? Do you know?"

"Not God's name; maybe the devil's," he whispered. "She's in there. She should be back by now. I told her to be careful. Tell her..." A breath rattled out of him as he passed out. I peered into the car. A blood-soaked shirt was tied around his thigh. He let out a low groan and breathed out one word, a name. "Rachel."

I turned to face the building.

"Is that who you sent in there? The blonde you were with?"

Only one way to find out.

Leaving the car behind, I sprinted for the old building, slamming through the main door. I didn't care who heard me now. If there was a human in here with

Caine, he could control her, make her free him. This was a disaster.

Her scent was heavy in the air, and with it, a hint of her blood. Which meant she was probably already dead. Rather than use the stairs, I leapt up and over the railing, falling through the open space all the way to the basement, the air whistling around me. Landing in a crouch, I took a split second to register the scene in front of me.

Caine was drinking from a woman's neck, but she had a gun trained on him.

Damn, he was about to get the last surprise he ever had.

The sound of the gun going off bounced around the room and Caine's body jerked hard. It wouldn't kill him, but it would bring him close enough that there would be no coming back from the injury.

I grabbed his leg and dragged him off her, spinning out a blade and cutting his heart out in a few swift motions.

"You alive?" I said over my shoulder as I guaranteed the job was done twice by removing Caine's head and pushing it away from his body. With the old vamps, they rarely turned to ash, which meant you had to take extra precautions to make sure they were really dead. "Hey, are you alive?" I spun on my heels and stared into the barrel of the gun that just sent Caine down the path to his fate.

I had to give her credit. The gun was steady. I slowly lifted my hands into the air. "You might not believe this, but I think we're on the same side."

Her eyes narrowed. "And what side would that be?"

"The side that feeds bastards like this to the fishes."
I thought she believed me.
Until she cocked the hammer of the gun.

Chapter 12

RACHEL

My heart raced and the bite on my neck throbbed, but all I could do was focus on the woman in front of me. I kept my gun trained on her. "What are you?"

A slow smile spread across her face. A predatory smile right down to the canines peeking past her lips. "You wouldn't believe me if I told you."

Probably not. But whatever she was, she wasn't normal. The way she'd ripped out the asshole's heart was proof enough of that. I couldn't let go of the fact that Derrick had told me to use his silver bullets. He'd said that Caine wasn't a werewolf, but that he was something else. Bile rose in my throat as I considered the implications, but I swallowed it. This was not the time to panic.

The woman tilted her head ever so slightly. "Maybe you should be asking what *he* was."

She took a slow step toward me and I kept my gun trained on her. "Come one step closer and I'll shoot."

She stopped and held up her hands in surrender, but I wasn't fooled for a moment.

"Okay," I said, taking the bait. "What was he?"

"A child molester. An abomination."

"Is that why you had him hanging in a net after you gutted him?" I still didn't understand how he could have survived that, and with enough strength to tackle me and drink my blood. "Is he some kind of pervert who thinks he's a vampire?"

She didn't answer, only stared at me with her dark, penetrating eyes.

But a new thought nudged its way to the surface. "Is he the one who's been killing people all over the city?"

Her left shoulder lifted into a slight shrug. "People get killed in this city every day."

"Yeah, but you don't see many of them with the blood drained from their bodies and occult symbols carved into their skin."

Her eyes widened slightly at that and I wondered which part had caught her by surprise. Why didn't I think it was both? Maybe because she'd found that pervert Caine drinking my blood. But if he was the one who'd committed the murders—and there was a good chance he was since the coincidence was too strong—that meant the woman in front of me had stopped the serial killer.

Only she looked more deadly than he had.

"Why did you want to talk to him?"

She raised an eyebrow. "Who says I did?"

"If you want to kill someone, you don't gut them and hang them in a metal net. Not unless you're a serial killer, and you don't look like a crazy serial killer." No, her eyes were too cold and calculated for that. "So if you went to that much trouble, I know you must have tortured him for a reason. You went to extreme measures to get the information he had."

Her jaw tightened; the movement was nearly imperceptible in the dim light, but I caught it.

Dammit. Derrick was desperate to get information from Caine, and this woman had just killed him. Then again, I'd shot the guy in the head, which likely hadn't helped matters. But what if this woman already had the information that Derrick and I needed? Yet I knew she hadn't gotten it all. Otherwise, I wouldn't have found him alive. "What does drinking people's blood have to do with bioterrorism?"

Dark eyes rolled upward, as if seeking an answer from the heavens above. "Do you just blurt whatever comes into your head?"

I lifted my left shoulder into a shrug, my T-shirt sticking to my chest. I really needed to get pressure on my wound or I was going to pass out soon. "Pretty much."

"Bioterrorism? What would *I* know about

bioterrorism? I'm just a vigilante seeking justice, remember?"

I released a sharp laugh, which sent a new round of pain to my throbbing neck. Blood trickled down my chest from the open wound. It was taking both hands to keep the gun steady. "If you're a vigilante, I'm the Queen of Sheba."

A genuine smile tugged at her lips. "I can fix that for you." She nodded toward my neck. Something flickered in her eyes...hunger.

"Yeah, I'm gonna pass on that." I had to get out of here. If I lost consciousness down here with her, I was as good as dead. I slid backward toward a wall and pushed my back against it, thankful that she stayed where she was. "I have a friend waiting outside for me."

"He's not going to be of much help to you." She said it as matter-of-factly as if she'd told me it was raining.

"I'll be the judge of that." She'd lie to me without one ounce of guilt. I could see that in her. But I'd left Derrick in bad shape. Why hadn't I called 911?

The look in her eyes shifted to something that resembled compassion, and it warred with the hunger residing in the dark depths. Maybe I could use it to my advantage.

A wave of dizziness washed through my head. I needed to get my answers and get them quickly. I pointed at the mangled body between us. "What was his name?"

She grinned again. "Caine. But you already knew that."

"What do you know about the bioterrorism?"

She took a step toward me. "I know that this matter does not concern you."

It was time to go for broke. I had to convince her

that I was a player in this game—someone worthy of confiding in. I decided to throw out the name from the text. "What do you know about the Asclepius Project?"

Genuine confusion drifted over her face, but it only took a second for her eyes to harden again. "Never heard of it."

That, I believed, but now it was obvious she wanted to know what I knew. I took a backward step toward the stairs, my legs shaking. I worried I'd never make the one-story climb. "Do you know where the facility is?"

That got her attention. "*What* facility?" She took two more steps toward me.

I jabbed the gun toward her. "Stay back. I *will* shoot you and I'm an excellent shot." She didn't seem to know much about *anything*, which meant she probably wouldn't be able to help me.

"I am sorry. I can't let you leave."

I released another short laugh, hoping my fear didn't seep into my false bravado. "My gun says you can't stop me."

She leapt for me and I pulled the trigger, aiming for her heart. I expected her to crumple to the ground, but she kept coming. The impact knocked the gun from my hand, sending it skittering across the broken tiles. The shiny glint of metal caught my eye, and I tried to flip over to grab it, but a pair of men's shoes appeared next to it and a wrinkled hand picked it up. I was about to beg the newcomer for help, but he handed the gun to the woman who was still holding me to the ground. My gaze shifted to her chest, blood seeping through her shirt directly over her heart. Her face was contorted with pain and rage, but just as I was wondering how she still had the strength to pin me to the floor, the butt of the gun headed toward my temple.

And then there was nothing.

Chapter 13

LEA

The bullet trail burned, the silver sticking to me even though the thing had gone straight through me. I clamped a hand over it and stared at Calvin. "How the hell did you get away from them and back here so damn fast?"

He shrugged. "I might be old, but I'm not feeble yet. And you know that taxis in this town are fast when you pay them well." He let out a breath and waved at the woman on the floor. "What are we doing with her?"

I couldn't help but stare at him. Something was off, something was different…and not in a good way. A subtle scent clung to him that made the hair on the back of my neck stand at attention.

He pushed at the leggy blonde on the floor with his foot. "If I were forty years younger, I'd be begging to take her home with us." His shoulders were tight and even the cadence of his voice was off.

What the fuck had happened to him?

I wasn't fooled for an instant; I knew his avoidance tactics well. "Wrap her neck up. I don't want to get too close."

Stepping back, I watched as he bound her wounds from Caine, checked her pulse, and then stood. Calvin moved faster than he had even a few hours ago. Only one explanation made sense.

Putting his hands on his hips, he gave a slow nod. "There, she's good to go."

I swallowed hard, fearing the worst. Fearing that I would lose my only friend if I was wrong. Calvin didn't like to be touched, even more so when it came to me, but I had to know, and there was only one way to know for sure. Before he could react, I grabbed him and yanked him to me. The reporter's blood was everywhere and my fangs itched to feel flesh under them. A poor excuse, but it wouldn't take much to push me over the edge if I ate nothing. His skin gave way with a quick pop and the warmth of his blood coursed over my tongue. Calvin struggled for a split second before the pleasure hit him and he slumped in my arms. "I hate you," he mumbled.

I took only a little of his blood, enough to tie him to

me. Rougher than I meant to, I pushed him away from me. "You taste like shit."

He glared at me and I drew in a deep breath, focusing my mind and putting power into my voice. I wasn't strong with this ability, but it would have to be enough. "Who took you from the restaurant?"

Calvin's eyelids fluttered and his breathing shifted. "I'm not supposed to tell you."

"Did they give you blood?"

"Yes."

Gods above and below, had he turned on me? "Did you...ask them to?"

"No. They forced me and told me to forget."

Someone wanted to control Calvin, but how did they even know he was my helper?

There was only one answer. That fucking asshole Victor.

"Forget that you took blood, forget that I bit you. It was Caine who bit you, but we killed him."

Calvin frowned and then nodded. "That bastard."

I let go of the power and he shook his head. Now to act as though nothing had happened.

"So what are we going to do with her?" I frisked the woman and pulled her wallet out of her back pocket. Flipping it open, I stared at her driver's license, her blue eyes seeming to glare at me even from the photo. "Rachel Sambrook." I turned the wallet upside down, but nothing fell out except for a single business card.

I caught it in mid-air and turned it over in my fingers. Some government official named Sean Price. Tapping it against my cheek, I tried to think past the burning sensation in my chest. Fucking silver bullets, someone had come prepared. Obviously there were more ties to this facility than Calvin and I had realized. The pieces were scattered around us and it looked like Rachel was about to become one of them.

"Why don't you just let her go? We can follow her," Calvin suggested.

I considered it for a split second before shaking my head. "No, that will take too long."

"We on a sudden deadline?"

The itch along the back of my shoulders and neck had nothing to do with the bullet hole that still burned inside me. No, it had to do with following my instincts for so many years. I knew when something bad was coming, long before it showed up. A trait of being a Cazador. "Yes, I think we are. Even if we don't know why or how long we have."

He put my bag of tools away, being careful with the blood on the silver netting and pincers. "Then what in God's name are we going to do?"

There was only one answer.

"You're about to get your wish, Calvin. She's coming with us." I tucked the business card into my shirt and scooped up Rachel. "Looks like we're going to get to know each other better after all."

Calvin pulled a small tin of gasoline out of my kit, poured it over Caine's body and struck a match. The whoosh of flames curled around me as I turned away.

Carrying her up the stairs should have been easy, but damned if my body hadn't suffered enough damage for the night. Breathing hard, something all but foreign to me, I reached the top and had to wait for my heart to catch up.

"Looks like I'm not the only one who's getting old," Calvin muttered. I glared at him as he walked past me, minus his trademark limp. The vampire blood coursing through his veins was making him stronger than he'd been in ten years. Whoever it belonged to could control him—even from a distance. The smart move would have been to kill him, end it fast and painless. Draining him at this point would turn him. He would hate me forever if I did that.

We made our way through the fence and to the car with no problem other than Rachel muttering in her unconscious state.

The sound of a gunshot echoed through the night and I ducked low, holding Rachel against my chest. Slowly, I stood and peered over the car. A dark figure stood beside Derrick's car, yanking his boneless body out and onto the pavement.

I had no doubt that Rachel's friend was dead. And somehow, she seemed to know it too, as if she'd lost a piece of herself.

Rachel stirred in my arms, her eyelids fluttering. "Derrick, I'm sorry. I tried."

Reflexively, I tightened my arms around her. "That makes two of us."

I climbed into the back of the car with her, stretching her out across the mangled backseat.

"Keep her head higher than the rest of her," Calvin said as he pulled onto the road.

I boosted her up against my shoulder, her breathing

a bit uneven but her heart strong and steady. I handed her license over the seat to Calvin. "Let's go to her place. She'll be more comfortable there."

"Since when do you care about a mark's comfort?"

"She isn't a mark," I snapped. "She's a part of this, though, and we can use her and the info she has to find the nest. There aren't a lot of old vamps left, Calvin. And if they're all holed up in some government facility, we could take them out in one fell swoop."

He was quiet for a moment. "You really think you can take them all out?"

"I have to. Or I might as well give up and just accept that I'm one of them."

Calvin sucked in a short, sharp breath but said nothing more for the rest of the drive. He pulled up to a smaller apartment building in East Harlem. The night was waning, and the humans were mostly in bed. I scooped her into my arms again and headed toward the building. The front door was locked, but Calvin picked it in a matter of minutes.

Rachel's apartment was, of course, six flights up. Damn. Gritting my teeth, my canines clinking against each other, I started the climb. This wouldn't be such an issue if I'd had a chance to feed. And that thought made me consider the scent of fresh blood wafting up off her wounds.

I jogged up the last few stairs, surprised to find the door partially open. Not waiting for Calvin, I pushed through the door and beelined for the couch, not even pausing to take in my surroundings. I dropped her onto the cushions and backed away.

The urge to feed swirled up in me, growing and groaning as my belly rumbled. I closed my eyes and sank to a crouch.

"Shit, how long has it been since you ate? You know you can't heal this many wounds without feeding." Calvin's voice seemed to come from far away.

I couldn't stay here. I ran for the door, letting my senses guide me as I bolted up the stairs to the rooftop. From there, I hopped my way to the next building and slid down the fire escape. When I landed in a crouch in the alley, I picked up the scent of a homeless man, his sleeping body slumped under a pile of cardboard. The odor of his unwashed body wasn't enough to deter me, not when I was this hungry. I took him to the point of death and stopped.

Tipping my head back, I licked my lips and let out a huge sigh of relief. "Thank you."

I tucked him back under his cardboard house and slipped a hundred-dollar bill into his shirt. At least he would eat for a few days. A week if he was careful. It helped to assuage my guilt over the fact he wasn't a willing participant. He probably wouldn't even remember my late-night visit.

Once more in control of myself, I climbed the building, hopped the roof, and was back inside Rachel's apartment in no time.

Calvin sat in a recliner across from Rachel, a beer in his hand. "Five minutes?" He lifted both eyebrows at me.

I shrugged. "I got lucky."

"Did you find anything?"

He snorted and took a slug of the beer. "Didn't even look."

"Lazy ass helper," I muttered, but there was no heat to the words. I was better at the whole search and destroy thing anyway. Lifting my head, I tasted the air. Rachel's unique scent was the top layer. But there were a few others as well.

I pulled the card with Sean Price's name on it. He'd been here—his smell of leather and gun oil was mixed in with the scents of several other men, including the now-dead man who was her friend. Derrick. Focusing on his scent and Rachel's, I followed them through the apartment, retracing their steps. The other men who had been here had tossed the place as thoroughly as any human might. I was betting on government boys based on how similar each of them smelled. Uniformed from top to bottom.

Rachel had gone into her closet several times, and there, under the floorboards, I could pick up Derrick's smell again. Something hidden away that belonged to him.

Bending down, I worked my fingers around the edge of a barely visible lip until I was able to pull up the wood slats of the floor. "Now that is interesting." A huge dark green duffel bag was tucked into the hiding place. Taking hold of the handles, I pulled it out and started snooping. Lots of government papers, a laptop, disks, and several binders with seals on them that made me think this was what the army men had been after.

Taking the bag with me, I left the room and sat across from Rachel's sleeping form. The sun rose as I stared at her, wondering how she fit into this mess. Regardless, I would find out and either she would become an asset…

Or a necessary casualty.

Chapter 14

RACHEL

The first thing I was aware of was the pounding in my head and the fact that every part of my body felt like I'd been run over by a truck. My mouth was dry, and judging from my crazy dreams, I realized I must have one hell of a hangover. Only I didn't remember drinking more than a couple of glasses with Derrick at dinner. Did we drink more after he came back from his meeting?

I forced my eyes open, not an easy feat considering

my eyelids felt like they were attached to ten-pound weights, and was surprised to find myself on the sofa. Had Derrick taken the bed? My clothes felt stiff, and when I looked down, I realized my shirt was covered in dried blood.

I bolted upright in alarm. Oh, God. It wasn't a dream.

"Derrick!" I tried to shout, but my mouth and throat were dry and it came out in a croak.

Sensing movement in my peripheral vision, I swung my gaze to the worn leather armchair, panicked to see the woman from my nightmare.

"He's dead," she said, sympathy in her eyes.

An overwhelming fear for Derrick along with fragmented memories of the torture dungeon returned to my memory, and I inhaled sharply. She had overpowered me after being shot point blank in the chest. I had no idea how I'd escape from her.

"I shot you."

She should be lying in a morgue, or at the very least in a hospital bed, not stretched out in my chair with her feet propped on the coffee table.

A sarcastic grin tilted up the corners of her mouth. "Yeah, and it hurt like a son of a bitch. But it's all healed up now."

A grunt of disapproval steered my attention to the kitchen. An older man stood at my island, holding a cup of coffee. I recognized him as her buddy from last night.

I was surprised to see her grimace. Did that mean the old guy was the one calling the shots?

"How are you still alive? Or not in a hospital?" She

looked perfectly fine, and her clean shirt was minus a bullet hole.

"I'm not like most people."

"No shit," I said, scooting several inches away from her on the sofa as I tried to assess the situation. She'd knocked me out with the gun, and then she and the old guy had brought me to my apartment. I knew they hadn't been holding a vigil, which could mean only one thing.

They wanted answers.

But I wanted answers too, so maybe I could use this to my advantage. Then I remembered she'd probably wanted answers from Caine. At least I wasn't in a torture chamber, dangling from the ceiling in a net with my guts spilling out. Score one for me, but I knew if I didn't tell her what she wanted, I was a hair's-breadth away from her unique brand of questioning.

Even the Taliban hadn't resorted to those measures.

The older man moved with more agility than he'd seemed to possess the night before, and handed me a glass of water. "Drink that. You're probably dehydrated after all that blood loss."

I took the glass from him, not liking the way he was staring at my chest. Was he some old pervert? Was that why he was with the woman who was still stretched out in my chair? I could see why he'd want to be with her. She was gorgeous. Her nearly black hair was pulled into a French braid, but tendrils had spilled out around her face. Her eyes were dark and exotic, the perfect complement to her darker complexion. She was tall and her body was lean, but she had curves in all the right places that men loved.

But for the life of me, I couldn't figure out why she was with *him*. His body was slightly stooped and his thinning hair was gray. Wrinkles covered his face, and the thought of them sleeping together made me sick, kind of like Hugh Hefner and all those hot blonde women in his Playboy mansion.

But maybe I could use that to my advantage, too. I'd study them both and try to figure out the dynamics of their relationship.

As I took a sip of the water—which turned into several greedy gulps—I tried to figure out how to play this. Might as well start from the beginning. I set the half-empty glass on the coffee table, then asked, preparing myself for the worst, "Where's Derrick?"

"Like I said, he's dead."

The ache of loss washed through me, but my distrust tapped it down. "I'm just supposed to take your word for that?" My tone was cold and harsh. I refused to believe her. This could be part of her ploy to convince me to share what I knew.

"He was nearly dead when I found him outside the building, but he was worried about you. He knew you'd been gone too long."

I couldn't hide my sharp intake of air. "So, he *wasn't* dead when you found him."

"No," she said softly. "Someone showed up and finished the job after we were out of the building. Which means they're probably after you now."

It made sense; in fact, I was surprised they hadn't shown up on my doorstep yet. Yet I still struggled to accept it. "Finished the job... How?"

"They shot him, then dragged his body away to tidy up."

Oh God. She could have been lying, but I knew it was true. There was little chance he was in a hospital somewhere—the men following us would never let him get that far—and he wasn't here with me now.

Pain, anger, and a thirst for revenge that caught me off guard flooded me. But I pushed down my grief. This woman had information that could help me find the people who had killed Derrick. I needed to focus on that at the moment.

She sat up and leaned over her legs. "Who was after you?"

"Why did you want to talk to Caine?" I countered.

She released a low growl that raised the hair on the back of my neck. "I think you and I want the same thing, if you'd just cooperate."

"You mean I spill my guts or you'll do it for me?"

She jumped to her feet, fast and swift, like a predator attacking its prey. But she didn't attack me, merely released a groan of frustration and began to pace. "You're not like him. I won't do that to you." She stopped and held my gaze. "I have other ways to get information from you, but I hope it won't come that. I think we can help each other."

"I'm not like him," I repeated. "Somehow I don't think you mean the child molester part."

She remained silent, but the old man shifted on his perch at the end of the sofa. "Lea, tell her."

Lea gave him an incredulous look.

"You know her history. She can help us."

"I don't think that's a good idea, Calvin," Lea said, shaking her head.

"You know who I am?" I blurted out without thinking. Obviously they knew who I was or we wouldn't all be in my apartment having this little powwow.

Lea held up her fingers, ticking one off for every fact. "Rachel Sambrook, age thirty-one. You spent seven years in the Middle East covering the war. You were known for your impulsiveness and courage. You covered quite a few stories most men wouldn't take. And you didn't just report the U.S. military line; several of your stories reported on their faults."

I wanted to ask her how she knew all of that, but she beat me to it. "You've been out for several hours, and Calvin here is good at getting information. It's why I hired him."

He snorted, but otherwise remained silent.

I gave a shrug, grimacing at the pain in my neck from where that bastard Caine had bitten me the night before. "So you know all about me, but I don't know the first thing about you other than that your name is Lea, you're handy with a knife, and you're apparently resistant to bullets."

She engaged in a several-second stare-off with the old guy before turning back toward me, uncertainty in her eyes.

"You're right. I am all those things, and one more. I was trained as a Cazador. A hunter of things that go bump in the night. I fought the darkness until it swallowed me whole. They thought they'd destroyed me by making me one of them, but all they did was make me strong enough to truly have a chance at wiping them out."

Letting her look down at me gave her power, so I stood, my eyes nearly level with hers. "Made you one of them? What do you mean? What are you?" I swallowed, suddenly unsure I wanted the answer.

Lea's eyes never wavered from mine as she said a single word. The answer that had been dancing in my head since this all began.

"Vampire."

Chapter 15

LEA

Rachel took a step back; involuntarily, I was sure. Human nature dictated that she run from something that could eat her. Her blue eyes narrowed as quickly as they'd widened.

"That's a crock of bullshit." Her words were strong, but her tone told me something else entirely. She believed me, she just didn't want to.

I folded my arms over my chest, a slow smile spreading over my face. "Then explain everything you just pointed out to me. The bullet not killing me, my speed and strength. Rachel, when you have eliminated the impossible, whatever remains, *however improbable*, must be the truth."

I didn't think it was possible that her glare could become any harder, but it did, her eyes becoming mere pinpricks of blue.

"Don't quote Sherlock Holmes to me."

I spread my hands wide, palms up, as if in supplication. "He might be fictional, but that doesn't make him wrong. To the majority of the world, I am also fictional. I do not exist, and yet here I stand. You felt Caine's fangs. You felt his power as he fought to control you. Your wounds from him are healed already, which to you should be impossible, yet the vampire saliva does just that. It hides the bites. You tell me what he is, if not a vampire."

Her scent changed as my words triggered the memories. She swallowed hard. "Let's say I believe you, for the sake of this conversation."

This was finally moving in the right direction. I decided to throw my information to her. If she proved sketchy, I could always drain her and dump her body in the river. "The vampires I am hunting are being protected by the government at a facility, at least as far as I can tell from my interrogation of Caine. You mentioned the Asclepius Project. Calvin tried to search for it while you were out, but didn't find anything on the project. The name, however, is interesting."

Her eyes shot straight to Calvin and the laptop that he now had in front of him. She was easily within reach of me if I'd been so inclined. No wonder she was an ace reporter—she was willing to walk right into danger. Unfortunately, the ones who were willing to risk it all to get the story they were after were also the ones who always ended up dead.

Calvin tapped the screen. "Asclepius is from Greek mythology. Turns out, he was all about raising people from the dead. Doesn't bode well for a project named after him, tied to vampires as it is."

Rachel looked from the screen to me. "Is that what you think they are doing? Raising the dead?" I could see the conflict on her face. To even ask the question had to gall her.

"More likely they are turning high-placed, important officials into vampires. Most vamps have the ability to control people to a degree."

She nodded. "Caine tried to do that to me."

I gave her a tight smile. "The force is strong with you. Those with extreme stubborn streaks and strength of character can resist. We can still force them, but we have to have our own tanks full to manage it."

"And now you're quoting *Star Wars*. Really?" Rachel headed into the kitchen and pulled a beer out of the fridge. She cracked it open and took a big swig before setting it on the counter.

Calvin lifted his hand. "I'll take one of those."

"You're on the clock, old man." I snapped.

Rachel took one out for him and tossed it to him when she was partway back to the couch. He beamed at her. Fucking ingrate.

"So we have a project named for a character who

raised the dead, and we have vampires and a government facility we think exists."

I put my foot on the green army bag and slid it forward. "And whatever may be in Derrick's bag."

Her eyes popped wide. "How the hell did you find that?"

I touched the side of my nose. "It stinks like him."

She pulled the bag closer to her seat and started to rummage through it. "I can probably break his codes and get into his laptop, but it will take time. I took a quick glance last night, but nothing made sense. It seemed a jumble of papers just thrown in the bag in order to throw people off."

"Or completely blacked out," Calvin said.

She glared at him and he looked away. I snapped my fingers, and her blue-eyed glare swung my way. An idea was growing inside me that Calvin would not like, especially when he understood my reasoning.

Before he had just been old and slow, but now he was a liability.

Rachel was young, eager, and as tough as any Cazador I'd ever known. She would make a great replacement for Calvin. But that meant I had to keep her around, keep her alive, and hope to hell we both survived whatever storm was brewing on the horizon.

"Here is what I'm going to propose. We both want to find the facility and expose whatever it is the government is doing." I held up my hand to forestall her as her mouth opened to argue. "Yes, we have different motives, but does that matter when the end result will be the same? You will bring your government to justice and I will kill vampires."

Calvin spluttered around his beer, and it was my turn to glare. "You are not a part of this decision, old man." He paled and clamped his mouth shut. No, it wasn't nice. But I had to be tough. I had to let him go before the vamp who'd fed from him turned him from the light completely. This would be his last hunt, whether he knew it or not.

Rachel leaned back against the couch, looking up at me. "Let me get this straight. You want me to work with you? Go in as a team and expose this Asclepius Project?"

I gave her my best smile. "Yes, that is what I am proposing."

I could almost see her weighing the pros and cons.

"I'll work on Derrick's notes, see what I can find. What are you going to do?" Her gaze swept between the two of us.

"I have a patron who has been a naughty boy," I said. "He's gone to ground, but I mean to find him and make him talk. I believe he has ties to this project."

A whiff of gun oil and two-day-old sweat wafted under the front door. I spun around and drew in another breath to be sure, then said, "We have company. Your friend Sean is back."

Rachel hefted the army bag and all but threw it at me, whispering, "Put this back where you found it and get the hell out of here. I'll deal with him."

I didn't move. "Tell me we have a deal. Until this hunt is over, you and I will share information and work together as a team. Until the vampires are all dead."

Calvin gave a little choking sound.

She nodded twice. "Yes, yes, now get out of here."

I grabbed her hand and brought the palm to my mouth, slicing it with my teeth. I did the same to my own hand and then slapped our palms together. "Now swear it."

Her brows tightened and she stared at our clasped hands for a split second. "I swear I will work with you until all the vampires are dead. Okay?"

I let her go and nodded. "Better than okay. Follow up with your leads today. I'll meet you back here at eight and we'll compare notes."

Calvin followed me into her bedroom and watched in silence while I stuffed the bag into her secret hiding spot. Grabbing him around the waist, I all but threw him over my shoulder and climbed out the window to the fire escape as I pulled my cowl up over my head. Thank God for dreary fall days with plenty of cloud cover.

"Put me down, Lea."

I did as he asked, then shut the window behind us and started down the metal steps.

"You replacing me?"

I stopped on the landing below him and looked up. For just a moment I could see the young man I'd taken on as my helper almost fifty years ago. Fifty years we'd worked together, and there had only ever been one slip-up. One moment of weakness on his part—a night I would not forget and he seemed determined not to remember.

"Yes. You knew it would be coming, so why are you surprised?"

"But her? Why her?"

I tore my gaze from him and leapt from the fire escape, letting my body fall through the open air. As I landed lightly in a crouch, I stared up at the figure slowly making his way down. Calvin would never understand, but the truth was I saw a kindred spirit in Rachel. A woman determined to make a difference despite the dangers around her.

That was what I needed at my side, as my teammate.

A force to be reckoned with.

And, if nothing else, Rachel was surely that.

Chapter 16

RACHEL

Sean repeated his knock, sounding more insistent, and the beer cans caught my eye. When I grabbed them and tossed them into the trash, the blood on my palm smeared a little, reminding me that I was still wearing a bloody shirt. I pulled it over my head and threw it in the corner, then dampened a dishtowel and swiped at my neck and chest, getting all the blood off. Lea was right; the bite wounds from Caine were completely healed.

I realized I had a dilemma—take more time to go grab a shirt or answer the door in my bra and jeans. If it really was Sean, I could use the latter to my advantage.

I tossed the dishtowel onto the counter, then walked over and opened the door.

Sean stood on the other side of the threshold, wearing several days' growth of beard. His eyes widened as his gaze was drawn to my black bra, but he quickly raised it to my face.

Several things struck me at once. One, Lea had identified my visitor correctly, which only gave her claim of being a vampire more credence. Two, I was taking the news that vampires really walked the earth remarkably well. Three, Sean looked like shit. And four, even looking his worst, Sean still had his hooks in me.

"Are you okay?" he asked, sounding worried. "You're so pale." He leaned closer. "Are those marks on your neck?"

Apparently not as healed up as I'd thought.

I pulled the hair tie out of my ponytail and let my hair fall around my neck. "I was clumsy. What are you doing here?"

He glanced over my shoulder. "Can I come in?" I hesitated and his eyes softened. "Please? I need to talk to you about something important."

I didn't really want Sean to come in—the chances were pretty high that he was behind the order to chase us through Manhattan and ultimately kill Derrick. It seemed undeniable that Sean had a connection with the Asclepius Project, and based on what Lea had said, this wasn't his first visit to my apartment. I could barely stand to look at him, but I might be able to get answers, or at the very least, a few leads.

"I was about to make a pot of coffee." I backed away and walked into the kitchen, fully cognizant I was still wearing just my bra.

He followed me into the apartment and shut the door behind him. "You always did know the way to a man's heart."

"Ha!" I said, filling the pot with water. "I thought that was food."

He moved behind me, his chest dangerously close to my back. "For me, it's sex and coffee, and you were always particularly good at the former."

I resisted the urge to turn around and beat the shit out of him even as I felt the tug of the chemistry between us. This man betrayed me two years ago, and he was most likely my enemy now. I couldn't let myself forget that no matter how he made me feel. If Derrick really was dead, there was a good chance Sean had played a role in that, as difficult as it was to believe.

I slid to the side and poured the water into the back of the coffee maker. "Ancient history, Sean."

"Why is there a bloody towel in your sink?" His voice was tight.

Dammit. "I cut myself," I said lightly as I scooped coffee grounds into the machine.

"That must have been one hell of a cut," he murmured, lifting his hand to my neck. "Was it from this?"

I brushed his hand away and showed him my still-bloody palm. "Just my hand, but it looks worse than it is. I'm fine."

He grabbed my hand and used his thumb to brush

open my fingers. I ignored the flutter of anticipation in my gut and tried to pull free, to no avail.

"See?" I asked as he studied the cut. Thank goodness Lea had sliced my palm instead of puncturing it.

He studied my hand, then looked into my eyes. "Want me to kiss it and make it better?"

I jerked my hand free. "No, thanks."

His fingertips slid down my arm, sending chills down my back.

"Are you cold?"

"Yeah, I need to get a shirt," I responded, but I didn't dare go into my room. He might follow me there and somehow find Derrick's hidden bag. I grabbed my jacket off the back of the chair and noticed the Google search on Asclepius was still up on my computer screen on the coffee table. If Sean was part of it, the less he thought I knew, the better.

After shrugging on the jacket, I walked over and scooped up the laptop, closing the lid and setting it down on the table. "Would you like to sit?" I asked, sinking onto the sofa. "It will be a few minutes before the coffee's ready."

He walked over and I waited to see where he would sit. I still wasn't sure why he'd shown up on my doorstep at 7:30 in the morning, but I suspected it wasn't to ask me for a date, or even to screw me. In fact, according to Lea he'd been here before. So when he sat next to me, I knew he was playing me, big time. The question was why?

"What brings you by my apartment, Sean?" I asked, pulling my afghan over my legs. "How'd you know where I live?"

A grin tugged at his lips. "Please…"

"Isn't using classified information for personal use against the rules?"

His grin spread. "Finding out your address doesn't exactly qualify as classified information."

"Okay…" I conceded. "That brings us back to my original question. Why are you here?"

His smile faded. "I'm afraid I have some bad news. I wanted you to hear it from me."

"What?"

"Derrick…" He grabbed my hand. "He was murdered last night."

A chill washed over me. I'd accepted Lea's word for it, yet hearing it from Sean made it feel more real. "How?"

"Shot. In the head."

That seemed to fit with what Lea had told me, but not entirely. I had to decide which one of them I trusted, and at the moment I was going with Lea. She'd said whoever shot him had dragged his body away. If Sean had these details, it meant he had been part of his murder. I resisted the urge to scoot away from him. I had to play this out. "Nothing else? No other wounds?"

His eyebrows rose. "That's not *enough*?" When I didn't respond, he said, "Yeah. That was all."

My shoulders tensed. I was right. He *was* lying. Why was I surprised?

"I tried to warn him, Rach. But like I told you—he was obsessed. He was on a bunch of Doomsday forums, telling people to prepare for a zombie apocalypse and that the U.S. government was behind it. He'd truly lost his mind."

Doomsday forums? Zombies? "So then who killed him?"

He paused, as though weighing his words. "I suspect the Russian mafia. He'd been digging around in their business. He thought they were backing it."

I was quiet for a moment, trying my best to stay seated next to the man who had likely been behind the order to kill our friend.

Derrick was dead.

The reality of it finally hit me like a two-by-four. My eyes burned and I swallowed the lump in my throat. For some reason the truth of it only sank in then, while I was sitting there with Sean. Maybe it was because the three of us had survived so many near-death experiences together we had begun to think of ourselves as invincible.

"Rach, I'm sorry." He took my hand, his thumb making a sweeping smoothing motion. "Were you two still close?"

I tried not to jerk my hand away. I had to play this as though I was clueless about what Derrick had learned, but I couldn't suppress a tiny flinch. I decided it could be easily explained as a scorned girlfriend flinching at the touch of her cheating ex.

But a flicker in his eyes hinted that he might know the real reason, although I saw no malice in his gaze, only concern.

Which side was Sean really on? Hell, I wasn't even sure what the sides even were. More reason to keep him around and find out.

I shrugged. "Like I said the other night, we hadn't talked for a couple of years. But you can't go through what the three of us went through together and not be close."

"I know." The way he said it sounded more personal than an empathetic agreement.

I looked into his eyes, surprised and confused by the emotion I found there.

"Can I do anything?" he asked.

I shook my head, reliving the previous evening. What could I have done differently to help Derrick? I should never have left him alone in that car. I should have assessed his injury better. I'd left him there weak and defenseless. His death was on my head, and I wasn't sure I could live with that.

Sean must have seen the guilty look on my face because something wavered in his eyes. "I want to find who did this to him, Rachel. I promise to make them pay, but first I have to figure out who murdered him. Do you know anything that could help me find them?"

"*You're* going to help find his murderer?" I scoffed. "Since when does the U.S. military hunt down Russian mafia? Doesn't that fall under the jurisdiction of the NYC police department?"

"It's personal," he said softly. "You're right. He was like a brother to me. He had some mental health issues at the end with all his crazy conspiracy theories, but I still loved him." He shook his head. "I can't believe he's really gone."

My mind whirled. Did he really think I'd buy the Russian mafia angle when he reminded me in the next breath about Derrick's conspiracy theories? How could I get him to talk about what *he* knew?

"Are you sure you didn't see him after that night I found you in the alley?" he asked.

I lifted my eyes to his, careful to conceal my thoughts. Lea said he'd been here and his—or someone else's—goons knew Derrick had shown up at my apartment the night before. "Yeah, he came by yesterday afternoon. Said he needed a place to crash. So I let him sleep on my bed, I fed him dinner, then he took off, saying he had to go to a meeting."

"And he didn't tell you anything about the meeting?"

"No. He said it was too dangerous for me to know anything about."

Ironically enough, I had told him the truth. I hadn't learned much from Derrick himself. But Sean didn't believe me. The look on his face confirmed it. "I know you don't trust me," he said. "And I understand why. You have no idea how sorry I am for hurting you, but this is different. You can tell me the truth." When I didn't answer, he licked his lower lip. My traitorous eyes followed the movement. "I'm worried about you. These guys Derrick was poking into…they don't like outside interference or attention. If they think you were associated with Derrick in any way…" His hand lifted to my upper arm. "Rachel, let me protect you."

Wrong choice of words. I scooted a few inches back, far enough to get my message across. "I don't need protecting."

Irritation narrowed his eyes. "Look, I know you're tough and strong. And I know you can kick most men's asses, but so could Derrick, and look what happened to him." His voice lowered and he reached for the back of my head, the heel of his hand resting on my cheek. "I love that you're strong. Since you, every other woman has been a pale imitation. I screwed up when I cheated on you, Rachel. I'll regret it for the rest of my life."

I jumped to my feet. "I have an appointment in the city in about an hour and I still need to get ready."

A sad smile filled his eyes. "Where's your phone?"

"Why?"

Orneriness spread across his face. "Are you always this suspicious?"

"Yes." There was no denying it, and I sure as hell wasn't apologizing for it. My suspiciousness had saved my ass too many times to count.

He laughed. "God, I've missed you. Now where is it?"

I continued to glare at him.

"I just want to make sure you have my cell number programmed into your phone. If you get into trouble, you won't have time to dig out my card."

"Fine. I'll put it in."

His body tensed. "I want to see you do it."

I groaned and pulled my phone out of my pocket. "What's the number?"

He rattled off the digits and I saved it into my contact list. "There. Happy now?"

"No. But it's a start." The longing in his voice caught me off guard. "I plan on seeing you again, Rachel. Whether it's about Derrick or something… more personal."

I tilted my head to the side, hating the small part of me that begged me to take him up on the latter offer, consequences be damned. I still had a hard time believing Sean would so callously have his friend murdered. "I guess we'll see about that."

He grinned, but it wasn't his usual cocky grin. He moved closer and pressed his lips to my forehead, leaving a lingering kiss. "If you see or hear anything about Derrick, call me—not anyone else—just me. Please?" When I didn't answer, he put his finger under my chin and tilted my face up to stare into my eyes. "You don't have to do this alone, Rachel. You have to let other people in. It's not such a bad thing."

My shoulders stiffened. "Well, look where it got me with you."

He dropped his hand and took a step back. "Did you ever consider that if you'd let me in—really in—I might not have been tempted to stray?"

He wasn't asking me anything I hadn't already considered, but between Derrick's death and the whole finding-out-vampires-were-real thing, I could do without an impromptu therapy session. "Cheating is still cheating, Sean. Which makes you untrustworthy."

He shook his head. "I'll do everything I can to prove that you can trust me."

I put my hands on my hips. "Why?"

"Because I think your life depends on it." He paused and his voice lowered. "And because I never stopped caring about you."

Then he spun around and walked out the front door.

I followed and turned the deadbolt, more confused than ever. Part of me wondered if Sean could be right. Had Derrick really lost it? If so, then how did I explain the people shooting at us last night? But Sean had always been able to slip through my bullshit meter. I couldn't trust him, no matter how many pretty words fell from his lips.

Derrick hadn't been killed by the Russian mafia, and I suspected Sean either knew who killed him or was involved himself. He was stringing me along to get Derrick's research.

I dug Derrick's bag from its hiding place in the closet. If I wanted answers, I needed to work Derrick's trail backwards, and as quickly as possible, so I flipped to the back of his ledger and scoured the last two pages. An entry quickly caught my eye. Derrick had set up a meeting with a man named Brian Morrison. From Derrick's notes, Morrison worked at a bar in Greenwich Village, but he hadn't shown for their meeting.

What if Derrick had scared him off?

I stood and arched my back, stretching my aching muscles. Brian Morrison might have been leery of talking to Derrick Forrester, but I had a feeling he might spill for Rachel Sambrook.

Sometimes being a pretty blonde came in handy.

Chapter 17

LEA

Calvin was, to say the very least, pissed. His knuckles bulged on the steering wheel, white from the tension in his hands.

"Head toward the city center. Victor's father had a safe house there. I don't think he knows I'm aware of it, so I suspect that's where he'll be." I spoke softly, the words just loud enough for him to hear.

He nodded, but said nothing. Yes, pissed was an understatement.

I leaned forward so I could rest my hands on the console between us. This was still not a conversation I wanted to have, yet I knew the time had finally come. "Cal, it's time. I need to take on a new Cazador. We both know that a part of you has hated me since that night in France, and that was thirty-five years ago."

He jerked the wheel to one side, parking the car by jamming it against a curb. His eyes stared straight ahead; his shoulders were slightly hunched. "Lea, we have a break in this, we might be able to find every vampire—"

"Calvin." Just his name, as soft as I'd only said it once before.

"Calvin, please don't turn away from me. Not this time. I can barely remember what it means to love anymore. If I lose that, I'm no better than the rest of them. I might as well hand you a vial of holy water to pour over me."

His hands slid up around my face. "No, this can't happen." But he didn't move away from me. Didn't walk away as he'd done so many other times.

The seat creaked under him. "Why now? Why are we having this conversation right now?"

"Because it might be the last chance we have. If this gets as ugly as I think...I don't know if any of us will survive." There, I'd said it. The feeling that had been growing in me for the last twenty-four hours had finally been aired.

He slowly twisted in his seat, reached over and took my hand. "I don't hate you," he said quietly. "I hate that I let anything happen between us. I swore that I would kill every vampire I met after my wife and son were taken from me. And not only did I not kill you, I slept with you."

Why, oh, why did Calvin have to be the one my heart picked? There had been other Cazadors, other helpers. Many who would have jumped at the chance to be in my arms. Yet it was Calvin, with his stoic nature and determination, who had caught my eye. And I hadn't been able to catch his for more than a brief blink.

I stared at the old man who sat before me, but all I saw was the young, strong man with jet black hair and piercing blue eyes who had stolen my heart even as he told me how much my kind disgusted him. Maybe I was the twisted one. I pulled my hand away. "I will never regret it, Calvin. For as long as I live, however that plays out."

A low grunt slipped out of him. "Then we stand on opposite sides of that divide, too, because I will never forgive myself."

If he had slammed a silver-tipped stake through my heart, I was sure the pain would not have been as bad. Leaning back in my seat, I struggled to breathe past the hurt in my body.

But I was disgusting. A monster of the worst kind. What did I expect from him? A sudden and undying devotion? Teeth clenched, I looked out the window at the slow-building storm clouds above us, the sudden splotches of rain on the glass making me wish I could let my own emotions unleash like the storm growing around us.

Then again, maybe I could.

Calvin pulled into an underground parking garage,

found an empty spot, and turned the engine off. "Am I coming up with you?"

He never asked. He always did whatever he wanted. "Go back to Rachel's. Give her a hand if she needs it. If not, see what you can find out about the Asclepius Project online. Surely there is something you can hack."

I slid out of the car, hands reaching down to touch the silver stakes tucked into the tops of my boots in a subtle gesture to ensure they were there. Adjusting the cowl around my head, I walked away from the car. The engine started up, and Calvin pulled away. But I didn't glance back, just went straight to the stairwell on the far side of the dim parking garage. I refused to give him one last look.

A few moments later, I slowed my steps as the sound of a heartbeat reached my ears.

Shadows flickered and moved to my right, a shifting of bodies in the darkness. I stopped and turned carefully, lifting one hand. "I know you're there." The air was stale and still, which made it hard to scent whoever was trying to hide. A scuttle of feet and a pair of glowing eyes peered at me from around a cement support column. It took all the willpower I had not to gasp and step back because what I was looking at was not human.

And it wasn't a vampire either. A bat face was attached to a tiny human body, grafted somewhere around the neck. The thing scuttled forward, bobbing and weaving, its hands held above its head in some sort of weird supplication.

I made myself hold still, though everything in me

wanted to back away. In my time, I'd seen monsters, but none had looked so alien as this being.

"What are you?"

Its head tipped to one side and its mouth dropped open to reveal needle-thin teeth. "Kill me." The creature reached out and touched my left leg. "Please. Kill me."

I pulled a silver stake from my boot, whipped it out and across the creature's upturned throat. The blade edge sliced the creature all the way to the spine, sending blood spurting out and over my hand. At the last second, it lifted its own hand to its bat mouth and then held it toward me. A kissing gesture of thanks, perhaps.

I brought my hand to my nose and sniffed the blood. Not human. Not animal. I dared a taste and my whole body convulsed in disgust. It was the vilest of blood, like an animal dead for a month, rank and old.

I grabbed the body and dragged it into the shadows. "Be at peace, little creature." I whispered the words in Spanish over it, knowing there was nothing else I could do. Instinctively, I knew that somehow this bat/human hybrid had something to do with the facility. The pieces were piling up, but where did they all go?

Wiping my hands off on the creature's body, I strode toward the stairwell once more. The door was locked, but a sharp kick was all it took to break through the flimsy attempt to keep people out. Inside the stairwell, it looked as if you could only go up. But I knew better. If you looked carefully enough, you could see a faint outline on the far wall. A door. I pushed in the top right corner of the outlined area while pushing on the bottom left hand corner with my foot. The whole door sucked in piece by piece, like a puzzle being opened up.

I stepped through the opening, and there was the soft hissing of air slipping out around me. The door closed behind me as motion sensors picked up on me. The near darkness of the long hall would have most humans fumbling for light, but there was enough that I could easily see. More importantly, I could see the dim glow of light thirty feet away at the end of the echoing hall. That, of course, was not something that Victor and his father had banked on when creating their failsafe.

The steel girder my feet were balanced on was only three inches wide and hung over open space. I walked forward, balancing on the balls of my feet with ease. Only two people had ever breached the safe house, and both were at the bottom of the pit, rotting away.

But since I was the one who'd helped Victor's father develop the safe house, it only seemed right that I should be the first one to bypass all the failsafes.

A few minutes later I reached the next door. Four feet thick and made of fire-hardened steel, this door would be harder to break through. It had to be hoisted with a winch from the other side. I crouched and dug my fingers under the tiny lip I'd made sure was built into the door. With a quick burst of energy, I heaved the door up and shot through the opening as it clanged to the floor behind me.

I stared into the bright space, taking the scene in at a glance. Victor lounged on a chaise with two of his bodyguards, one on either side of him. A polar bear rug lay on the black tile floor at Victor's feet, the mouth open and snarling my way.

"Lea, I'm surprised you managed to find me here." Victor stood and took several steps back, flustered. He waved his guards back, though the scent rolling off him was full of fear, the flavor heavy on the back of my tongue. The guards melted against the wood grain of the walls, almost as if they weren't there.

"Your father never told you?" I slipped the cowl back and off my head, shaking my hair loose, watching from the corner of my eye as Victor stared, his eyes wide and the throb of his heart apparent in the hollow of his throat. At least I still had that card to play if need be.

Victor seemed to regain his composure, remembering that I'd asked him a question. "Told me what?"

I waved a hand as if to encompass the whole room. "I helped him design this place. It was part of the deal we made. Part of my end of it, anyway." I took two steps forward and dropped into the only other seat in the room, a lovely overstuffed chair that allowed me to lean back. As if we were having a chat instead of a deadly repertoire that would likely end with Victor dead.

His green eyes, cold as ice, raked over me. "I want far more from you than my father did. This silly game of yours, hunting your own kind, needs to stop. You do realize that you will never wipe them out? I want to be like you, Lea. And one way or another, you will give me what I want."

I stayed where I was, breathing slowly, but my eyes fastened onto his. "Really? Is that how you seduce women now? Demand they give in?"

He strolled toward me, circling to the back of my chair. There was a moment of hesitation, and then he slid his hands onto my shoulders, up my neck, and into my hair, massaging my scalp. "Is this more to your liking?"

"Hmm." The sound came out like a purr. How long had it been since someone had touched me like this? Knowing what I was, and still wanting me?

Since Calvin and I had our single night together.

I leaned back into Victor's hands. The idea of fucking him was not so repulsive. He was handsome, and if the massage along my neck and scalp was any indication, he had some skills with his hands.

And he wanted me. More than any other man I'd ever known.

I leaned my head back and he dropped his lips to mine. Skilled, indeed. He slanted his mouth, his tongue darting in and out in a rhythm that hinted at other things. His one hand slid over my collarbone and down the front of my shirt while the other—

A knife sliced across the side of my neck, the sudden pain snapping me out of the sexual daze I'd stupidly allowed myself to tumble into. The two bodyguards rushed forward, moving with a speed that almost matched mine.

Almost.

I pushed off the floor, tipping the chair backward and smashing against Victor, who struggled not to stab himself with his own knife. "You fucking dog," I snarled, kicking out at him as my knees hit the floor, making contact with his ankle.

He crashed down with a cry and I scooped up his

knife. Slashing upward as I stood, I took out the first bodyguard's stomach with a single slice. His guts spilled out and he tried to catch them, but they slid through his fingers to the floor in a slippery mess. His buddy hit the brakes and tried to backpedal, but he hit the blood and gore next and went down beside his buddy.

Flipping the knife over in my hand, I threw it at bodyguard number two, driving the blade into his throat.

That left only Victor.

I turned and scooped him up as he tried to get away, his blond hair pink in places from the blood.

Holding him by the jaw with one hand, I raised him over my head. His feet dangled and his face went white, red, and purple.

I gave him a slow smile, showing him my fangs. "One way or another, Victor, you are going to tell me what I want to know. Every. Last. Thing."

Chapter 18

RACHEL

I took a shower and washed off the last remnants of blood and grime. Even after a year of being back in the States, showers still felt like a luxury. With my schedule, I had few luxuries in my life, so I refused to let myself feel guilty about taking long showers. Besides, I did my best brainstorming in the shower, and I definitely needed some major brainpower to sort through the crazy puzzle that had become my life.

I grabbed a bath crayon I kept in my shower caddy

and wrote what I knew on the shower door—the occult-like murders, the Asclepius Project, the U.S. government's involvement, and bioterrorism. And what about the pile of ash in the alley behind the last murder victim's place? What did that have to do with it all?

And, of course, there was the most bizarre piece of all. Vampires.

Had Caine been the murderer responsible for the six strange deaths or was it someone—or *something*—else?

And if I let my mind accept the possibility, which I was coming around to, like it or not, it wasn't a leap to think the pile of ashes in the alley might have been the remains of a vampire. But I realized I really didn't know anything about vampires other than what I'd learned from horror movies and books. I suspected Lea didn't sparkle in sunlight, which meant my information was sadly lacking. Why hadn't I thought to quiz Lea?

Maybe because I was still in shock.

Unfortunately, I had no way of contacting her, and I had a couple of hours to kill before I could drop by the bar Morrison worked at without looking suspicious. It was a long shot that he was even working today, but I was determined to make an effort.

After my shower, I pulled out all the contents of Derrick's bag, going through everything again, then going through files in his computer, which was frustratingly bare. But there was a file, buried within the applications folder, that turned out to be a journal. While he hadn't given details about what he'd found, he recorded his concerns about the things he was finding.

The first was dated two days after our huge fight two years ago.

All my life I've struggled with the concept of fate. I felt the undeniable pull to investigate these medical experimentation rumors, but if this turns out to be as deadly as I suspect, my life and anyone close to me will be in danger.

I knew it was a stupid move to tell Rachel how I felt, especially on the heels of her finding out about Sean's cheating. But I had to go into the investigation with no regrets, knowing that I wasn't giving up a chance with the one person who could make me feel complete.

But it's better this way. Was it my fate to investigate these rumors and save the world? Or was it my choice to walk away from the only woman I've ever loved?

Tears stung my eyes. Had I been the one to condemn Derrick to his fate? If I'd only loved him, he wouldn't have chased this story.

I scanned further into the document, finding vague notes about how he felt about what he'd discovered, although no facts. He'd been to Syria, Iraq, Pakistan, even Iceland. But he'd been in the States for six months.

I walked past Rachel's apartment today. I almost pressed the buzzer to see if she'd let me up. She walked by the window, her hair up in the messy ponytail she always wore when she was hard at work on a story. She stopped and looked outside and for one brief moment, I thought she'd seen me. My heart stopped and I waited for recognition to spread across her face, but she turned and walked away.

Then so did I.

I couldn't bring her into this madness, for that is surely what this is, madness.

I'll protect her at any cost.

I continued to scan the journal, the words blurry

through my tears. Until I reached the end, my breath catching.

Rachel,

If you're reading this, then I've failed. I wish you hadn't found me. I wish I could have protected you from this. But now you must protect the world. I need you to go back to the place you found me, where we found the pile of ashes. Right before you showed up, I was looking for a glass vial. Its contents, or more likely what it contained before the ashes, is important. Find someone you trust to test the contents. I'm sure it's key. I would have gone back earlier but the alley was being watched. Be careful.

And yes, I knew you'd figure out my password—I created it with you in mind.

I had to get back to that alley. And I had to ignore all the emotions bubbling up inside me. I didn't have time to cry. I had to make sure that Derrick hadn't wasted two years of his life.

I stored his bag under the floorboard again, then headed back toward the crime scene. The fall air had a bite to it as I walked around the corner to the alley, making sure I stayed aware of my surroundings. It was a fairly good neighborhood, being on the Upper East Side, but there was no sense being stupid. Especially since Derrick was sure it had been watched, but today the only threatening thing was a three-legged dog being walked by its owner.

I wasn't surprised to find no sign of those strange ashes, but there was a faint outline of what appeared to be a human body. Since the body had been ash, I would have expected the pavement to be blackened from the intense heat. But it was a pale gray, almost the same color the ash had been, if memory served me right. I squatted to examine it more closely, then looked around the area, even holding my nose to look under the Dumpster. That's where I saw a tiny glass vial with a red capsule inside.

Derrick was right.

I tried to temper my excitement as I knelt and reached under the trash bin to grab the bottle at the top with my gloved hand. It was about two inches tall and less than one inch wide. It was missing its screw cap, but the red capsule seemed to be wedged against the sides of the bottle.

As I examined the vial, I wondered why Sean and his crew hadn't found it while searching the crime scene. But it had been dark and the vial was a couple of feet under the trash bin. When I held it up for closer inspection, I saw gray ashy fingerprints on the glass. I stood and stepped back several feet as I studied the outline of the body. The arm on the right was raised; it was conceivable that the person could have been holding the bottle in his hand when he turned into ash.

I pulled a tissue from my messenger bag and rolled it around the bottle. To give it more padding, I added my glove around it and packed it inside my bag. Then I pulled out my phone and called Tom, my friend at the coroner's department.

"I don't have any new information, Rachel," he said, sounding irritated.

"I might have some information for you, actually. On the last occult murders."

"That might have been helpful yesterday. Before the Feds took it over."

"Well, shit." But the news didn't actually surprise me.

Tom laughed. "That was our thought, too."

Since I didn't trust Sean, I had no plans to hand this vial over to him. And if Sean was watching me, he was probably listening, too. I couldn't tell Tom anything over the phone. "Say, Tom. Can we meet in person?"

"Sure..." His voice shook a little when he made his response.

"I'm headed your way now. How about I take you out to a late lunch and we'll discuss it."

He groaned. "I can't leave for lunch. We're backed up today. But I can get a quick cup of coffee. The shop around the corner from my office."

"I'll be there in twenty minutes."

Tom was already sitting at a table when I walked into the shop, his face red and his hands trembling as they gripped his cup. Another cup sat in front of him.

The first time I'd met Tom was at a party soon after I arrived in the city. I was going out with a cop at the time—a very brief fling—but I flirted with Tom enough to convince him to exchange professional information.

The second time was when I "accidently" ran into him at a bar. I bought him several drinks and convinced him to give me inside information on a case I was writing about. We'd worked out a deal. He gave me inside info on cases and I occasionally appeared as his date at social functions. But this was the first time I'd ever given him physical evidence.

"Sorry I couldn't meet you at my office," he apologized, looking embarrassed. "Too much going on today."

He was lying, but that was okay. It was better that very few people knew about our working relationship. We weren't seen in public enough for me to casually drop by his office. In fact, I probably should have waited until tonight to contact him, but I was anxious for information.

I ordered a muffin since I hadn't eaten yet and then sat myself in the chair in front of the waiting coffee cup. Tom looked down at his hands. "So what's this about?" Then he looked up at me with wide puppy-dog eyes that made me instantly feel like a bitch. I hated manipulating people, especially people I actually liked. Like Tom. And I knew that before this conversation was done I was going to get my way, one way or another.

"I have some information about the case."

He grimaced. "Like I told you, the Feds took it over."

"You might not still be working on it, but I am. And I think I found evidence they missed."

"What are you talking about?"

I told him what I'd found—the ash and the vial—and I mentioned seeing Sean on the scene the other night. But I kept everything else to myself.

"So you want me to do something with the vial?"

I took a deep breath and looked into his eyes. "Can you run the print? I have a feeling it was the murderer."

"Why would you think that?"

"Call it a hunch. Can you run the prints?"

"No." Then he grimaced. "But I have a friend who can."

I leaned forward, looking into his eyes. "So will you?"

"I don't know," he said. "Maybe you should just give it to your boyfriend." I wasn't surprised to hear a hint of jealousy.

"He's not my boyfriend. And there's no way in hell I'm giving it to him." I tried to curb my frustration.

"Tom, I'm on the cusp of breaking a huge government cover-up. I have a gut feeling this could be a huge break in the case." Then I added, "*Please*."

He didn't answer, which I took as a good sign.

"Look at it this way, this could be a big 'fuck you' to the Feds."

He laughed and then took a sip of his coffee. I used the opportunity to pinch a piece off my muffin and stuff it into my mouth.

"So, is that a yes?"

"It won't be easy," he warned. "I can handle the print, but the pill…" He sighed. "I might know a guy in toxicology who will run it for me, but it'll cost."

I tried to hide my grimace. "How much?"

"Not money. He'll want an invite to my D&D tournament next weekend."

"And that's bad?"

He grinned and made a face. "He's annoying as hell."

"So you want something from *me*?"

"How bad do you want it?"

How bad indeed. "What do *you* want?"

He blushed. "There's a work thing."

"You need a date." He'd never been nervous about asking before, so I had to wonder what was so heinous about this one. Not that it mattered. I'd agree. "Okay. Where and when?"

"Next Friday. One of my coworkers is getting married. We'll go to the wedding and the reception. Semi-formal."

Work? He'd always kept it to dinner and drinks with his friends and his fraternity brothers who came in from out of town. But he'd never crossed the work line. It was dangerous to start now. But who was I kidding? "Will we play it off as a first date or pretend to be an established couple?

"First date. Everyone I work with would know I couldn't keep it a secret."

"Okay. It's a deal."

"So let's see it."

I opened my bag and carefully pulled out the glove and set it on the table. "It's in here. I wrapped it in a tissue. I hope I didn't screw it up."

He picked it up and stuffed it in his pocket as he stood. "I'll let you know what I find out."

I picked up my to-go cup and walked out with him. He stopped outside the door and turned to me, catching me off guard when he stooped to plant a kiss on my lips.

He grinned when he pulled back. "I figured we should make our date look legit." Then he walked away, whistling a happy tune.

At least somebody was happy.

It wasn't that I didn't like Tom. I just didn't like him like *that*. But leading him on made me feel like scum. Then again, after everything I'd done over the last seven years, maybe I *was* scum. But I had a feeling my last shred of humanity was about to be ripped away with this story.

Figuring it was still too early to check out the bar, I headed out to look at the alleys behind two of the other murders, but there was nothing. No gray figures on the pavement. It only corroborated what I had begun to suspect: The murderer was a vampire who had been interrupted during his last kill, and was murdered himself as he tried to get away.

It was five o'clock when I walked into the One Toed Monkey bar. There were a few patrons at tables and an old guy sitting at the counter. I picked a seat on the opposite end, relieved when I saw a guy working behind the counter. Chances were better that Brian was a guy's name, though you never know in Manhattan.

He walked over with a towel over his shoulder. No nametag, of course—it couldn't be that easy. I had to figure out how to play this.

"What can I get you?"

I sniffed and pretended like I was about to cry. "A glass of wine."

His expression softened. "What kind, honey?"

I waved my hand. "Oh, I don't know. Something white."

He pulled down a wine glass and began to pour. "Want to talk about it?"

I took a sip, then set the glass down and purposely toppled it over, making it look like an accident. "Oh," I whined. "He's right. I can't do *anything* right."

He yanked the towel off his shoulder and started to mop up the mess. "It's just a glass of wine. No harm done. I'll pour you another. On the house."

"Thank you," I said, grateful for the three seasons of summer theater I had done in college. "You're so nice… What's your name?"

"Brian."

Bingo. "Thank you for being so nice, Brian. I'm Larissa and I seem to have the crappiest taste in men. You've given me hope."

"I can't imagine a pretty girl like you having problem with men."

"You'd be surprised." I spent the next ten minutes making up a bullshit story, trying to figure out how to lead this fluff into the kind of questions Derrick wanted to ask this guy.

"And to make matters worse, my boyfriend is a conspiracy nut."

His smile froze. "What kind of conspiracy?"

I shrugged and picked up my glass. "Something about the government, but don't most conspiracy theories involve the government? It had some funny name that started with an A."

He stood upright. "You don't say?"

I was hitting too many right buttons. I needed to take the heat off him. I waved my hand. "He read all about it on some weird website."

He released a breath, then said again, "You don't say."

My phone buzzed in my pocket. I set it in my lap and peeked down at the screen, relieved to see it was a text from Tom.

No ID on the print, but I have some interesting results on the pill. Call me.

I gave Brian a pleading look. "Can you point me in the direction of the bathroom?"

"Yeah. It's down the hall."

As soon as I rounded the corner I called Tom's cell. "I got your text."

"I've got some results on that pill."

"Already? I thought it would take longer."

"The guy working on it was intrigued enough to keep going."

"And?"

"It's nothing they recognize, but from what they

could tell, it looks like a suicide pill of some sort. *Nothing* could take this and survive."

Could the vampire have offed *himself*? Was it even possible? I needed to talk to Lea as soon as possible. I wasn't sure this could wait until our prearranged time.

"Where did this thing come from?"

"That's the question of the hour." I'd already told him about finding it under the Dumpster, but I was sure that wasn't what he meant.

"I'll let you know as soon as I hear something else."

"Thanks, Tom."

I hung up, figuring I should go home and hope that Lea showed up soon, but just as I headed back to the bar to pay Brian, the front door opened and a man walked in.

And damned if it wasn't the last person I wanted to see.

Sean.

Chapter 19

LEA

Victor held his hands up in surrender. "Okay, okay, I'll tell you what I know." If he'd been any other person, I would have just bitten him and read through his memories. But that would be giving him exactly what he wanted. With the vampire blood he'd been drinking, if I drained him now he'd turn. The last thing I needed was Victor as a vampire.

I tightened my hold on him.

"You have exactly one minute to tell me what I want

to know, and then I'm going to start removing body parts." I grinned. "Actually, please stay silent. It's been a long time since I've had a blood bath."

He paled and his mouth dropped open. "You wouldn't. I'm your patron. My father helped you for over fifty years!"

"You can be replaced, Victor. Forty-five seconds left."

"I'm funding a government project. I don't have all the particulars." His eyes darted with the lie, but I knew I would get it out of him later, so for now I just let him talk. "There have been some problems."

"Because they are using vampires?"

His throat bobbed as he tried to swallow. I tracked the movement with my eyes.

"No, that's not a problem."

"Then what is?" I had a hard time believing that whatever vampires they were working with weren't a problem.

"Security mostly, guards going missing, they can't seem to keep the staff together. Issues with leaks. If this gets out to the media, the whole project could be pulled. I can't have that. The work is too important, and too many lives are at stake." His eyes were almost sincere enough for me to believe him.

Almost.

"Where is all this taking place?"

"Little town called Johnsonville in Ohio."

I tightened my grip on him, pulling his face close enough to kiss. Or bite. "Bullshit. Where in New York is it happening?"

His body shook. "I can't tell you. I don't even know myself."

"How does Rikers Island play into this?"

His eyes twitched and darted away from mine again. "I don't know."

I pushed him, sending him flying across the room. His body smashed hard into the far wall and he slid down without even a whimper. "Lying prick."

Taking my time, I ransacked the room. Secret compartments were a specialty of mine and it didn't take long for me to find the one in the pedestal, under what had to be a three-hundred-pound, half-century-old vase. I lifted it and the tiny button below it depressed, opening a panel within the pedestal.

There was money, which I took, and a few jewels, which I also removed. Payment for all the shit he'd put me through. I didn't need the money, but it would be nice if Calvin could retire in style.

But none of that was what I wanted. Under it all was a single file folder. I pulled it out and opened it.

Asclepius Project was stamped on the inside of the folder.

But there wasn't a single fucking sheet inside it. "Son of a bitch." I slapped the paper down and ripped the pedestal out of the ground, throwing it and the vase across the room and through the main door.

Two guards came flying in, guns raised. I knew they would have silver bullets in the chambers. It looked like my time with Victor was up.

I had no choice but to leap toward them. Rushing them, I went for the guard on the left with the missing teeth and the dead eyes. Driving my elbow forward, I slammed it into his throat, taking him out with ease. The second guard swung toward me and I kicked back with my right leg, sweeping the weapon out of his hands.

He backed up. "Please, don't hurt me."

It occurred to me that these two might have some information I could use. "You won't feel a thing." I grabbed him and yanked him to me. Burying my fangs deep in his neck, I took a huge gulp of the coppery warm blood. His memories flickered through my mind: sex with his girlfriend, sex right after that with her best friend, standing on guard, masturbating while on his last lunch break. Nothing about the project, though, nothing at all.

I let him go and he slid to the floor, his eyes closed. "I hope your girlfriend caught you."

He smiled in his sleep and rubbed at himself, then slowed his movements as his heart slowed. Even as he died, he was trying to get himself off. Pig. I shook my head and left the underground bunker. Whatever information I needed I wasn't going to find here. But if not here, then where? Rachel was pumping her leads for information, but my gut said it wouldn't be enough. The only way we would crack this conspiracy was if we both gathered information from our individual sources.

I strode along the street as the night fell. Calvin had headed back to Rachel's place like I'd asked, so I was on my own.

I scanned the thin crowd around me. While I was dressed in an unusual manner with my tall leather boots, leather molded chest armor and hooded cowl, no one in New York even batted an eye at me. "Great costume," one guy said. "You here for Comic-Con?"

I nodded, and kept moving. Whatever they thought was fine with me.

The streets blurred as I walked, my mind going over the miniscule details we had collected. A government conspiracy involving vampires. There could be no good end to that. But where were they hiding the old vamps? And who was making all of these young, inexperienced vamps?

Peter could be behind this whole game. It was his style to work from the shadows. My maker would find a great deal of humor in watching me try to find him. Games were all the bastard knew.

I clenched my fist, barely resisting the urge to smash the wall beside me.

"Where are you?" I whispered into the empty night air.

A faint whisper tickled at my nose, like a perfume I could almost smell, could almost taste. Blood and chocolate and cologne.

Drawing in long deep breaths, I scented the air. There it was, a vampire. And a relatively new one by the scent rolling off him; still very human under the vamp smell. Tracing the scent, I wove through a box-filled alleyway to a less busy street on the other side of the block. There he was, twenty feet ahead of me. Sauntering like he didn't have a care in the world. Young and blond and built like a linebacker. He seemed to be searching for someone. Most likely, dinner.

My natural instinct was to rush him, take him down fast and hard, but I held back. Maybe these new vampires were the key to whatever mystery surrounded Victor and the Asclepius Project. So what if I befriended one, made him believe I was with him, and then pumped him for information? Young as he was, he probably hadn't even been warned about me yet. It was a chance I was willing to take. Worst-case scenario, I would just torture him for the information.

But this way, he would spill his guts without effort. Especially if he thought he was going to impress not one, but two pretty women.

A slow grin spread across my face. Yes, that would work.

Following him was easy, and I let my steps take me at a slow pace so I didn't close the gap between us. The last thing I needed was for him to get suspicious while I worked the details out in my head. I tucked my weapons away so they weren't visible, and swept the cowl off my head so my long dark hair flowed around my face and down my back. I knew the effect it had on men.

At the next corner he paused to lift his head and scent the air. This was my chance.

"Hello, my friend," I called out and he slowly turned to face me. I let my hips sway as I approached him, even going so far as to run my fingers through my hair. "I see you're looking for a place to eat?"

He was young, even in human terms. Maybe nineteen at the most. Baby-fine blond hair dotted his chin. It wasn't helping him look any older, if that had been the intention. He rubbed a hand over his shaved head. "Yeah, maybe. You want to eat together?"

I slipped an arm around his waist and he put one across my shoulders. "I have the perfect place to eat.

You'll love her." I gave him a wink and he laughed. If I could get him back to Rachel's place, we could interrogate him, maybe even make him think Rachel was going to be turned. Yes, that would work well.

"God, I love this life," he said as he tightened his arm around me.

"Don't we all," I whispered. "Don't we all."

CHAPTER 20

RACHEL

I hid around the corner of the hall, watching as Sean methodically began to check the booths and tables. Had he followed me? Or did he know the connection between Derrick and Brian? I felt bad about ditching the bartender without paying, but there was no way I could deal with Sean right now. I literally had seconds before he'd turn the corner to the hall. I had to act now.

I hurried to the door marked Private, thankful the

bar's security measures were lax. It was easy to slip into the alley. I pulled a wool scarf out of my bag and pulled it over my head, tucking the ends under the collar of my jacket. My first priority was to escape Sean, but I still really wanted to find out what Brian knew.

I hid behind a trash bin, not surprised when the back door to the bar opened and Sean's head popped out of the opening. He glanced around before heading back inside.

So he knew I was here. He'd had me tailed.

Shit.

I should have known better. I should have been prepared for it. Did he know I'd talked to Tom?

I pulled my phone out of my pocket and quickly called him. "Tom," I whispered as soon as he answered. "I'm being followed by the Feds."

"What?"

"I don't know if they saw us together or not, but you need to be prepared."

"Okay." His voice was tight.

"If they come to you, blame it all on me," I said, trying not to sound panicked. "Do whatever it takes to clear your name. Tell them I blackmailed you."

"Rachel, I'm not going to do that."

"Tom, listen to me. I'll sort it out on my end. Just take care of yourself."

"Call me later. Let me know you're okay."

"Okay."

I hung up and stuffed the phone into my front pocket, then waited for fifteen minutes before heading back inside. By then, a light drizzle had begun to fall and the sky was getting darker. Keeping my scarf wrapped over my head, I inched down the hall and peered around the corner. No Sean.

Brian was surprised to see me when I sat at the opposite end of the bar, still wearing my head covering. I pulled it lower and his eyes widened.

"Oh, fuck," he groaned. Panic filled his eyes and he backed up, banging into the counter behind him and knocking over a glass. The one guy in the place, sitting at the opposite end of the bar and nursing a beer, never even looked up.

I held up my hands. "Brian, I'm not going to hurt you. I only want to talk."

That only pissed him off. He slid back over, leaning down toward my face. "I'm not worried about *you* hurting me, little girl. It's the big bad wolf that's gonna get us. Literally."

My chest tightened. "What's that mean?"

He released a bitter laugh and shook his head. "You don't know shit, do you?"

I put my arm on the bar and lowered my voice. "I know you know something about the Asclepius Project and I know you're scared because the government is running it."

"You still don't know shit."

"Then enlighten me. What do you know?"

"The less you know, the better."

I banged my hand onto the counter. "They killed my friend, Brian, and there's no way in hell I'm going to let them get away with it. I need to know what you know. What you refused to tell Derrick."

He blinked. "Wait a minute... You know Derrick Forrester?"

"I've known him for seven years...knew him. They killed him." I swallowed the grief that followed those words.

But Brian seemed dazed by my news. "Derrick..." His reaction to Derrick's death seemed a little strong for a stranger.

"You two were friends?"

He shook his head with a blank look. "Sort of. I started talking to Derrick about a year ago...all online. We met in a forum."

"What kind of forum?"

He shrugged, trying to gather his thoughts. "Conspiracy theory stuff. I'd gone there looking for answers about things I'd seen."

"What did you see?"

He sucked in a breath, then released it. "I used to work at a place owned by a man named Victor. *Amore Sangre*. It was upscale, tips were good, but the clientele was...eccentric."

"How so?"

He grimaced. "I know this is going to sound crazy, but some of them liked to drink blood."

"They were vampires." Did I really say that un-ironically?

He nodded, then moved on. "But that wasn't even the strange part."

Of course it wasn't. "Then what was?"

He licked his lower lip. "Some of them disappeared, and I'm pretty damn sure Victor had something to do with it. I didn't think much of it, until I saw something in storeroom."

"What?"

"One of our clients, but a non-vamp. One of the vamp tramps…" He shrugged at my blank expression. "Women—or men—who hung out with vampires for the thrill of it. They get off on the whole blood-sucking thing."

I shuddered recalling my own up close and personal experience with Caine. No thank you.

"I hadn't seen her in over a month, but the vamp she hung out with hadn't come to the restaurant for at least that long, so I didn't think anything about it until I saw her."

"Why would she be in the storage room?"

"She wasn't there of her own free will. She was locked in."

"Why?"

"She wasn't herself. They changed her."

"Changed her how?"

He licked his lips again. "She was a monster."

I was about to ask him what in the hell he meant when Sean burst through the front door, his eyes wild.

Goddammit. This really wasn't my fucking day.

I expected him to give me a hard time, but I wasn't prepared for him to grab my arm and drag me down the hall.

As I recovered from the shock, I tried to pull loose. "Get your hands off me."

He gave me a hard shake. "I'm trying to save your life. Come on."

"What are you talking about?"

"They know you're asking questions. You have to go!"

"I'm not going anywhere with you until you give me answers."

"Rachel, listen to me. You have to go." He pushed the back door open and shoved me out, then I heard crashing and shattering glass from the front. The yelling started next.

"Too late," he said, rushing into the alley with me. "Come on!" He grabbed my hand and took off running toward the street.

"Where are we going?"

"Somewhere to hide."

I didn't have time to wonder if I should trust him. There didn't seem to be much of a choice. Self-preservation kicked in and I pushed to keep up with him as we crossed the street and continued on down the alley.

He stopped next to a derelict door and threw his shoulder into the wood, busting it open.

"Why are *you* running?" I asked. "Weren't those your people back there?"

He turned back to me in surprise. "No. They definitely were *not*." He pulled me into the backroom of what appeared to be a bakery, then into a windowless office in the middle of the building.

Adrenaline had kicked in, making it difficult for my complex reasoning skills to work, but I knew none of this made sense. "Do you know about the Asclepius Project?"

He groaned. "Oh, fuck. You know about the Asclepius Project?" He kicked the desk. "Damn it all to hell. I prayed Derrick hadn't told you about it."

"So you're not denying it?"

His face hardened. "It's a little late for that now, isn't it?"

"Then what do you know about it?"

He grabbed my hips and pulled my body in front of his, not touching but close enough to spike my hormones. "It was created by a terrorist group. The ultimate bioterrorism—taking civilians and turning them into fighting machines."

"How so?" I asked.

"We don't know. But people started to go missing. Inmates started to die at a fucking crazy rate. And then the murders…" He paused. "We think the group has taken their experiments out of the lab and into the wild."

"Wait. Inmates? What inmates?"

"They've been buying inmates and using them for experiments."

I let out a shaky breath. I had never dreamed my two stories might be connected. If I could get the work order from the guard tomorrow, I might be able to track down who'd ordered it. But there was no way in hell I was going to share that with Sean. "They've been creating vampires."

He looked surprised. "Yeah, but not just any vampire. Out-of-control vampires that aren't right in the head."

Was Sean right? Derrick had been certain that the government was behind this, but what if Sean was really out to stop them? "So that's why you were in the alley that night?"

He nodded. "I knew Derrick was on the case too, and I tried to get him to back off. I warned him the group would find him and kill him to keep the information secret. But you know Derrick…"

"I still don't understand why we're hiding in this room."

"My agency doesn't trust anyone with this information. They think you know what's going on and they want to lock you up. I can't let that happen." He looked into my eyes and I felt my resolve weakening.

"Why not?" I whispered.

"Because I still love you." His lips lowered to mine, soft and tentative, but when I didn't resist, the kiss became harder and more urgent. He cupped my face with both hands and pulled back, fear in his eyes. "I can't let anything happen to you."

What was I doing? But if Sean could help us in any way, maybe it would be best to see how this played out. At least that's what I told myself. "I can take care of myself."

"I know that, Rach, but I can't help feeling protective of you."

"Then what do you want me to do?"

"Back off this case. If you stop digging, I think I can convince them to leave you alone."

I lifted my eyebrows.

"But I know you," he said with resignation. "You're incapable of backing off."

I knew he was playing me like a Stradivarius violin, and it wasn't hard to figure out that I was much closer to the truth than he liked—because I knew there was more to the story than he was letting on. But he was right. He did know me, and he would have been suspicious if I'd caved too fast.

"I can't do that. I can't let those people get away with murdering Derrick."

"And I promise I'll do everything in my power to make them pay for what they've done."

I took a step back, breaking free from his hold. Free from his spell, more like it. I sucked in a deep breath to clear my head.

He grabbed my hand. "What can I do to earn your trust?"

"Why don't we—"

A muffled metallic sound clanged in the backroom.

Sean's back stiffened. "Dammit. They found us."

"Who?"

"The terrorists." He pulled a handgun out of the shoulder holster inside his coat and loaded the chamber. "You still carry a gun?"

"Yeah."

"Get it out."

Shit. I'd suspected—no, hoped—the whole terrorist story was a ploy to sway me. I pulled my gun out of my bag and turned off the safety.

"Shoot to kill," he said quietly, his voice tight. "These boys won't be playin'."

My heart slammed against my ribcage. Had I gotten him all wrong? Why was he trying to protect me if he was part of the conspiracy? "What's the plan?"

"I'm going to distract them and you're going to run."

I shook my head. "No. I'm not leaving you here."

"I didn't just find you to lose you. *Please*. Just do as I say. This is my area of expertise, remember?" I started to protest, but he interrupted. "That wasn't a sexist statement and you know it. I'm a trained soldier. Your martial arts aren't going to protect you from bullets."

He had a point.

He grabbed the back of my head and pressed his mouth to mine, his tongue finding my own. He pulled away, leaving us both breathless, and me more confused than ever.

We heard another sound, closer this time.

"They came in through the back door," he said. "Just like we did. I'm going to distract them and you find a way out the front." He dug into his coat pocket and pulled out a card. "There's an address on there. Meet me at this location in two hours. And if Derrick gave you any information, bring it with you." A hard glint filled his eyes. "Then we'll go after the bastards. Together."

"Sean."

"I know I haven't given you much reason to, but I'm begging you to trust me. Just this once. We'll work on the rest later."

Did I really have a choice in the matter? If he wanted me dead, we wouldn't be having this conversation. "Okay."

"Thank God," he muttered. "Now, on the count of three, I'm going to run across the hall to the prep area. You run to the front door. Shoot the lock if you have to."

"Be careful. I want to see you in two hours." I was surprised how much I meant it.

A ghost of a grin tipped the corners of his mouth. "That's the best thing I've heard all day." Then he bolted across the hall, shoving a metal rolling cart into the wall.

Within seconds I heard gunfire as I ran to the front door.

It was locked, which didn't give me a lot of time to figure out how the hell I was getting out of this mess. A brush of air on the back of my head turned me around. There was a vent right above me...just big enough for me.

I had a feeling things were about to get ugly.

Chapter 21

LEA

The young vampire's name was Louis, and he was a fan of Anne Rice—his mother had named him after the main character in her books. How was I not surprised?

"You see, the vampires in her books were really just tortured souls that..." he rambled as we climbed the steps to Rachel's apartment. God he was young, in so many ways.

"What made you want to be a vamp?" I asked

suddenly, for the first time in a hundred years curious about what would motivate someone to do such a thing. Rarely did I actually talk to any of them, I just killed them and was done with it.

Louis grimaced and tapped his right thigh. "I had cancer. It was in my bones really deep, and they were about to take my leg to the hip. Then they found it in the other leg, and both my arms, too. They said that it was a long shot, but they could take everything off and maybe I'd live. Maybe."

I frowned, wanting to believe I wouldn't have taken an out if faced with those odds. "And?"

He laughed, but it was a nervous sound. "You need more of a reason than facing the rest of your life—short as it may be—with no limbs? I don't believe Ms. Rice was right, you know. I don't think we're tortured souls unless we want to be."

Now that was way too fucking deep for a kid of nineteen. I had to force myself to smile at him. "Well, I guess you might be right."

"Why did you turn?"

His question caught me off guard, and I answered without thinking. "I didn't have a choice."

Louis sucked in a sharp breath and stopped on the landing in front of me, Rachel's door behind him. "That's against the rules. You should complain to the council."

Rules? Since when did vampires have rules? And what was this council he was talking about? I shook my head. "Happened a long time ago. Don't worry about it."

I stepped past him and tapped on the door. Three

rapid-fire knocks followed a slap of my palm against the wood.

Calvin opened the door. "What the hell took you so long? I've been back here for—"

"Calvin, we have a guest." I stepped sideways so he could see Louis. Louis gave him a big grin, his fangs hanging long in his mouth. The young pup hadn't even figured out how to properly hide them.

Calvin froze, his eyes flicking between Louis and me several times. "I see. Is he...staying long?"

"Long enough to meet Rachel and have dinner."

Louis laughed and pushed past me. "Is she here? You said she was beautiful, but I have a hard time believing she's prettier than you." He looked over his shoulder and winked at me.

"No," Calvin said, "she isn't back yet."

I stood in the doorway, doing a quick calculation in my head. She was overdue by at least half an hour. Maybe in another situation that wouldn't be so bad. But with the assholes we were dealing with...I knew I couldn't chance it.

I grabbed one of the coats hanging on the back of the door and breathed in her scent, settling it into my brain. Earthy like a heavy incense, with more than a hint of gun oil. Very unique.

I pointed at the young vampire. "Louis, you stay here with Calvin. Don't eat him, he's mine."

Louis held his hands up. "I can wait for Rachel. I don't like old dude blood anyways. They taste like hemorrhoid cream."

Calvin spluttered. "Listen, you little shit—"

I shut the door and ran down the stairs. Calvin could take care of himself around a newbie like Louis, I wasn't worried. But Rachel was a whole other can of worms.

Her scent was still fairly fresh and I followed it, running as fast as I could along the streets. She'd stopped in an alleyway first in the Upper East Side, her scent lingering as if she'd stayed for at least a few minutes. I swept the alley, looking for what might have caught her attention. The faint ghost of ash caught my eye and I crouched over it, breathing it in.

Vampire.

So...this was one of the murder sites she'd talked about. I paused, thinking about the ash. The same as the vamp I'd hunted in Montreal when he'd swallowed that pill. There was a different smell to it than when I staked them. An undercurrent of antiseptic.

But what would make the vamp here down a suicide pill?

There was only one obvious answer and it made the hairs on the back of my neck stand up.

Another Cazador. A hunter like me.

The implications were huge, but at the moment, I had to find Rachel. I'd deal with the possibility of someone like me later.

I jogged along her trail, tracing her next to a coffee shop. The night had fully fallen and my eyes adjusted accordingly. The coffee shop was hopping with hipsters, many of them with silly moustaches that so resembled the men of my bygone era.

"Stupid then, stupid now," I muttered under my breath. Rachel had met a man at this coffee shop.

Someone I didn't recognize, but I was betting he was a contact of hers, someone who provide her with information.

Maybe a lead. But if so, why hadn't she come back to wait for me?

Because she's more like you than you want to admit, my inner voice said. Damn, I hoped it was wrong because if she was that much like me, I had no doubt she was in trouble.

I picked up my speed, running fast enough that people did a double take as I passed them, unsure of what they'd seen. Rachel's scent trail took me to two more alleyways, both with the residual odor of death and vampires. More murder scenes then. Damn, she was determined.

From there, she headed back into Harlem to a bar called the One Toed Monkey. I pulled my cowl up, tucking my hair underneath it, and stepped inside.

Quiet for a Friday night, that was my first thought; the sign said 'Closed', which I ignored. My second thought was that there was blood everywhere.

It had been cleaned, but if the smell was any indication, it hadn't been cleaned well. My nostrils flared and my fangs descended. I strode up to the bar. The man behind the bar had a brand-new shiner and his lip was split, but he still managed to give me a smile.

Until I smiled back.

His face paled, making the shiner stand out. "Shit."

"Where is she?" I leaned forward. "I can smell that she was here. I don't like all the blood that's been spilled; it's making me antsy as hell. So I suggest you speak quickly so I leave and don't act on my...urges." I ran my tongue over my lips and fangs.

I hadn't thought he could get any paler, but I was wrong. "A guy took her. Army dude grabbed her and ran. Then a bunch of his friends came in and smashed my place up." He held his hands up to either side of his head.

I leapt up onto the bar in a crouch so we were almost nose-to-nose. "Where'd all the blood come from, then?"

With a shaking hand he pointed at an empty white pail on the bar. "They poured a bucket on the floor."

The only reason they'd do that was to chum the waters to draw in what they were fishing for. Why did I get the feeling I was the one they were trying to hook?

I inched closer. "You recognize me. What I am. What do you know about vampires?"

He swallowed hard, his throat bobbing. "Derrick told me about the project. He was hoping to confirm all the rumors. All I know is that it's in an underground bunker somewhere in the city. I swear that's all I know."

I reached out and patted him on the cheek, feeling the truth of his words. "Good boy."

Sliding off the bar, I started toward the back door, picking up a trace on Rachel again. Army dude had grabbed her, and his friends had busted the place up.

Out the back door I went, then across the street and into another alley. Rachel was with Sean, the man who'd ransacked her place. I smelled him now, the same scent that had permeated his business card and her apartment. Damn, what was he up to? Was it possible they were friends? No, it couldn't be. Friends didn't tear apart each other's places. Even I knew that.

The front and back doors of the bakery were both smashed in, but Rachel hadn't left and the smell of gun oil and rank man sweat was thick in the air. I crept in through a side window, keeping to the shadows as I searched for her.

The creak of a floorboard ahead of me stopped me in my tracks. I lowered myself to my belly and waited. Listening.

There it was, the soft exhale of a breath and the distant beating of several hearts. As I lay there, the glint of a gun winked at me from a side door in the shop. I watched the shop, eyes flicking from place to place as I counted the slightly darker shadows indicating feet blocking the miniscule light. There were at least six men waiting for me.

A trap with Rachel as the bait.

They had to have been watching her apartment; they had to have seen me with her. The blood in the bar was only a failsafe to draw me in if I did indeed follow her. This was their chance to catch the elusive Cazador by taking out her new associate.

Very fucking clever, Sean.

Slithering forward on my belly, I kept searching for Rachel, following her trail into the main room. They'd blocked her from escaping forcing her to go to ground.

I rolled onto my back and looked straight up into the vent above me.

Rachel stared down.

"On three," I whispered. She nodded.

"One." I tensed my body, ready to grab her and run out the front door.

"Two," she mouthed at me as she lifted the vent's grate to the side.

"Three."

She dropped out of the vent at the same time as I sprang to my feet. I grabbed her wrist and leapt forward, pulling her through the air with me and out the broken front bay window.

Shouts erupted behind us, and shots shattered the night air.

I bolted into the alley, taking her with me. "What the hell were you doing with Sean?"

"How did you know?"

"I can smell him all over the fucking place," I snarled, running as fast as I could while dragging her behind me.

The sound of a howl drifted into the night air, followed close behind by four answering howls, one right after the other. I skidded to a stop as a creature that should not have existed stepped into the alley to block our escape.

It had four legs, a head, and a tail. But the rest of it bore no resemblance to man's best friend. Its loose, mottled, furless skin looked like a costume three sizes too big. The head was far too human for my liking, except for the fact that its jaw seemed to be able to unhinge.

"What the fuck is that?" Rachel breathed out. She lifted her gun and squeezed off a shot before I could tell her it probably wouldn't do any good.

Perfect aim, she hit the thing square in the chest.

It didn't even flinch.

"I don't know."

"You're a vampire. What do you mean, you don't know?" Rachel yelped as we turned to run the other way.

"When it comes to monsters, this is not on the list of natural species."

We slid to a stop as another of the demon dogs stepped into view, blocking the other end of the alleyway. Closer than the first, this time could see the oh-so-human eyes blinking up at us.

For the first time, I considered that we might be in over our heads.

Spotting a fire escape ladder, I pushed Rachel toward it. "Climb."

"We'll be trapped on the roofs."

"No, we won't," I said, right behind her. By the time we were halfway up, the two creatures had gathered at the base of the ladder.

Where were the army dudes?

Something whizzed by my head and slammed into the brick wall, sending mortar and dust into the air.

"They've got silencers," Rachel gasped as she pulled herself up the last few rungs.

I pushed off and leapt the rest of the way, landing beside her. "So they do. Your Sean has asshole friends."

"Those aren't his friends. Those are the bad guys. I can't believe Sean would be a part of this," Rachel said, with more than a little defensiveness in her voice. But I could see in her eyes, even she didn't believe her own words.

I looked over the edge. "*Mierda.*" Shit, this was getting

worse and worse. The two creatures were climbing the fucking wall like spiders.

Rachel took a quick look and then stumbled back. "This has got to be a nightmare. This can't possibly be happening."

I eyed up the buildings next to us. "Do you trust me?"

"I don't think I have a choice, do I?"

I shook my head as her blue eyes met mine. "No, not if you want to survive."

I motioned for her to follow me as I ran to the far side of the roof. There was only one way this was going to happen. Before she could protest, I grabbed her arm and threw her over the gap between the buildings. She let out a squawk, but I was impressed. She didn't scream. I backed up, took two running steps, and leapt across the divide.

Rachel was standing there glaring at me when I landed. "A little warning would have been nice."

"I wasn't sure you'd let me toss you."

A shot zipped by us again, but it went wide.

"They have to be on the roofs by now, too." She shook her head. "This must go deeper than I thought if they're willing to go to these lengths to keep me quiet."

It was my turn to shake my head. "I don't think it's just you. You were bait, Rachel. They knew I would come looking for you. You can't think they didn't know you were in that vent…"

She was silent as we jogged to the far side of the roof. This one she could jump on her own. We jumped three more rooftops before I stopped her. "Time to double back."

"Those creatures are back there."

"I doubt it." I took a deep breath. We were downwind of where we'd started and I was getting nothing. Retracing our steps, I stopped her when we reached the building I'd originally thrown her onto.

"Time to get back to your apartment." I kicked open the rooftop door and peered inside. Steps led down to a second door, which was unlocked. I ducked my head in and then motioned for her to follow me. The long hallway of apartment doors was silent.

"My apartment is going to be the next place they look," Rachel said.

"I know. Which is why we have to hurry. I left Calvin there with a hungry vampire."

"You did what?" She grabbed my arm. "A hungry vampire?"

I flashed her a smile. She was a protector of others. Just like me.

"Like I said, that's why we have to hurry."

Chapter 22

RACHEL

What I really needed was a few minutes to clear my head, but Lea was right. Time was not on our side. I wouldn't be surprised to find Sean's friends—or the supposed terrorists—waiting behind my front door.

I turned and looked at the woman next to me. I'd met her less than twenty-four hours ago, yet here I was, literally trusting her with my life. Letting her make major decisions that could get me killed.

All I had to go on were my instincts. They'd served me well in Iraq. I'd be stupid not to listen to them now. And everything in me said she was my best option—at least at the moment.

"You don't seemed too fazed by any of this," I said, hustling to keep up with her brisk pace. "This must be just another day at the office for you."

"I could say the same about you." She glanced over her shoulder. "Nice shot, by the way."

"It helped having a dad and brothers who were all about teaching me self-defense."

"That was well past self-defense."

I grinned. "Let's just say I'm an overachiever." We were silent for a moment, then I asked, "So this is what you do? Run around catching monsters?"

"Something like that."

"And Calvin…he's your…" My voice trailed off.

Her back stiffened. I was slightly worried she'd turn around and literally rip my head off, but hopefully our girl-time with monsters would protect me. I was surprised when she answered, "He has been my partner for over fifty years."

Partner? As in business or significant other or both? I wanted to ask her, along with how old she was, but I figured that would be pressing my luck. Besides, I wasn't sure I wanted to know. "So…just you and Calvin? No one else? No family?"

"No."

Her answer caught on the wind, but I still heard the loneliness saturating that one word, which seemed to carry centuries of desolation, and I felt a tie to her I'd never felt with anyone.

For the first time, I felt like I'd found someone like me.

Raised in a house full of boys, I'd never fit in with the girls in school. I was too much like the guys, which was one of the reasons I'd adapted so well in Iraq. But it was a lonely existence, and after Sean cheated on me and Derrick left, I never let myself get close to anyone.

When we were close to my apartment, I grabbed Lea's arm and pulled her to a halt.

She obviously wasn't a touchy-feely person because she jerked back and her dark eyes flashed at me with a feral wariness that quickly faded. Note to self: refrain from touching the vampire hunter.

"I have a way into my apartment that might keep us from being seen."

Her eyebrows lifted slightly. "I'm listening."

"We head down this alley and sneak in the back door of the apartment building next door. Then we take the stairs to the roof, leap over to my building, and take the fire escape stairs to my apartment."

Her eyes narrowed. "Why don't we just go straight to your fire escape? It seems much easier."

"Because they'll be watching the ground. They won't think to look up."

A slow smile spread across her face and I got the distinct impression I'd passed some kind of test. She swept her arm toward the alley in a graceful flourish. "Lead the way."

I hung to the shadows while I dug out my lanyard

of keys, finding the right one with the help of the streetlights. When we were close, I stopped, my back hugging the side of the building. "Do you see anything suspicious?"

"Do you?" There was a hint of challenge in her voice.

"No, but I figure you probably have a special skill set I don't. Might as well combine our assets, right?"

She smiled again.

I strode to the back door of the neighboring building, looking like I owned the place, then slipped the key in the lock and opened the door.

"Where did you get a key?" she asked as we headed into the hallway.

I snuck up to the front entrance, looking out onto the street for any obvious signs of surveillance. "The maintenance guy."

"And he just gave you one?" I heard the smile in her voice.

There were no signs of Sean's buddies, or whoever they were, but they knew I'd be looking for them now, so they'd be more discreet.

I turned back to give her a wicked grin. "Like I said, skill sets." She probably thought I'd slept with him, but all it had taken was a little flirtation and some sleight of hand.

I led her to the stairwell. No sense taking the elevator and risking witnesses in case Sean's guys were smart enough to figure out my secret route. I was in great shape, but I was out of breath when we reached the roof. Lea acted like she'd done nothing more strenuous than stroll down the hall. She looked around the skyline, then at the gap between the buildings.

"Smart."

I shrugged. "Always have an alternate exit. Or two." I looked over the edge to make sure no one was looking up at us, then leapt over the edge, landing on my feet. I turned back to look at her, but she had already landed and was walking toward the door to the stairwell. Damn vampire speed.

"So, it's true," I whispered as we descended the one flight to my apartment. "Vampires are fast."

"You've seen it for yourself."

"I have no idea what's fact or fiction, so I'm just making a list for future reference. I have to say I'm relieved you don't sparkle."

To my surprise, she chuckled.

"No sparkling. But as you've probably figured out, our sense of smell is very acute." She paused as we reached the door to my floor. "No fresh scent of your friend."

"Sean? He has a distinct scent?" But then she'd told me so earlier today.

"Everyone does. How do you think I found you?"

Well, shit. I hadn't even considered that part yet. I'd been too busy trying to not get killed. God, I was getting sloppy *and* stupid.

She opened the access door and strode toward my door, her grace and confidence assuring me of what I already knew—she was a deadly force to be reckoned with. I had no desire to see her skill set turned on me. Lea currently considered herself my friend, but I needed to think about how to defend myself if she changed her mind.

She rapped on my front door with a series of knocks and hand slaps and the door opened, revealing Calvin. At least Lea's vampire friend hadn't eaten him. Yet.

Shit. What if he wanted to eat *me*?

Lea looked over her shoulder. "You're perfectly safe."

Could she read minds too? Or could she smell my fear? I hoped it was the latter as I followed her into my apartment like I was the fucking guest.

A handsome young man was reclining on my sofa, his arm extended across the back. His eyes lit up with excitement as his gaze traveled up and down my body before landing on my face. "Lea, you didn't exaggerate about your friend." He actually licked his upper lip, his fangs hanging out in what I figured was the equivalent of a vampire hard-on.

Great.

Rather than respond to the kid, she directed a pointed glance at Calvin. "Any trouble?"

"No."

If Lea could smell fear, then her boy-toy could, too. This was *my* goddamned house. My anger superseded my fear. Forcing myself to release the breath I was still holding, I headed to my fridge and grabbed a bottle of water. Holding it up, I said, "I'd offer you guys one but…" Then I shrugged and screwed off the cap. "Lea, care to introduce us?"

"Louis, Rachel."

He patted the seat next to him, keeping his hungry, albeit slightly confused, gaze on me. Good God. How old was he? Of course, that was probably a complicated question.

I rolled my eyes and perched on a barstool. "I'll pass. I gave blood last night."

He turned a confused look up at Lea.

She gave him a patient grimace. "A little pre-dinner conversation first."

I leaned forward. "That means the grownups are going to talk now, sweetie."

His smile was gone in a flash, replaced by a snarl of anger.

Lea sighed. "Rachel. Please."

I sat back on the stool and took another swig of water. "What are we doing? We need to get out of here before the people from that bakery show up at my front door."

"We need to figure out where to go next."

"That's easy. We get the fuck out of the city."

"But I think what we're looking for is here *in* the city."

"The lab?" I asked, incredulous. Would someone—government or terrorists—actually build a dangerous lab in such a populated area? That seemed insane, and far from inconspicuous. But then I thought again about what we'd seen in the alley and what Brian had told me. He'd seen a monster. For that matter, so had we.

I stood and began to pace, no longer afraid of the danger on my sofa. At this point, he was low on the ladder of life-threatening concerns. "We need to pool our information." I stopped and looked her directly in the eye. "You first."

Her eyebrows rose in challenge.

Calvin began to laugh, a deep phlegmy sound. He

sat on the side of my armchair, trying to recover. "You really have met your match, Lea."

She studied me for a moment. "I found my patron. Victor."

I held up my hand. "Wait. Brian, the bartender, used to work at a place owned by a guy named Victor. He said it was frequented by vampires. *Amore Sangre.*"

She gave a slight nod. "It's his place."

"Brian said he saw a monster there. A former patron. He said she was a vamp tramp, but her vampire stopped coming to the restaurant. He found her locked in the storage room." So much for letting her spill her information first. "He met Derrick online a year ago in a conspiracy theory forum."

"A year ago?" she asked in surprise.

I thought about the creatures in the alley. "Brian was able to recognize her. But those things we saw…they were not even close to human."

"I saw another creature when I found Victor. It had a tiny human body, but a bat-like face. Definitely unrecognizable as a former person."

"So maybe the woman Brian saw was an early experiment?" I shuddered at the thought. "I'd been chasing a story about disappearing inmates. Sean said they'd been buying inmates and using them for experiments. But it's like we have two separate events going on. The blood-drained bodies. What do they have to do with the lab and the monsters?"

"The blood-drained bodies…I think they were to get my attention. The journalists specifically called them 'Vampire Murders.' Not exactly subtle, but it worked."

"And why would they want you exactly?"

She gave a half shrug. "Probably to off me. If I'm gone, they can come out of hiding."

It seemed like a lot of work to kill one vampire hunter, but we had no other theories at the moment.

"Back to your patron—Victor. We know he had something to do with the creation of the monsters. Why would he do that?"

"Power. Respect. He wanted to be a vampire, but I refused to turn him."

"So why didn't he just get someone else to do it?"

"The council," Louis said. "The way I understand it, if you ask a powerful vampire to turn you and they turn you down, you can't ask someone with less power." He shrugged. "Not to mention the council regulates the more powerful vampires. They don't want them to upset the balance of power."

I shook my head. "Wait? There's a council? A *vampire* council?"

He gave me an exasperated look. "Of course. Someone has to run things."

I shot Lea a wide-eyed look of disbelief, then turned my attention back to Louis. "So if Victor wanted power, he'd have to find another, even more powerful vampire to turn him."

"Yeah, but lately the council has lifted the quota ban on new vamps because so many are getting killed. The older and more powerful ones are disappearing."

I cocked my head. "Disappearing how?"

He shrugged. "The council doesn't know. They thought it was the Cazador, but now they think it's something else. That's part of the reason they let me be turned."

"How old are you?" I blurted out.

He looked surprised. "Nineteen."

"You've been a vampire nineteen years?"

"No. I've been a vampire for a month. I guess I'll forever be nineteen, huh?"

"Enough," Calvin barked. "Back to what's going on here."

I turned to Lea. "Why don't we ask the council to tell us what they know?"

Lea's eyes darkened. "Think about our vow."

Louis looked from her to me. "What vow?"

"Shut up," she snapped at him. His jaw closed with a click and he sat quietly. Well trained, at least.

Oh, my God. I'd vowed to kill all the vampires. Which included the man on my sofa. Nausea turned my stomach. He was a baby. Literally. When I'd made the vow, I'd met one other vampire—Caine, a true monster. What had I agreed to?

She saw the horror in my eyes and held my gaze. "We can't go to the council."

Of course we couldn't. She wanted to kill them all.

You're the Cazador, I mouthed, not daring to say the words out loud. If Louis heard them, he'd be gone.

She continued to hold my gaze, practically daring me to judge her. But I couldn't. Not until I had more information.

"So you found Victor?" I asked, breaking her hold on me. Had she tried to use her vampire voodoo to get me to do what she wanted? If so, it hadn't worked.

"Yes, he tried to tell me the facility was in Ohio, but I saw through his lies."

"What *did* you find?"

"Money, a folder with Asclepius Project stamped on the inside. The folder was empty. He admitted he was helping fund the government project."

"Sean said it was conducted by terrorists."

She lifted her eyebrows in a look of strained patience.

I'd known Sean was likely lying, so why did the confirmation stab me in the gut? Dammit. "Why would Sean come up with that elaborate setup?"

"Me," Lea said matter-of-factly. "They want me."

"No offense," Louis said. "You're pretty and all, but why would they want you? I know there's a group who put a price on the Cazador's head. The council is trying to find her and turn her over to them in some type of exchange. They've tried to lure her out."

Lea turned her now deadly cold eyes on her guest. "What does your council," she spat the word in thinly veiled disgust, "tell you about this Cazador?"

"She's been a vampire hunter for hundreds of years. Even after being turned into a vampire herself, she chose to hunt us instead of joining us."

"And they would murder innocent people to find her? Enough to make the news?" Lea asked.

His eyes widened in fear as he started to connect the dots. "Oh fuck," he whispered, scrambling to his feet.

I had to defuse this situation. "Sean's not done with me. He gave me a card with an address on it, and told me to meet him in two hours with Derrick's information."

I glanced at the microwave. "Which gives us about twenty minutes."

Lea turned her attention to me.

"I have to meet him," I said.

"It could be dangerous."

"*Could be?* I know it will be. But I have to find out what's going on."

Her jaw ticked. "I'm coming with you."

I started to protest, but I had to admit I liked the idea of someone having my back. Especially someone as powerful as Lea. "We need to leave now, but I have to grab some things first. I suspect I won't be back here for a while. If at all."

Louis was pressed against the window, terror in his eyes. I couldn't go without dealing with him first.

"Lea, I'll let you come with me, but you have to agree to let him go." I motioned to Louis.

"He knows too much," she snarled.

"Can't you spell him into forgetting this ever happened? And maybe convince him that he can have a snack without killing his food?"

"It doesn't work that way with vampires." But I saw her resolve slipping.

"The council already knows you exist. What does it matter if he saw you?"

Calvin stood, his gnarled fists clenched at his sides.

"Lea," I edged toward her until there was only a foot separating us. "I want to trust you. If you let him go, I'll help you until this thing's over. No questions asked. Blind trust. Please."

She hesitated, then nodded sharply.

Louis let out a sound of gratitude, but Calvin looked pissed.

I didn't care. Let the old man gnaw off his cheeks with his dentures. My agreement was with Lea, not with him.

"Get your stuff. I'll take Louis to the roof and see him off, you head to your meeting and we will follow."

"Deal."

I hurried to my room and tossed some clothes and toiletries into a duffel bag, then pulled Derrick's bag out of its hiding space.

"You can't just hand that over to him," Lea said, standing next to my bed.

"I'm not stupid." I pulled out a folder and plucked out two pieces of paper I'd taken photos of earlier in the day. "But if I'm going to play this out, I have to give him something."

"Good thinking." Lea reached for Derrick's bag and I hesitated before handing it over. I'd just told her I was going to trust her. It was time to live up to my word.

Chapter 23

LEA

With one hand I gripped the duffel bag containing all of Derrick's gathered evidence; in the other, I held onto a now-shaking Louis.

"You really are the Cazador? Shit, how could I not have figured that out? I'm so stupid." His words tumbled off his lips. "The council hates you. They said you were a cold-blooded killer who had no idea what it even meant to be a part of the vampire family, but you're going to let me go. Which means you aren't as bad as—"

Calvin slugged him in the back of the head. "Shut the fuck up."

Louis cringed, which made me want to cringe. I couldn't kill him, no matter what Calvin was thinking. And I knew my helper well enough to know it was going to be an argument. Maybe it really was time to say a final farewell to my long-time partner. The money and the jewels from Victor would be enough to see him through his final years in comfort.

"Calvin—"

"No, we aren't discussing this." He looked at Rachel. "Where are we meeting you?" As soon as she opened her mouth to speak, he growled at her. "You would disclose information about a meeting with a potential mark in front of this vampire?"

He'd done that on purpose, to trip her up. Jealousy already? Yes, that sounded about right for him.

Flushing, she grabbed a notepad off the kitchen counter and pulled off a piece of paper. "Actually, no, I was going to ask you how long I should wait before I worry about you and Lea."

With a quick flourish, she scribbled something on the paper and handed it to Calvin. His jerky movements told me all I needed to know. He was pissed about this whole situation.

I tightened my hold on Louis and started him toward the door. "You won't see me, Rachel. But I'll be there. You'll hear the cry of a night bird. That will be me."

She nodded. "Be careful."

Her concern surprised me. "I'm not the mortal one. Don't let him corner you, no matter what happens." I couldn't resist throwing her own words back at her. "Have more than one exit."

A sharp laugh escaped her. "Goodbye, Louis. I'd say it was nice to meet you but I'm not sure it was. If I can give you a piece of advice?"

He nodded. "Sure."

"Don't believe beautiful women won't drive a stake through your heart. I think you'll last longer."

Hustling him ahead of me, I forced him out the way Rachel and I had come in. "The roof, Louis. I'm going to show you a trick of the trade."

"You're going to teach me something?"

A slow breath escaped me. What was wrong with me? I should just kill this vamp and walk away. But his story hung inside of me, like a picture I couldn't stop looking at. Sick, scared, dying. Who wouldn't take an out that gave them back a chance at life and immortality?

To top it all off, he did seem like a nice kid.

I dropped the bag and advanced on him. "I'm just about the only hunter left, so if you see me coming for you again, run."

He nodded, but didn't back up. "You said you were going to show me something."

"You ever jumped a roof before?"

"Shit, you mean like in *The Matrix*?" His eyes widened with distinct pleasure and I fought not to smile at him.

"Never heard of it, but pay attention." There were

two buildings next to Rachel's apartment. One was snug against it with a barely three-foot gap which I'd been across several times. The other was about fifty feet away. I ran toward the roof's edge and pushed off at the last instant, sending myself flying over across the larger gap.

I landed in a crouch and looked back at him. He gave a holler and fist-pumped. "That was freaking awesome!"

My lips twitched and I beckoned him. "Come on, kid, let's see what you've got."

Calvin popped up on the fire escape and I spared him a glance and a shrug. I'd promised Rachel I wouldn't kill the kid.

And for some reason that promise meant more to me than my vow to kill all vampires.

Louis sprinted toward me and pushed off. There was a soft pop and his body jerked mid-air, losing momentum. He hit the roof's edge and I grabbed his hands, hauling him up. "What the hell?"

Blood pumped out of his shattered heart, bits of silver glinting against the deep red. As he spluttered in my arms, his blue eye sought mine. "Do you think I'm going to hell?"

Another breath burbled out of him, and then his heart stopped. I laid him down on the roof as the final stage of death took him, his body turning to ash in a blinding burst of light.

"No, Louis, I don't believe you are. But I might be." I looked up in time to see Calvin duck back down the ladder. I paced the roof, more to give myself time to calm down than to give Calvin time to get to the car.

"Son of a bitch, he heard me give Rachel my word!" I snapped into the night air, my movements getting progressively more violent. What the hell was he thinking?

The vow, he was holding to the vow even if I wasn't. The fight went out of me and I bowed my head. In my heart, I was torn in two directions. Toward the life I'd built with Calvin, which revolved around hunting vampires and nothing more, and toward Rachel. A friend who could help me find a glimmer of humanity in myself. In my kind.

Something I hadn't even known I was craving.

I leapt across the building and scooped up the bag.

Rachel's head popped up from the escape ladder. "Louis left already?"

"He's gone." I helped her up, then watched as she made the short jump to the closer building.

"Thank you for not killing him, Lea. I know it goes against your vow."

"And yours," I said softly, unable to look her in the eye.

When I glanced up again, she was slipping into the adjacent building, her hair now concealed by a baseball cap. She'd still be hard to miss, but at least she was trying.

I grabbed Derrick's bag and jumped off the edge of the building. Dropping like a stone, I hit the ground hard, bending my knees to absorb the impact. I caught up to Calvin two blocks over at the Camaro. How the hell had he moved so fast?

I bent closer to smell him and he swatted at me. "Keep your nose to yourself."

Frowning, I slid into the car and said nothing.

"You aren't going to yell at me for shooting the kid?" His eyes flicked to the rearview mirror.

"Not going to change anything." I opened Derrick's bag and riffled through his things, looking for key words or something that would jump out at me. My fingers grazed a bump in the bag. I ran my fingertips over the large area again and realized what it was—a compartment sewn into the bag. Finding the lip carefully hidden in the top stitching, I ripped it open. A thin sheaf of papers looked up at me, three words shining at me like a beacon.

Lieutenant Sean Price. His name was signed at the bottom of one of the documents. I pulled the papers out and flipped my way to the beginning. Security detail for the Asclepius Project. Confirmation that he was in on the whole show. Shit, and now I had to tell Rachel. I could tell she didn't trust him, but I could also tell she liked him. More than liked him—I could smell him all over her.

"*Mierda*, this is going to give us grief." I tapped the paper. I wanted to read more, but Calvin was already pulling to a stop.

"We're here."

Here was an abandoned hotel with a single burning light on the ground floor. Calvin parked us behind a rusted-out garbage truck, giving us good cover. I watched as a dark SUV pulled up and parked in front of the building. Four men got out. Four men with big guns, headpieces for communication, and an attitude that had nothing to do with being excited to see Rachel.

Sean was the last one to get out of the car, his scent unmistakable. I slid out of the Camaro, waved at Calvin to stay where he was, and crept closer.

I managed to catch the tail end of what Sean was saying to his men.

"Do not engage. I want to talk to Rachel before we decide what to do."

The men all laughed and I narrowed my eyes at the casual misogyny. They needed a good lesson on what women could do, and I was just the person to give it to them.

The four men spread out, and I marked their positions. Two went in with Sean on the first floor; the other two headed to the second floor to keep watch, one in the front, one in the rear.

I slipped around to the back first, using the rubble of leftover renovations gone wrong as my cover; a beaten-up couch, the remains of the original front desk, and what looked like a knock-off replica of the statue "David"—minus the best part, which had been broken off. The walls of the old rundown hotel were slick, but handholds were plentiful. I was sliding through a second floor window just as the soldiers were getting into position.

The interior of the building was blown out other than a few walls that held it together. No rooms, just a wide-open expanse with support beams here and there. I couldn't see the second soldier, the one watching the front entrance, but I didn't waste time looking for him. I'd find him soon enough.

I picked up a piece of old tile and flipped it past the

soldier's head. The clatter spun him around, and I used his distraction to creep up behind him. I grabbed his head in one hand and his gun in the other. A sharp twist snapped his neck. So easy.

Holding his body, I slid him down to the floor without a clatter, then scooped up the headpiece and slipped it on. Just in case Sean decided to change things up.

Hurrying, I raced to the other side of the blasted-out hotel. The few remaining walls provided perfect cover. Headlights appeared and the soldier on my headset confirmed her arrival.

"I see a car, sir."

"Excellent. She's on time," Sean said. "Well trained, I will give her that. Keep an eye out, I expect her vamp to tail her in." The men laughed in chorus.

Interesting. His words only confirmed what I'd guessed. They *were* baiting me. But why? Just to protect the vampires? Or was there something more as per Caine's hints at my blood being pure? Why did I get the feeling it was the latter possibility?

"No one touches a hair on Rachel's head," Sean added, much to my surprise. Perhaps he wasn't as much of a bad guy as I'd thought. I snorted; I was going soft.

I watched from my spot as Rachel slid out of a taxi before it spun and pulled away. She approached the hotel. The solider watching the front entrance was so focused, I didn't have to use any sort of distraction. Just snuck up behind him and cracked his neck like I'd done to his buddy.

No biting, though. The last thing I wanted was for

Sean and whomever the fuck he worked for to get more of my DNA. As he slid to the floor, a piece of paper waved at me from his back pocket. I pulled it out, my eyes going wide. This would be the final nail in Sean's coffin, but I had to play it carefully. I tucked the paper into my vest.

I raced to find a stairwell, searching the rubble for a good three minutes before I found something that would work. An old elevator shaft.

"Good enough," I whispered, forgetting all about the headpiece. One of the remaining soldiers snorted.

"What are you talking about?"

"Quiet," I growled, hoping to hell I sounded manly enough. Apparently it worked, as the others went silent. I shimmied down the shaft, using the old cables as ropes. The elevator doors hung open down below. I peered out to see one of the soldiers was right in front of me. Too damn easy.

I slid out one of my knives and worked my way back up the cable so I was suspended at the height of his head. Slamming the knife forward, I drove it through the back of his skull and held it there while he twitched and jumped like a fish on a line. There was a sharp clatter of his gun hitting the floor, but that was it.

"What the fuck are you doing? Sean's going to have our asses if you blow our fucking cover."

I didn't answer the last solider. He was the lucky one. He was the one I was going to catch and hold for that perfect moment.

The moment I'd show Rachel what a complete and total traitor Sean was.

I couldn't help the grin that slid across my face.

Chapter 24

RACHEL

The taxi's taillights faded as I eyed the run-down, abandoned hotel. This was a setup and I needed to be prepared. The papers were tucked in my bag. My gun was loaded and in a holster strapped to my chest, hidden under my jacket. But he'd be ready for that.

God, I was such a fool.

But he wouldn't expect the knife strapped to my leg under my jeans and the one up my jacket sleeve.

I opened the car door and stepped out, taking in the black SUV parked in front of the entrance and a garbage truck to the side. I didn't see any of Sean's men lurking around, but then, he'd never been sloppy.

The heels of my boots clanked against the pavement as I made my way to the broken front door. I pulled out my gun and held it up in front of me. After the ambush at the bakery shop, Sean would expect me to come prepared.

The glass was busted out of the front door. I eased through, keeping an eye out so I wouldn't be blindsided. The place looked ransacked, and there were pieces of tile and chunks of drywall everywhere. I turned a corner and saw Sean leaning against a pole, holding a flashlight.

"Rachel." Relief filled his eyes. "I was so worried." He reached for me and I resisted the urge to stiffen as I lowered the gun. He pulled me into a hug.

"Why are we meeting here?"

"It's best we lie low. You can put your gun away. We're alone. Did you bring Derrick's research?"

I stuffed my gun into my holster, thankful that it bought me some time. Should I play stupid or ask questions? He knew I wasn't a fool. Asking questions was built into my DNA. "How did you get involved in this?" I asked.

His shoulders relaxed slightly. "There are reports of terrorists in Ohio. But we think they're running trials here in the city. I'm here to investigate."

"You said they were trying them out in the wild. Do the terrorists want to kill or infect?" He gave me a surprised look. "Bioterrorism lends itself to infection. But what is their particular focus? Death or infection?"

"Both."

"I saw some. When I escaped. The terrorists must have brought them when they were tracking us."

He looked alarmed. "They didn't bite or scratch you, did they?"

"No. Is that how they infect?"

He studied me for a second. "We don't know."

"So we need to capture one."

"We?" he asked in surprise. "You're not capturing anything."

"Then what am I doing here? I want to help put a stop to this."

"I'm trying to keep you safe." He put a hand on my shoulder. "In addition to the terrorists, I think the vampire is targeting you next."

"Me?" My shock was genuine. "Why?"

"Our sources say she knows you're getting close and she wants you out of the way."

"She?"

"Yes, she's a very old, very powerful vampire. She likes to play with her victims, pretend she wants to work with them. It's her MO. You can't go against her alone. I'd like to put you under my protection." He paused. "But you can also help us."

"How?"

"We know she's coming for you. We'd like to use you as bait."

"To kill her?"

"No, to use her."

"That doesn't make any sense."

"We've found the location of the lab and we're about to raid it. We can't just shut it down, so we think we can use her blood as an antidote, if you will."

His excuse was such bullshit. Did he really expect me to believe him?

"And if I don't agree to your plan?"

"Rachel, don't be stupid. Not only will you be getting protection, but you'll be helping us get a monster off the streets. How can you even consider not going along with this?"

"Because I don't trust you."

I heard a soft bird's cry. Lea was here.

I took a step back. "I think you're a liar."

He looked shocked. "How can you say that?"

"Perhaps because your men had her surrounded," Lea said as she stepped out of the darkness, holding a knife to a soldier's throat.

Sean lost his composure and stepped away from the pole. He made a move to grab me, but I pulled the knife from my jacket sleeve, holding it in a defensive stance.

He glanced down at the knife, then up into my face. "That's a new trick."

"Just keeping you on your toes." I took several steps back toward Lea.

"So you're working together?"

"That's none of your damn business, Sean."

"She's using you, Rachel. I'm telling you she's done this before. She is *not* your friend."

"Using me? The only person I see using me is you."

The man in Lea's grip made a move. She gave him a

sharp jerk and pressed the knife into his throat, drawing a trickle of blood. "I have no qualms about slitting his throat."

Sean looked like he wanted to rip her head off. "Keep your bitch on a short leash, Rachel."

My pulse throbbed in my temple. "On a leash? She's not an animal."

"Rachel. *Open your eyes.* She hunts and kills. That's pretty much the definition of an animal. You've picked the wrong side."

Lea released a low grunt, presumably in response to his insult.

"You don't have all the facts," Sean said, holding out his hand and advancing toward me. "You think I've betrayed you, but she's the one who will kill you before this is all over. I love you, Rachel. I only want to make sure you're safe."

I cast a quick glance to Lea, whose expression was hard, her eyes cold. I turned back toward Sean, lowering the knife slightly. "You're exactly right, Sean. I'd be insane to choose the side of an animal."

A grin lifted the corners of his mouth.

I could feel the anger radiating from Lea.

I cocked my head and sneered. "And the only animal I see in this room is you. I'm passing on your offer."

He clenched his fists at his side. "You'll regret that decision."

"The only decision I regret today was kissing you earlier. I think I need to be tested for STDs."

"Enough," Lea barked, moving a few steps forward. "We need to decide what to do with him."

I had a few ideas, but Sean wasn't going to like any of them.

Chapter 25

LEA

I held the soldier tight against me, his heartbeat echoing in my ears. His vain attempts at struggle only made my fangs drop. "Don't force me to kill you," I whispered into his ear.

Rachel glanced at me. "Just talking to my friend here," I explained.

Her eyes widened as she took him in. "I know him. He and Ben worked with Sean in Iraq. Justin, what are you doing helping this asshole?"

Justin tensed. "We're saving the world, Rach."

Rachel looked over his shoulder at me. I shrugged. "They'll tell them anything to get them to do the dirty work. Saving the world, stopping terrorists, whatever it takes."

His whole body shook under my hands. "Fuck you, bloodsucker. You're the one causing all the problems."

"What do you mean by that?" Rachel stepped closer, her tone softening. Cajoling. Damn, it was no wonder she was such a good journalist. I could feel Justin softening. He opened his mouth, but all it took to silence him was a swift look from Sean. A look of sadness flickered across Rachel's face. I couldn't help the sigh that slipped out of me. I had no doubt she'd ask me not to kill Justin.

"Don't kill him. Just knock him out," she said.

I rolled my eyes as I wrapped an arm around his neck and tightened it over his carotid artery. He gurgled and gave one last violent struggle before the fight slipped out of him, and with it, his control over his bladder. The hot scent of piss filled the air. I curled my lips and stepped away from him. Slowly, I smiled at Sean. "So are you going to do this the easy way, or the hard way?"

Rachel laughed. "Oh God, he only knows the hard way."

"Excellent, that's my favorite choice."

Sean's head whipped from side to side as he tried to keep us both in his line of sight. But that was impossible. We moved with him, always keeping him between us like an unspoken signal. We were the hunters now, not him.

Sean had finally become the prey.

"Rachel, you don't know what you're getting into. You can't trust her." He pointed at me. I snapped my teeth at him.

"A little closer, I could use a snack," I said.

Rachel laughed again, but there was a bitter tone to it. "Yeah, get a little closer to Lea."

"God, it sickens me that you would give it a name," Sean growled.

Rachel gasped and I narrowed my eyes. Then again, he had a point. As a Cazador, I had been taught that all vampires had to be wiped out as quickly and efficiently as possible in order to keep the rest of the populace safe. We no longer saw them as the humans they'd been before they were bitten. So while I didn't like what he'd said, there was truth underlying his words.

I was a monster, and had been one far longer than I'd been human.

Rachel pointed her knife at him, her arm not wavering for even a second. "Sean, you are going to take us to the facility and help us get in."

"No."

I burst out laughing; I couldn't help it. "You think saying no is going to stop us? Delusional. They must be handing out good hallucinogenic drugs at the base."

Sean turned his attention fully to Rachel, his eyes and face softening. "Rachel, please, please listen to me..."

I didn't let him go much further than that. I leapt into the air, straight up above his head and landed directly behind him. Grabbing his shoulders, I yanked him back so that his ass slammed into the floor. After his head snapped back, I cupped his throat with one hand and his forehead with the other. "There's a good boy. Now behave or I'll rip your throat out and dance in the blood."

His eyes rolled up to look at me. "Bitch."

I smiled down at him. "Thank you."

Rachel cleared her throat. "Since you two are getting on so well, how about we move this along? Sean, you are going to escort us to the base. The cover is that we are bringing in Lea since that was your plan all along. I will be your helper, and of course, the reason you were able to capture her."

"They'll never believe it."

I gave him a shake. "Don't be an idiot. You told us they're after me. That's why Rachel was used as bait. That's why they committed those murders. To draw me to New York. Keep your own stories straight at least, eh?"

His jaw tightened. I looked at Rachel. If her expression was any indication, we had him. The plan would work.

Rachel hurried over to Justin's prone body and pulled off two pairs of cuffs. "One for Sean. One for you later." She flipped a pair to me, which I caught and slid onto Sean, tightening them until he grimaced. I dragged him to his feet and frisked him, finding several knives and a small gun tucked into the small of his back. I checked the safety and handed it to Rachel.

"We don't need anything else, do we?" Rachel asked.

I shook my head. "No, we can take Sean's SUV from here. Calvin can follow us in my car."

Sean cleared his throat. "Rachel, you can't trust her."

"You keep saying that, but you are the only one who's lied to me," Rachel said. Her words sent a twinge of guilt through me. Louis's death might not have been at my hands, but Rachel wouldn't see it that way if she knew.

Sean smiled up at me from where he sat. "I'll bet she

killed my two other men. One of them was Benjamin. You remember Ben, don't you?"

Rachel swallowed hard. "Tell me he's wrong. Ben was my friend. We were in Iraq together."

There could be no compromise here. "And if he was your friend, why didn't he warn you? Why would he help Sean stake you out?" I said. "I'm sorry if they were your friends. But I won't lie. They are dead."

"She would have killed them even if she'd known. That's what she *is*, Rachel. She's a fucking killer." Sean's Adam's apple bobbed against my hand, and for just a second, I considered doing as I'd said. Then again, without him, we'd be stuck without a proper escort.

Rachel pulled herself together. "People die in war, and that's what this is, isn't it? War."

A breath of air I didn't realize I had been holding slipped out of me. Sean let out a low laugh. "You think that's the worst of her sins? She promised to let the young vamp go, didn't she? Tell me, why is there a pile of ash outside your building then?"

Rachel sucked in a sharp breath. "You had my building bugged?"

He nodded. "I had one of my men watching. He watched while Louis had his heart blown out of him with silver shot. I keep trying to tell you that I'm on your side. I'm trying to protect you from the monsters, Rachel."

Her blue eyes sought mine and I didn't look away. I wouldn't lie to her, not even to make this happen an easier way. Whether she realized it or not, she'd sworn an oath to me. I needed her trust fully and completely, no matter how hard won it was going to be.

I nodded slowly. "He's right, Louis is dead."

Jaw tightening, she stalked over to Sean, grabbed his arm, and helped him stand. "Then I guess I am the fool here."

"Rachel—"

"No, just fucking give it up. I wanted to trust you, but obviously I can't trust *anyone*. Don't you follow us, Lea. Not for one fucking second." She glared at me as she pushed Sean in front of her. But then she tipped her head to me ever so slightly. She might not trust me fully, but I was the only backup she had.

Maybe she was pissed at me about Louis and the others, but she was a smart girl.

She needed me to get this job done.

Rachel stalked to the front door and down the rusty steps. I waited until I heard the engine start and the wheels of the SUV pull away before I sprinted after her. I reached the Camaro and leapt into the backseat. Calvin was so fast asleep he didn't even twitch. Some helper.

"Calvin, wake up, old man."

He startled in his seat and opened his eyes, starting up the engine before he was even fully awake. "Did it work?"

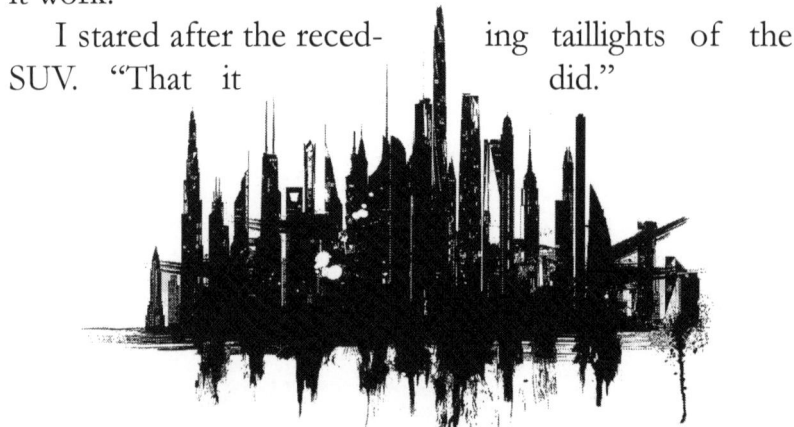

I stared after the receding taillights of the SUV. "That it did."

Chapter 26

RACHEL

A fine mist fell from the sky as I shoved Sean into the backseat of the SUV, then climbed behind the steering wheel, my mind reeling. She'd lied to me.

Why had I been so stupid?

Yet I still needed her. Damn it.

The keys were still in the ignition, so I didn't have to dig them out of the pockets of any dead bodies. Bodies of men I had thought were my friends.

Like Ben.

He, Derrick, and Sean had been close back in Iraq. It didn't make sense that Ben wouldn't have tried to help Derrick.

What if Sean was right after all?

I was questioning everything.

I started the vehicle and backed it up, then pulled on to the street. "Which way?"

"Rachel," he pleaded. "Think this through."

"I *am* thinking this through, you asswipe. *That* was why we never worked. You always underestimated me."

"How was cheating on you underestimating you?"

"You thought I was too stupid to find out."

He was silent.

"Where are we going?"

He released a sharp laugh. "You really think I'm going to tell you?"

I cast a glance over my shoulder. "If you're smart you will."

"You think I'm *scared* of you?"

"No." I shook my head. "I think you're so stupid that you've underestimated me once again. *God.*" I shot him a look of disgust in the rearview mirror. "Do you *really* think Lea's just going to let you go?"

Surprise filled his eyes.

"She's going to follow us, you fool. I'm delivering her for you with a nice tidy bow. That's exactly what you want, right?"

He sat up, his jaw slack with surprise. "You're helping me?"

"I'm here in this damn car with you and she's not. What does that tell you?"

His eyes narrowed. "Why the change of heart?"

"God, you really don't know me, do you?" I asked with a sneer. "She not only lied to me, but she also broke a vow."

He snorted. "That's always been your problem. You're so damn idealistic. When are you going to figure out the world doesn't work that way?"

I was starting to ask myself the same thing.

"I'm only trying to help you, Rachel."

"Stop. Don't pretend you give a fuck about me or how I feel. I'm here for self-preservation, nothing more, nothing less. You can bet your ass I'm not doing it for you."

"I'm not the one who lied to you."

I snorted. "Don't insult me." I glanced at him in the mirror. "But I need you to tell me the truth now."

He studied me for a moment before I glanced back at the road. "You've changed."

"I'm not sure if that's a compliment or not."

"You're wiser."

"If I wasn't, I wouldn't still be alive."

"Why do you want to turn her in? It can't be because she lied to you. Why not just let me go and be done with this?"

"For one thing, do you really think someone like her would just let me walk away? I know too much. Besides, I turned my back on her. She'll hunt me down to the end of the earth to find me." I searched the mirror for his eyes again. "Just like she'll find you," I said in a low, ominous tone.

He swallowed, betraying his fear.

I sucked in a breath. "But mostly it's for Derrick. He deserved more than what he got." I paused. "I think she did it. She knew it would motivate me to search for answers, which would lead her straight to you and the facility." I found his eyes again, so he would know I meant every word I was about to say. "Because I vow to find Derrick's murderer and I will *make them pay*."

His gaze softened. "Then let's make her pay. Together. We can do this as a team. We used to work pretty well together."

I released a harsh laugh. "Working in bed does not count."

He leaned forward, his mouth in my ear. "I disagree," he whispered huskily. "We were always quite in sync."

He wasn't lying there.

The mist turned to a drizzle and I switched on the windshield wipers. "If I pull over and un-cuff you, then what?"

"Then we do this together. And I can only hope it's the beginning of more togetherness."

I shook my head. "This is just a job for you, Sean, so quit bullshitting me. You've been using me from the start. Just. Like. Lea."

"Rachel, pull over."

"Do you think I'm stupid?"

"I want to tell you the truth. Can I do that?"

"Nothing's stopping you."

"I need you to look at me while I tell you."

I groaned.

"Rachel. Please."

I didn't see Lea tailing us. I had a gun and two knives, and he was unarmed and cuffed. "Fine, but I'm keeping my gun on you the entire time and I won't hesitate to shoot."

"You need me to take you to the facility."

I pulled off the road and parked behind a building. "I never said anything about killing you."

He laughed as I put the car in park. I pulled out my gun and shifted in my seat, pointing it at his crotch. "Back up all the way in the seat. You make one move toward me, and I'll shoot off your favorite body part. Understand?"

Grinning, he shook his head and sat back. "Is this good?"

"It'll do. Start talking."

He pushed out a breath. "I've been chasing this group for a year. It became obvious Derrick was on to the same thing, which was no surprise. He'd been in contact with the scientist who'd been heading up the program, but the scientist stopped all contact. Derrick realized he was missing and was trying to track him down. But it was Derrick, all alone, against all of them. Like I told you, I tried to warn him, but he refused to listen. My superior officers," he leaned his head back and sucked in a big breath of air before letting it out and lowering his gaze to mine. "Once they figured out the Cazador was interested in you, they decided to see how it played out."

"So you decided to use that to your advantage?"

His expression became pained. "My superiors' plan

was to capture you and use you as bait. We made our move earlier today—at the bar. I was dead set against it, but then I realized it would be easier to protect you if we brought you in. That's when the terrorists showed up and I knew I had to get you out."

I groaned. "Don't insult me. There are no terrorists. The government owns the lab. You're protecting a government facility."

He watched me for a moment. "The government *does* own the lab, but there is a terrorist group set on using the research for harm. They kidnapped one of the scientists—the one Derrick had made contact with—and forced him replicate his research. And they were there at the bar and the bakery this afternoon. They were after you and Lea. The monsters are theirs."

"More lies," I said in disappointment.

"I swear. I'm telling the truth."

"Which time? When you were molesting me in that bakery or now? Or how about this morning? You tell so many lies I don't even think you can keep them straight."

"Call Justin. If he's even still alive. Ask him." His eyes narrowed. "I'd tell you to ask Ben, but that monster vampire killed *him*." When I didn't respond, he forged on. "He volunteered for this mission. He found out we were protecting you and he was the first man to jump on board. He died trying to keep you safe. Don't let him die for nothing."

"Even you can't deny you've lied to me."

"To protect classified information. To keep you safe."

"Save it."

He slowly tilted his face forward. "I know you have

every reason not to trust me, but I'm begging you. Take off my cuffs and let's avenge Derrick's death together. The key is in my coat pocket."

I watched him, the rhythmic thud and squeak of the windshield wipers making an eerie sound. I wasn't sure what to believe, but I knew I didn't trust any of them. Not Sean. Not Ben. Definitely not Lea. I only had my instincts to keep me safe, and I was listening to them now. I only hoped they didn't steer me wrong.

"I'll un-cuff you, but you're driving and I *will* shoot you if you make a wrong move."

His coat pocket buzzed and he glanced down at it. "If I don't answer that, they'll start looking for us."

I slowly reached into his pocket and pulled out the cell. Recognizing the name, I answered.

"Justin?"

"Rachel?" he asked, his voice sick with worry. "Are you okay? Is Sean with you?"

God, I hoped I hadn't made the wrong choice. I switched the phone to speaker. "He's with me."

"Justin. What's the damage?" Sean asked, all business.

"The team's gone. I'm all that's left." He paused. "Sean. I need you to take me off speaker."

Sean gave me a knowing grin. "Okay, Justin. I'm off speaker. What's up?"

My eyes widened in surprise.

Justin's voice lowered. "There's been a change in orders. Command says to take out the bait."

Take out the bait? That was *me*.

"Why?" Sean's tone was brisk.

"We don't need her. The vamp knows how to find the facility. She's headed there on her own. Tracking you."

Sean's eyes found mine. "So why take out the asset?"

"I don't like it any better than you do, Sean, but they want to clean up loose ends. What are you going to do?"

Sean's gaze still held mine. "I didn't find her just to lose her. Command can go fuck themselves."

"I was hoping you'd say that," Justin said. "So what do you want to do?"

"I made a vow to Rachel to help her avenge Derrick's death and that's exactly what I'm going to do. We'll sort out the rest later."

Justin hung up and Sean continued to stare at me. "I meant every word, Rachel."

"And so do I," I said reaching for the handcuff key in his pocket. I wouldn't stop until the person who had killed Derrick paid for his crime.

Even if that meant I had to face down Lea.

Chapter 27

LEA

Calvin kept the Camaro at a perfect distance, all the lights off. A pang of regret circled my heart. I was going to miss him, no matter how much of an ass he could be. Not to mention the fact that I knew he was being fed vampire blood. That alone made him a danger to this mission. I pulled out the things I'd taken from Victor's safe. I placed them on the seat between us.

"When we get there, drop me off and go."

He glanced at the small fortune piled up next to him. "Just like that?"

"I release you from your vow." My jaw snapped shut on the last word as the back of my eyes prickled. If I'd had any tears left, they would have been on my cheeks. Fifty years, and I was saying goodbye. Damn, it never got any easier.

"You still need me—"

"I've got Rachel now. Whether she likes it or not, she made the blood vow. I will train her." I stared straight out the window at the blinking taillights of the SUV ahead of us. I rubbed a hand over my face. "One of us isn't going to make it out of this alive, Calvin. And we both know I'm the one who's harder to kill."

"Lea, you don't know that. You don't know."

"I do, dammit! *Madre de Dios*! I see death coming and it isn't looking at me. And I can't do it. I can't be the death of you." I was yelling, screaming if I was being honest. All the years between us, all the fights, and then that one night...I loved him as much as he would let me, and at least I could do this one last thing for him. "Swear it to me, you will drop me off and leave. Take this money and the jewels and go."

His jaw tightened, reminding me again of the young, broken man he'd been. We never talked about it, but I was the one who'd found him that night, cradling his wife as she died in his arms.

"If I die, then it's my damn time to go. You think death scares me? I know she's waiting for me on the other side. My boy, too. I have no reason to run from death." He let out a sigh. "Why do you keep trying to protect me? Because I'm old?"

Now or never. "Because I will always try to protect those I love."

The words hovered in the air between us; things that had been left unsaid for fifty years.

"Kind of a shitty time to spit that out, isn't it?" he grumbled.

I tried not to smile. "Yeah, but my timing has always been suspect."

"You think it's going to go that badly in there?" Calvin motioned at the car in front of us with one hand.

The facts Rachel and I had gathered swirled around my head, like pieces of a puzzle I could almost see if I looked hard enough. "I think no matter how it turns out, it's going to be our last hunt together. The likelihood of us all getting out alive is...not good," I said the last two words softly, but I knew he heard me.

"And you would go in anyway."

"I have to. Even if it weren't for the vampires waiting somewhere in there, and whatever testing is being done on them, I have Rachel to think about." I drummed my fingers on the edge of the door.

"That bonded to her already?"

I let out a soft sigh. "She has potential. When I look at her, I see the person I once was, and I...I want to find that person again. She can help me, Cal."

He snorted and gave a bitter laugh. "You aren't ever going to be human again."

"No, I know that. But I can be better than what I am. I want...more than this life of a never-ending hunt."

"And all this deep conversation is because you think we're going to die." Not a question, a statement.

"Yes, I think there's a chance. And I don't want to leave certain things unsaid." I didn't reach for him, but my fingers itched to touch him. "I know why you killed Louis. I didn't realize at first how much he looked like the vamp who took your wife and boy. I'm sorry."

His hands tightened on the steering wheel. "They're slowing down."

I nodded. The SUV was pulling over, but there were no buildings. Nothing to indicate a base of any sort. "You don't have anything to say to me before we do this?"

Calvin let out a slow breath. He opened his mouth as if to say something, but then shut it again and shook his head. "No."

It shouldn't have hurt, that single word.

Yet it did, more than I cared to admit.

So I focused on something that was within my power. Rachel and Sean slipped out of the SUV.

And Sean wasn't wearing his handcuffs. What the hell was she thinking? Or was she really fool enough to think she could trust that asshole?

"Here," Calvin handed me a cell phone. "I can trace it. You go after her and make sure she doesn't get herself killed. If I'm getting replaced, at least it's by someone who's worth your time to train."

I took the phone and tucked it into my back pocket. "Be careful."

A big breath slipped out of him. "You, too. You're about the only vamp worth saving on this planet."

My lips twitched. That was as close to an admission of affection that I was going to get from him. "Thank you, Cal."

I rolled down the window and slid out the opening, not wanting the light from the door to alert them to my presence. Wherever they were going, they wouldn't know I was there, but I'd be watching. Waiting for Sean to try and hurt Rachel.

My fangs lowered of their own volition at the thought. Rachel was in my circle now and I wasn't about to let him lay a hand on her.

Chapter 28

RACHEL

"We're close," Sean said, pointing to the forest in front of us. "We'll slip in the back door, through the hangar. Very little security there, and I think we can rappel down. We need to try to beat her there."

I'd holstered my gun when I uncuffed Sean. I wasn't exactly thrilled about it. Despite the conversation between Sean and Justin, I still didn't completely trust him. I was either getting smarter or just cynical. Either way was an improvement over my previous naivety where Sean was concerned.

"What happens if she gets there first?" I asked.

"You know what she is, right?"

I suspected he wasn't just talking about her being a vampire. I might not trust her, but there was no sense volunteering any information he might not already have. Then again, I didn't know very much myself. "A monster."

"And the murders? They were ordered by the vampire council." It wasn't a question. "But why were the bodies carved with symbols?"

"If you can let yourself believe there are vampires, then why not believe in the power of symbols?"

"You mean magic?"

He shrugged. "Call it what you will."

I headed to the back of the SUV. "We're taking weapons with us."

"Of course, I wouldn't think of going in without them."

I sorted through a bag in the back of the SUV, sorting through the different guns and ammo.

"Care to tell me where we're going?"

He cast a glance at me before taking the Glock I handed him, checking the safety, and sliding it against his lower back. "Fort Tilden. On Rockaway Beach."

The abandoned military base. It was brilliant. That part of the peninsula was pretty much uninhabited.

"We can contain...*research* there."

"Monsters of your own."

"No. Not monsters, Rachel. Or, rather, only a special type of monster. Vampires."

"Why?"

"Their blood…it's special."

"What does it do?"

"I'd rather show you."

That remained to be seen. "And you're keeping vampires here?"

"Yeah."

"So, Lea…the symbols…they're for what? To make her stronger?"

"We don't know. But we do know she's a dangerous rogue vampire and we need to test her blood." He cast a glance at me.

"Are you using vampire blood to create the monsters?"

He released a short laugh. "No. Their blood is going to save the world."

I started to ask him how, but my phone vibrated in my pocket. I wasn't surprised to see Tom's name on the screen when I dug it out and took several steps away, keeping my eye on Sean as I answered. "Yeah."

Tom hesitated. "You're not alone."

"No."

"Then I'll keep it short. I have more information on the pill."

Sean was pretending to focus on the gun in his hands. "Go on."

"I told you we thought it was a suicide pill, but I don't think it's for humans."

"Then who—" But I didn't finish. I already knew what it was for.

"The chemicals are overkill for a human. I would say it's for an animal, but it would sure be a strange way to kill one. It's full of a variant of VX, a nerve toxin that was supposed to have been wiped out by now."

"What do you mean, 'wiped out'?" I cast a quick glance at Sean, but his eyes were sweeping the area.

"VX was a nerve toxin used in the '50s. All the stockpiles were supposedly destroyed. Tell me you used gloves when you picked up that bottle." His tone made sweat break out all over me.

"Yes, but they were thin."

"Shit, Rachel, this is bad. Wherever you are, you need to get tested to see if you have any of that stuff on your skin. Now."

"Thanks." I hung up and stuck the phone in my pocket. I swallowed hard. There was nothing I could do about it now.

"Business?"

"Yes and no." I debated how much to tell him, but my skin was already crawling with the thought of that nerve toxin. "I may have come into contact with a substance similar to VX."

Sean's jaw tightened. "Then it's a very good thing you're coming with me. We have the antidote in the lab."

I would have felt relieved. If his superiors hadn't just told him to kill me.

He didn't ask any more questions and I didn't volunteer any more information. We walked in silence through the forest the rest of the way to Rockaway Beach. I tried to guess where his allegiance truly lay. Or if there was an antidote for the VX...and if I would actually be given it.

When we were close, he motioned for me to slow down. We were in a forest in the middle of nowhere, and he wanted me to be quiet. A shiver of unease crawled up my spine.

"We need a plan," he said.

"You know the facility. I presumed you had one."

"I wanted to sneak in through the hangar, but I think we should be more straightforward. We'll go through a security checkpoint. They know me, so they won't question me being there. I want you to pretend to be unconscious. I'll bring you in as a bite victim."

I lifted my eyebrows, keeping a blank expression.

"I know. You'll have to trust me. Do you?" His face gave nothing away.

"I don't trust anyone, right now."

He took my hand. "Fair enough." His free hand cupped my cheek. "I know we've had our differences, but I loved you once, Rachel. I still do. We have a second chance, you and I. Let's avenge Derrick's death and then we'll start over."

"It's not that easy."

"Why not? We *have* something. You feel it." He leaned forward and kissed me. I tried hard to resist, but Sean had always had a pull on me that defied logic.

I pulled free, panting. "Now isn't the time, Sean. I could be covered in that toxin shit."

He blew out a breath. "You'd be dead already if you'd touched it, Rach. Just tell me there's hope. Please." His thumb stroked my cheekbone.

"Why?"

He inhaled deeply, then pushed out a breath. "Dr.

Stravinsky's research is dangerous. The public needs to be protected. I can't leak the information, but you can. I want to sneak you in and show you where it's located."

"Why didn't you tell me that two hours ago?"

"I wasn't sure how you'd take it. I didn't think you would trust me."

He knew the carrot he was dangling. I leaned forward, my lips lightly brushing his. "Let's get going."

Chapter 29

LEA

Following Rachel and Sean through the forest was a snap. Their voices slid back to me as they walked, their conversation making me more than a little crazy.

I hissed in frustration as Sean continued to push Rachel to trust him, cajoling her and teasing her with bits and pieces of info. And the way he didn't tell her right away that she was clean of the VX shit? "Fucking asshole."

Of course, VX was what was in the suicide pills. Something that would literally light a vamp on fire from the inside out. And of course, Sean had the antidote.

They paused in a small clump of trees, and Sean continued to try and convince her to see his things his way.

"Dr. Stravinsky's research is dangerous. The public needs to be protected. I can't leak the information, but you can. I want to sneak you in and show you where it's located," Sean said. I knew what he was doing, holding the ultimate prize in front of Rachel. The chance to break a story that would rock the very beliefs of the human existence. Heady stuff for a journalist of any sort, but especially one of her calibre.

The doctor's name shouldn't have shocked me.

Stravinsky. The monster maker. I'd never met him, only heard about him through reputation. And even that was enough to make me wary. He'd be able to manipulate the humans into believing him, making them think he was really a doctor. But if this was the same Stravinsky I knew by reputation...he'd understand all too well how to make vampire blood into a cure-all for every disease they had, at least enough to get the humans to believe they needed him.

"Why didn't you tell me that two hours ago?" Rachel said, irritation plain in her voice.

"I wasn't sure how you'd take it. I didn't think you would trust me."

There was silence, and then she breathed out a sigh. "Let's get going."

That was my cue.

I slid out from behind the tree, but my dark clothes

still allowed me to blend into the darkness. If Sean thought he was sticking her in there, he had another think coming. It worried me, though, that she thought she could trust him. I shook my head and waited.

They stopped two trees ahead of me, and Sean grabbed her around the waist. "One more time, for good luck."

She gave him a soft smile, far too soft. Shit, she *did* believe him. Damn love and the strings it pulled. He jerked her tightly against him and they wrapped around each other. Behind her back, his right hand slowly slid up her spine, then back down to his hip and a square metal thing waiting there.

She'd let him have weapons back? What. The. Fuck.

His eyes slid sideways as he kissed her and I stepped to the side so he could see me. He stumbled back and whipped out his weapon. It wasn't even a real gun.

"Seriously, that is not impressive. A stun gun? You think that would work on me?" I put my hands on my hips and stared him down. It would work, all too well, but I was hoping he didn't know that. Electricity would fry me almost as much as the bright sun would. "Rachel, you cannot trust him."

"And you think I *can* trust you?" Her blue eyes flashed with anger.

I spread my hands. "I've never lied to you. Not even when the truth made you angry. I didn't lie to you about Louis's death, either, but I could have quite easily manipulated you into believing whatever I wanted."

Her eyes flickered and I saw the doubt there. "Why did you kill him?"

"Calvin did it before I could stop him. Louis looked like the vamp who killed Calvin's wife and boy." The only way she was ever going to even halfway trust me was if I continued to tell her the truth, even when it wasn't mine to tell.

Sean snorted. "Please. You're a killer, a Cazador. *The* Cazador."

I nodded. "I am. But I gave Rachel my word. That means something to me. I will protect her, with my own life if I must."

I kept my eyes on Rachel, watching her for signs of understanding.

She took a step toward me. "I want to trust you, I do. I want to trust both of you."

I shrugged my shoulders. "One of us is lying to you." I pulled out the paperwork I'd found in Derrick's bag, and more importantly, the paper I'd pulled off the solider at the hotel. "Proof it isn't me."

With a quick scoop, she grabbed the papers from the ground, her eyes widening. "These are orders to have me killed as soon as Lea is tagged and bagged."

Sean shook his head. "You heard me and Justin. I'm not going to follow through."

Rachel slowly lifted her head. "You're the one who made the order. This is in your name."

"Rachel, it isn't like that. Those papers are probably forged." He was still trying to get her to believe him. I had to give him credit for persistence. Sweat broke out across his forehead. A sinking ship if I ever saw one.

Rachel threw the papers at him and they fluttered to

the ground at his feet. "I recognize your signature, Sean. You made the orders, you signed these fucking papers."

Sean lifted his hand with the Taser in it and pointed it at Rachel. "Damn, I was really hoping to fuck you one more time."

He pulled the trigger and I leapt forward, putting myself in the path of the prongs. They bit into my left side, driving through my jeans. Bolts of electricity rocketed through me. My whole body arched and I hit the ground as Sean hit the trigger again and again.

I was useless, and completely at the mercy of Sean and his one little finger.

Chapter 30

RACHEL

I sucked in my breath when Sean aimed the stun gun at me. He'd pull the damn trigger, of that I was sure.

Then there was a blur in front of me and Lea was falling to the ground, her back arching as electricity shot through her.

Why had she done that? Her vow? Even after I'd turned my back on her? But I didn't have time to puzzle out the answers. Sean was still shooting electricity through her body.

I considered pulling out my gun and just shooting the

fucker in the head, but we probably still needed him to get into the facility, which meant I had to do this the hard way.

He was so busy concentrating on zapping Lea and ignoring my demands that he stop—a perverse gleam in his eyes—that he didn't notice I was gearing up for a roundhouse kick until the box was flying out of his hand. His mouth flew open in surprise and he shook out his fingers, cursing.

I grinned, knowing it had to hurt like a son of a bitch.

He turned a murderous glare on me. "You'll regret that." He took a step sideways, assessing me.

"Not nearly as much as I regret letting you kiss me. I'll never make that mistake again." I circled away from Lea. It worried me that she hadn't moved or made a sound. The electricity couldn't kill her, could it? I stuffed down my rising panic. My initial concern was that I needed her to get into the facility, but that wasn't the only thought that seeped fear into my blood. She might be a vampire, but I could finally admit I felt a kindred spirit in her. Someone who totally understood me.

I didn't want to lose her.

He reached into his coat and pulled out the gun I'd returned to him. A grin spread cross his face. "You never were very bright."

I continued backing away from Lea. "You won't shoot me. You need me for something, but damned if I know what it is."

"Her." He waved the gun toward her prone and unmoving body.

"To lure her in?" I shook my head in disgust. "I'm not buying it. She was coming anyway."

"Then I guess it will be a surprise."

I refrained from rolling my eyes. No need to give myself away. "Truth or dare, Sean, and I get to go first. Truth."

He laughed. "A game?"

I cocked my head and moved to the other side of Sean, away from Lea. "Sure, why not? You're a huge fan of games. Setting me up. Making me believe you wanted to avenge Derrick's death when we both know you were the one who ordered him killed."

His eyes lit up. "Clever girl. But I did more than issue the order. I pulled the trigger myself."

My hands clenched at my sides and fury coursed through my blood. "You fucking bastard."

"It was so easy. Caine was the trap. He lured Derrick in so we could contain him." A smile spread across his face. "You should have seen the look of surprise on his face when I pulled out my gun and held it to his forehead."

I wanted to hurt him. Fillet him. My breath came in heavy pants as I held myself back.

"I asked him if he had any last words. Do you know what he said?"

I wasn't sure I could stand it if Derrick had said something about me, but to my surprise, Sean released a chuckle.

"He told me to go to hell."

"Then, in his memory, I'll speed your journey along."

I whipped the knife out of my jacket sleeve and leapt toward him.

He wasn't prepared for a physical attack, which is what I'd been hoping for. He fell to his side, my knife slashing the arm of his jacket. The asshole was wearing leather, so I doubted it sank deep enough to do any harm.

He rolled and jumped to his feet, aiming his gun at my stomach. "Oh, Rachel. You've made it so easy." Then he pulled the trigger.

His eyes flew open in surprise when the only sound was the clicking of the empty chamber.

"You really think I trusted you enough to give you a loaded gun?" I gave him a condescending glare. "Like I told you. Your biggest mistake has always been underestimating me."

He tossed the gun to the ground and rushed me, but I was prepared. I slashed with my knife, aiming for his abdomen. I didn't want to necessarily kill him—not yet, anyway—but that didn't mean I couldn't make him suffer before I subdued him.

Sean would fucking hate getting beaten by a woman.

The blade sliced through his shirt, connecting with his skin as he tried to wrench the weapon from my hand. But I twisted away from him, freeing my wrist from his grasp as I spun around to face him, crouched and ready to pounce. "Looks like you're out of shape."

He reached for his stomach, then examined the blood on his fingers. "You're gonna regret that."

I grinned. "You keep saying that, but you're the only one I see with any regrets."

He lunged for me again and I whipped to the side,

slashing at his arm. I reached deeper this time, making sure I got through the leather.

"Son of a bitch!" He spun around, grabbing his arm.

I laughed while I waited for him to attack again.

This time he lunged for my legs, intending to tackle me. I jumped far enough backward for him to miss, but not enough to escape his reaching hand. I stomped on it with my boot, making him cry out in pain. I wasn't prepared for him to react so quickly, though, and he managed to grab my leg with his other hand.

As soon as I came down on top of him, he grabbed the knife from me and rolled me onto my back. He slowly pushed the knife to my neck. I pushed as hard as I could against him, but he outweighed me by a good seventy pounds. We both knew there was no way I was going to win this battle of strength.

"You draw one drop of her blood and I will rip your head off," Lea's deadly cold voice rang out behind me.

I resisted the urge to breathe a sigh of relief. She was alive—or as alive as a vampire could be. "Listen to her," I said, still pushing on his arm. The blade was six inches from my neck. Too close for my liking. "I've seen her do it. Ugly business."

He gawked at her in surprise. "That amount of voltage should have killed you."

"I'm harder to dispose of than that."

I filed the voltage news away for future reference and then switched my focus to getting this asshole off me. I rolled to my side, catching him off guard, and lifted my now-free leg, ramming my lower thigh into his crotch. It didn't have the force I would have liked behind it, but it was enough to get him off me. His hand came down out of reflex to support his falling weight, and I pushed it to the side. It missed my carotid by a matter of centimeters, but it still nicked through the skin of my collarbone.

Lea inhaled sharply, then released a low growl. "I warned you."

Fear filled Sean's eyes. He leapt to his feet and took off running for the scrub brush behind us.

"He's getting away!" I scrambled to my feet in frustration. There was no way I could catch up to him on foot, and even though he was injured, I was pretty sure his adrenaline would push him quite a distance.

"He's not going anywhere."

Then she disappeared like a flash.

Chapter 31

LEA

Sean crashed through the bush like a rhino on steroids; easy to follow. But my reserves were low after that fucking Taser and I didn't have time for games. I bolted after him, using the last of my energy to tackle his ass to the ground. We rolled twice and I let him end up on top of me.

His eyes were wild with fear and adrenaline. "Fucking vampire."

"Not even if you were the last man on earth." I

bucked him off with my hips, sending him flying over my head, straight into a tangle of thorns.

He grunted and cursed, but the more he fought, the more twisted up he became. I stood and brushed myself off and moved to stand just in front of him. "You do know I'm going to kill you, don't you?"

Sean stopped fighting the bush. "Rachel might be pissed at me, but she's not a killer. She won't let you. Same way she didn't want you to hurt that young vamp. She's always been too soft."

I rolled my shoulders. He could be right; she might ask me not to kill him. I reached out and grabbed his arms, yanking him out of the bush. The thorns dug in and tore through his skin, drawing even more blood. "Could be that you're right. But then, I don't have to kill you myself to make sure you're dead. I could just drain you to the brink and leave you here in the bush." I dragged him along with me, his fighting and squirming bringing me to the brink of exhaustion. I had to feed or I would be useless.

Kicking him in the back of his legs, I dropped him to his knees while still holding his hands tightly secured against his back. Rachel stood in front of us, her gun steady on him.

"Rachel, you aren't a killer," Sean said, his voice going back to that smooth, silky tone he was so good at. I snorted, not bothering to try and hide it.

"She doesn't have to be a killer, Sean." I leaned in close to his ear. "That's why I'm here."

He blanched and Rachel lowered her gun. "You look like shit, Lea."

I let out a deep breath, the burn from where the prongs took me in the leg flaring up and hitching said breath. "I have no doubt. I need to feed. And if I take him to the point of death I'll get his memories too, which will give us what we need to break into the facility." Giving Sean a pointed shake, I looked at her. "You going to be okay with this?"

"You aren't seriously asking Rachel's permission to bite me? You are a stupid bitch if you think she's going to say—"

"Yes, fine by me." Rachel tucked her gun into the back of her jeans. "You need me to do anything?"

I grabbed Sean's hair and jerked his head hard to the left, baring his carotid. "No, but I may not be able to stop. The hunger is like that. This could be goodbye for you two for real." I wanted to make very sure she understood I was going to drain him.

And to make sure she wasn't going to freak out on me later.

Rachel's eyes didn't give anything away. She would have made a good cop. "I've said my piece to him. He deserves this, for what he did to Derrick at the very least." And she turned her back to us.

Sean fought in earnest, but I had a good hold on him. He wasn't going anywhere. I snaked my head out and drove my fangs deep into his neck, not bothering with the niceties. Adjusting my mouth, I made sure my fangs went in at a bad angle, hitting nerve endings as well as the carotid.

He screamed for five of his already slowing heartbeats and then settled into a low-grade whimper. His memories crashed over me and I picked through them as if I were deciding which book to read at a library.

Skipping over his time with Rachel, I focused on his knowledge of the base. Fort Tilden was supposed to be abandoned, but based on the many-layered structure I saw in Sean's memories, it was far from it. Fifteen levels below ground, the base stretched out for miles. The best entry point that I could pick out was the aircraft hangar that peeked out of the forest a short jog from where we stood. No guards were posted there because they thought no one could get in because of the layout. But Sean had left rappelling gear there for just such an emergency, and his memories confirmed that he hadn't just been blowing smoke up Rachel's ass.

A hand touched my shoulder. "Lea, is he dead?"

Blinking, shaking myself from the feeding stupor, I looked up at Rachel. "His heart still beats, but it's slowing. I won't drain him all the way, that will take him too close to becoming a vampire. I can taste a vampire on him that he's been swapping blood with, and that is the last fucking thing we need."

I stood and Sean's body flopped forward, already a dead weight. "Other than that first few seconds, he won't feel—"

"I want him to suffer." She bit the words out and I caught the glimmer of tears in her eyes.

"Then we'll leave him here. There are enough animals in the woods to finish him off, and he will likely still be alive when they begin to eat him," I said, walking away. I wasn't sure of that, but there was one thing I knew very well. Revenge was not something that let you sleep at night once you'd dabbled in it.

I went to the bag of weapons I'd grabbed out of Sean's SUV, and she followed. "Let's get as much gear as we can," I said. "The entrance he mentioned isn't far from here."

Rachel crouched beside me as we opened the bag. The thing was loaded with anything we could have wanted. Guns, knives, crossbows, grenades. "Where's Calvin?"

"He's going to hang back. He'd just slow us down." I couldn't tell her the truth, that he was gone from my life for good.

We went through the weapons quickly, taking everything we could, along with as much ammo as possible. Still, I felt like it wouldn't be enough.

Rachel stopped at Sean's body. I thought she was going to say goodbye to him, for old time's sake. She dropped to one knee and frisked him. After a minute, she yanked out a keycard and held it up to me. "We're going to need this."

Better and better.

We started into the woods once more, only this time I knew exactly where we were going, using Sean's memories to guide us.

"You saw inside his head..." Rachel said softly.

I nodded. "A gift or a curse, depending on how you look at it. I gain a victim's memories as I drink them down."

"Was he always like this? Did I just not see it, or was he fooling me all along?"

I flipped through Sean's past, stumbling over the

memories of him and Rachel. "I think he cared for you, but that changed. He saw you as an obstacle to the power and prestige he wanted."

I held up a hand, stopping her. "We're close. Our entry point is just around this clump of trees."

I thought she would be done with the questions. Wrong again.

"Why did you jump in front of the stun gun?"

There was no way around it now. "We made a blood vow. It's my duty to protect you."

She sucked in a sharp breath. "Why didn't you tell me that sooner?"

"You humans need to figure this shit out on your own. It was the same with Calvin. Until he saw I really did value his life over my own, he didn't trust me."

Rachel laughed. "Damn."

I held a hand out to her as we approached the drop-off. Below us was the entry point, but it was a wicked climb with a free fall of at least fifty feet tacked on at the very end. "And now I need you to trust me again. It's going to be faster if we do this my way."

Without hesitation, she put her hand in mine.

I swung her onto my back. "Hang on tight."

As her arms tightened around my neck and her legs cinched around my waist, I adjusted my body to the additional weight. After checking our position, I slid one foot over the edge and dropped us both over. Snagging the edge with my hands, I stopped our fall and started to move us sideways.

I had to give Rachel credit—she didn't even gasp.

"Tell me when I can open my eyes."

I laughed as I worked us down the sheer face. "You can't be afraid of heights. We jumped rooftops together."

"Those heights had cement and buildings under them. Here, there is nothing."

I glanced down. "Well, not nothing. There are trees, probably a stream or two."

"Shut up, Lea. You aren't making this any better."

I reached the spot where I had to let go. "Just don't open your eyes yet." She tightened her hold on me as I pushed off into open space. The fall lasted only a second, two at the most.

Bending my knees as we hit the cement, I was able to cushion the worst of the fall. Rachel's hold slipped a bit, but it didn't matter anymore. I swung her off my back. "We're here; you can open your eyes."

I started into the building, my eyes adjusting to the dim light with ease. The hangar had been built into the side of a tiny mountain and the opening was barely visible with all the overhanging vines and plant growth. But the interior was far bigger than I'd expected. Rachel caught up to me and flicked on a small flashlight. I didn't need it, but it did help.

Our boots echoed through the empty hangar.

"Just me, or does this feel creepy as hell?" Rachel asked, pitching her voice low.

"Not just you, and I've seen some creepy shit in my life." I picked up the pace. The sooner we were in and out, the better.

There was a single metal riveted door at the back of the hangar. I was expecting it to be locked. It had been locked at one point, but the door was bent outward, as if something large had slammed into it.

Repeatedly.

I carefully opened the door, scenting the air. The blood of an animal of some sort, layered with a trace of human blood. A red light flicked off and on above our heads. Glancing back at Rachel, I blew out a sharp breath. "What do you want to bet the monsters they've been making got the better of them?"

"Oh, that can't be good," she muttered.

"My gut tells me we need to hurry." The hallway in front of us was narrow and painted gray from top to bottom, but there were a couple of bare bulbs burning bright enough that we no longer needed the flashlight.

There was another door to our right. Rachel opened it and stepped in before I could say anything.

"Look at this," she called out softly.

The room was twelve by twelve and loaded with filing cabinets. Rachel held a piece of paper out to me.

Two holding facilities, one on the thirteenth floor for the blood recipients. One on the fourth level for the blood donors. I handed the paper back to her. "Want to guess who the recipients are?"

She snorted. "I'll find the donors, you deal with your friends." We had brought Sean's walkie-talkies with us, and Rachel handed one to me. "Channel four."

I didn't like that we were splitting up, but there was no way around it. I flicked my walkie-talkie to channel four. "Be careful. If you see anything that looks like it was human once, don't wait to have a chat. Run."

"Always."

I started out of the room.

"And Lea?"

Stopping, I looked back. "Yeah?"

"You be careful, too. I know you're a vampire and can kick some serious ass and all...but..."

"I'll be careful." And I would be.

Unless Rachel's life was on the line. Then all bets were off.

Chapter 32

RACHEL

Lea left the room and I hooked the walkie-talkie to my jeans, trying to decide whether I should head straight to the fourth floor or investigate these file cabinets. Despite the time crunch, my curiosity won out. That was part of the reason I was a journalist. I couldn't stop asking questions, even though it often got me into trouble.

But less than a minute of riffling through files told me there was nothing here to interest me. It was mostly supply requisitions and personnel files dated from the 1920s to the 1960s. If something *was* here, it would be like looking for a needle in a haystack. I needed more current information.

I headed down the hall, slipped into the stairwell, and descended the stairs. Though I was worried about running into one of the staff, it was late, which was on our side. As I made my way down the dark stairwell, my thoughts drifted to Sean. I knew I should have felt more remorse over leaving him out there like that, but I couldn't find it in me. Not after everything he'd done. Did that make me like the monsters Lea hunted?

I couldn't let my mind go there. At least not yet. There'd be plenty of time to think about it later.

When I reached the fourth floor, I peered through the small window and checked out the hallway. It was empty and late enough that the lights had been dimmed. I left the stairwell, then tried to figure out which way to go. I stood in the middle of the hallway, studying the numbers on placards next to the doors. Directly in front of me was 416, Supply Closet. I grinned. The signs would be helpful. I tested the doorknob. Locked, which meant the others would be, too. Thank God for Sean's key card.

I needed room 452, so I turned left, following the rising numbers and staying close to the wall. When I came to room 429, Records Room, I sucked in my breath. This certainly deserved a detour, but as I reached for the handle, something else caught my eye. About twenty feet down the hall was a large six-foot-wide window, its glass laced with wire. A heavy-duty window meant they either wanted to keep something out or keep it in.

Color me intrigued.

I stalked toward it, stopping just next to it, and carefully peeked around the corner to look inside.

It was a lab. Two people in lab coats sat at a table, their backs to me—a man and a woman. They were packing things into plastic crates, pausing now and again to make notes on the tablets next to them. Centrifuges and test tube racks covered most of the counters extending from the peripheral walls, and two rows of long worktables filled the center of the room, covered with microscopes and computers.

There were chairs for six lab technicians, but I only saw the two employees. Whiteboards covered the walls. I was too far away to make out all the writing, but the word diabetes was legible on one of the closer boards.

Sean had told me so many lies, I had no idea what was going on, but there was usually a nugget of truth to every deceit. Someone was creating bioterrorism weapons, and Sean said they were using vampire blood to create medical cures. Was it happening in this room? From the scientists' lack of safety equipment—no protective suits or even latex gloves—I suspected something else entirely was going on here.

I needed to get inside.

The man and woman appeared so intent on their work, I suspected I could slip in without them noticing.

I was considering how to get in when a buzzer went off. The woman groaned. "You're not going to get that, are you?" I could just barely make out her words.

"I'm the senior-ranking scientist," he said in a flippant tone. "The grunt work falls to you."

She got up and walked over to the corner. I decided to use the moment to my advantage. I opened the door, thankful it didn't squeak, and slipped into the room, making sure the door closed quietly behind me. As soon as I was inside, I hunched behind a worktable.

The woman turned off the buzzer, then opened a centrifuge and pulled out some tubes.

"We're down to less than an hour. Step it up," the man said.

His partner sighed. "We need more totes for our stuff. I'll set up these test tubes, then head to the supply room. You want me to grab you a coffee?"

"You know we're not allowed to have food or drink in here."

"And you're not allowed to make personal phones calls, yet we both know you're going to call your girlfriend as soon as I leave."

He laughed. "Are you saying I have secrets?"

"Says the man who works in a secret lab," she said, pipetting what looked like blood from a large test tube into smaller ones. "Why are we packing everything up anyway? I thought they said it was just a drill."

"McPherson says we've got to play by the rules. And the rules say when the red light starts blinking, everybody clears out." He pointed at the ominously blinking red light over the door. "Besides, we're close enough, they're thinking about going public. The powers that be are threatening to kill our funding, so they need proof we're onto something. Which means we need to get it all out."

"Public with all of it?" she asked in disbelief.

"What do you think?" he snorted. "Of course not. Just the cure."

"Which one?"

He shrugged. "Good point. But I hear they're only

releasing the one for acute lymphoblastic lymphoma. No sense giving it all away."

"It seems so wrong, though." She sighed again. "We have the cure for every cancer. Why not release it all at once? Why tweak the blood to pretend each form of it requires a specific, targeted cure?"

"The reason is as old as time, Lillian. Money."

I pulled out my phone, made sure it was on silent, then started to take photos of the whiteboards lining the walls.

They weren't just curing cancer. They were curing *everything*. Diabetes. Arthritis. Lupus. This was unbelievable. I needed to get my hands on one of those test tubes and get it to Tom.

"All done," Lillian said. "Can I get you anything in the kitchen?"

"See if they have any pastries. The cream-filled ones."

"I'll check." The worktables each featured a stack of drawers and enough space for three chairs. I ducked into one of these spaces and waited for Lillian to leave.

Maybe Lea was wrong about the monsters breaking out; these two scientists sure didn't seem worried, red alarm or not.

It only took a few seconds after Lillian left for lover boy to call his girlfriend. "Yeah, she's gone," he said. "What did you do tonight?"

I hoped I didn't have to suffer through a litany of his night, too.

Then, to my surprise, he got up and walked toward a door labeled *closet*. He went inside, shutting the door behind him.

Did I dare risk it? I had to.

I got up and started taking photos of everything. The work tables, the trays of microscope slides. The whiteboards I hadn't been able to photograph from my hiding place. The screen of the guy's tablet. I considered taking it with me, but I couldn't risk it. The tablet would be missed and the whole place would end up in lockdown. But maybe I could grab the woman's. It had been turned off and shoved to the side. They might think she'd misplaced it.

I started grabbing tubes, one from each rack. They were labeled with names like *Lyme Disease, Patient B2, Donor 32*. I didn't have my bag, so I found a quart-sized Ziploc bag and crammed them inside it. There was a messenger bag resting on a chair. It did not, as far as I could tell, belong to one of the two scientists, so I commandeered it and put the plastic bag and the swiped tablet in it.

Time to get the blood donors and get the hell out of here.

I ran down the hall to room 452, scanned Sean's card, and popped the door open.

What I saw made me gasp in surprise. The room was dim, but there was enough light for me to see it was large and full of cages that reminded me of small prison cells. Inside those cells were *people*.

Several men lay on cots, but those who were awake turned to look at me.

"What is going on here?" I asked, advancing toward them.

A man in one of the closer cages stood and grabbed the bars. "We ain't going. No more tests." His shirt was open and I could see a medical port on his chest.

"I'm not here to conduct any tests. I'm here to get you out." There was an electronic pad near his cage. I tried scanning Sean's card, and the door popped open.

The man's eyes widened. "Is this some kind of trick?"

"No. We need to get everyone out and quickly. I don't know how much time we have left. What's your name?"

"Rowland."

I opened the first two cells, but there were dozens more. There had to be close to fifty people in the room.

"Don't leave yet," I told Rowland, who seemed to be taking charge of the released victims. "We need to leave together in small groups." I figured there was safety in numbers. Besides, if they all started wandering off, it might alert security sooner.

The walkie-talkie attached to my pants let out a shrill sound.

God, I'd forgotten all about the stupid thing. I was lucky it hadn't gone off while I was waiting for the lab coats to leave.

"Rachel." Lea's voice squawked out of the box.

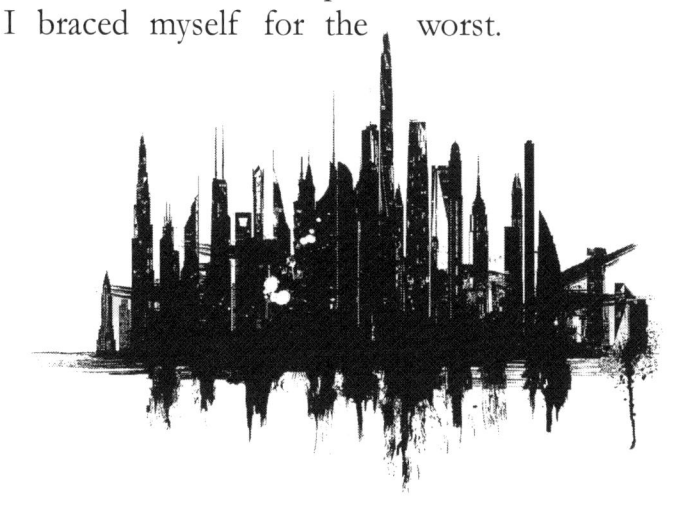

I braced myself for the worst.

Chapter 33

LEA

I jogged down the hallway, then paused when I came to a T. To the left was a stairwell. Peering in and down, it looked like it would take me to the sixth floor at the best. I stepped back and glanced in the other direction. An elevator with "Out of Service" plastered on it all but beckoned.

Perfect. I jogged to it and pulled a knife from a sheath on my leg. Sliding the blade between the two doors, I pried them open enough to slip in a hand. From there, the doors only offered a few minor protests. The twisted cables hung silently in front of me and I reached for one, gripping onto it as I stepped into open space, the elevator doors sliding closed behind me.

Seemed like me and old elevators were having a serious love affair lately.

Using the cables, I shimmied down, counting the floors as I went. I assumed we started on the first floor. But that would be easy enough to check. I could always pry another of the doors open and—

The click-clack of nails skittering above stopped me in my downward movement. I looked up, and while the light in the shaft nearly pitch black, I could still see.

And what I saw was not good. Three pairs of glowing neon-green eyes stared down at me. "*Mierda*," I muttered under my breath as an image of the bat creature I'd killed outside Victor's underground hideout flickered through my brain. How many monsters had these idiots created?

The scurrying of feet on metal, the snap of teeth, and a low hiss got me moving again. I could fight them—whatever they were—but not while I hung suspended from cables. I slid down to the next floor and swung hard, gripping my toes on the edge of the elevator doors' lip.

A furry, screaming body slammed into me from above. There wasn't time to escape through the doors, as I'd hoped, but I managed to wrap my legs around the cable. At least my hands were free. It was the best I could do.

The light from under the elevator door gave me a glimpse of dark red fur, a long whip-like tail, and claws that extended farther than they should. But the head was the real freak show. The creature's eyes were human, wide and terrified even as its alligator-like snout snapped at me. I got a protective arm up just in time and the creature bit down right to the bone. I snarled, wrapped my free hand around its neck, and jerked its throat out. The teeth gave way and the body fell down the shaft.

The creature's buddies scampered closer, hanging upside down as they clung to the walls with their claws and tails.

"What in God's name are you?" I whispered, horror flickering through me. I wasn't afraid. I could kill them with ease. But I was struck by absolute revulsion that anyone could do this to another living creature. It was like Dr. Frankenstein's monster all over again.

And yes, that is a story for another time.

I swung toward the doors again, hooking my toes once more on the ledge, and worked my knife in between the doors. I managed to slip through the doors before the remaining creatures could drop down on me, hissing and snapping their teeth. Pushing the doors back together, I turned to see just where I'd ended up.

A sign pointed away from me. "Rooms 1075-1045." The tenth floor. Not exactly where I had wanted to end up, but at least it was closer. I lifted my head and scented the air. A heavy overlay of cleaners and detergents, but under that was a darker smell. Formaldehyde. Embalming fluid.

Another deep breath brought traces of decomposing bodies. I was in the morgue.

I took the walkie-talkie from my hip and pressed the call button.

"Rachel."

There was a pause and I wondered if she'd gotten into trouble. Who was I kidding? She seemed to have a knack for it.

"I'm here," she answered, and I turned the radio's volume down.

"Did you find them?"

Another short pause. "Yeah, but I got detained."

In other words, she had been snooping for evidence. Or maybe someone had seen her, and she'd had no choice but to take care of them. "Trouble?"

"No, the opposite, but there's over fifty people in here, Lea. We're never going to sneak this many out."

"Just get them upstairs," I said. "With whatever is going on here, the security is seriously lacking. This might work."

"Where are you?"

"I'm on the tenth floor," I said, the sound of distant people talking getting my attention. "Let me know if you get into trouble."

"You, too."

I slipped the walkie-talkie back onto the waistband of my jeans. Settling into a stalking crouch, I moved down the hallways, looking for cameras, or anything that might have set off an alarm. Maybe more of the rats from the elevator shaft. But there was nothing except the red flashing lights above every door. A silent alarm system that someone—or something—had set off.

I turned the corner and the voices went silent.

Narrowing my eyes, I stopped moving and listened. Nothing. Ahead of me, a door on the right was open a crack. Moving swiftly, I jogged over to it and slipped inside.

The room would have made Rachel light up with glee. It was full of paperwork on the dead bodies that had come through the morgue. I picked up one of the top sheets.

To whom it may concern,
Please be sure to give appropriate reasons on the death certificates that are plausible causes of death except in the case of the Rikers Island patients.
*Anything less will be reason for immediate **termination**.*
Dr. Stravinsky

Well, that was interesting. So, no one was supposed to know how these people were really dying? Like having their bodies pulled apart and reattached in weird ways to animals? And there was yet another mention of Rikers Island. Inmates being used for experiments…the thought pinged through my mind and I couldn't push it away. It fit all too fucking well.

"And they call me the monster," I snorted softly to myself, spreading the papers around. I took a few, knowing Rachel would want them for evidence.

The sound of voices again, low and melodic. Almost like someone was singing under their breath. Two someones, to be exact.

Back in the hallway, I followed the singing to a closed door with a single word painted on it.

Morgue.

Frowning at the door as if it would answer my questions, I wrapped my hand around the doorknob and turned. While it stuck, it wasn't locked, and I pushed the door open, fully expecting to see a human I could interrogate.

But there was no one. Or at least, no one alive. Three bodies covered in long white sheets lay splayed out on the tables in front of me. Their chests were still, but I knew from experience that didn't mean shit.

I stopped at the foot of the closest body and grabbed the sheet, yanking it off with a flourish. A woman in her late fifties lay on the slab, her long dark curly hair pulled back from her face in a tight ponytail. I did the same to each of the bodies. Each one was female, and each seemed to be around the same age. They even looked alike. Though they looked very human, the smell in the room told me they were anything but.

A soft humming started and I stared at the first body as her eyes opened. As if on cue, her two companions started to sing a song I recognized all too well.

Ring around the rosie
A pocket full of posy
Ashes, Ashes,
We all fall...down.

They sat up in unison with the word 'down.' Dead eyes stared at me.

Zombies if ever I had seen them.

"*Madre de Dios,*" I whispered, backing right into a large set of arms that wrapped tightly around my upper body.

"You're going to die, Cazador."

"Someday," I kicked out behind me, nailing my would-be captor in the kneecap and snapping his leg backward, "but not today."

Chapter 34

RACHEL

After I finished my conversation with Lea, I hung the walkie-talkie back on my jeans and continued releasing the captives with my key card.

I was almost done with the first row and about to start on the second.

"You have to save the people back there. Please. My friend Valerie's back there," pleaded one of the women I had released. She was pale and could barely stand.

"What's back there?"

"I don't know. People go in there and they never come out. Sometimes we hear their screams."

I resisted the urge to shudder, but she must have sensed my hesitation.

"Please. She saved my ass when I first got to prison. We got each other's backs."

I nodded. "Okay. I'll try to find her."

When I'd gotten everyone out—many of them weak and ill—the corridor between the cages and the small open area by the door was crammed with people. I searched for the man who'd taken charge. When he met my eyes, I nodded. "Let's do this."

Rowland grinned, then turned to the crowd. "Okay, we're doing this in groups of ten. Amber, you take the first group up to the first floor."

"I'm going to check the back room." I scanned my card and reached down to turn the handle and push the heavy door inward. There was another door at the end of a short four-foot corridor. I looked back at the people gathered in the area behind me, then scanned Sean's card on the door. The lock clicked, and I pushed it open, then closed the door behind me.

The overhead lighting was dim in the large room, but it was plenty bright enough for me to make out the horror within.

There were close to a hundred naked bodies arranged on medical tables, each surrounded by machines with multiple tubes coming from their noses, mouths, and arms.

I walked closer to a table and looked down in horror. This person wasn't human. His facial features looked melted, like a blank slate waiting to be created. The fingers on his hands had fused together and his skin was slightly scaly.

What the hell was going on here?

Then the man's eyes opened, revealing red pupils.

I jerked backward.

The man sat up, panic in his eyes. His lips pulled back, allowing me to see the multiple rows of pointed teeth in his mouth.

"Let me help you," I said.

He hissed and ripped the tubes out of his face and his arm.

"Oh, shit," I mumbled, then turned to run back to the door.

He leapt off his medical table. I rushed to the door, desperate to make my escape.

Then I saw something out of the corner of my eye. "Derrick?" I could have sworn it was him—standing behind a machine, an IV pole trailing behind him. But I didn't have time to get a closer look, because the creature I'd awoken was determined to hunt me down.

Was that why he had been created? As a hunting weapon for the U.S. government?

But I could think about that later. Now I needed to get the hell out of there, especially since several of the thing's buddies had been roused from their slumber.

I swiped my card and made it through the first door, which closed behind me. I breathed a sigh of relief when the second door opened, but the sound of shattering glass startled me. I looked back to see the monster's hand punching the window, then it leapt through the opening. I ran through the second threshold but was tackled from behind, the impact shoving me through the door and into a metal cage wall.

People behind me screamed as the creatures rushed into the room and grabbed their prey, ripping out flesh with their teeth. I swung my horrified gaze to the monster who had me pinned to the metal bars. I spun around and tried to dart to the side, but the creature grabbed a handful of my hair and pulled me back, pressing me into the bars.

His mouth opened, his teeth looking even scarier than they had from a few feet away. A burst of anger exploded in my chest.

I'd be damned if it ended this way.

Chapter 35

LEA

The bastard who'd grabbed me from behind was more than familiar. He was a vampire from my past...one of the few who'd gotten away. The one who made me into a monster.

"Peter. Long time, no see."

I spun, flinging him off my back toward his three undead lady friends as they rose from the tables. His body knocked down two of them, but the first lady, the one with the curls, managed to dodge the impact.

Curly Sue slunk toward me, her body hunched and

twitching as her muscles jerked in an odd rhythm. In a blink, she was right in front of me. Faster than a vampire? This was not good.

Stumbling back, I barely avoided her first swing as she swiped a clawed hand toward my face. Her speed more than matched mine. In truth, she was faster.

"What's the matter, Lea? Finally met a vamp who you couldn't take out?" Peter spoke in my native tongue, the Spanish rolling fluently from his lips.

I dropped to my knees and struck at Curly Sue, dragging her legs out from under her and jerking her to me. She bucked and fought as I climbed up her body. Snagging a stake from the top of my boot, I yanked it out and drove it through her right eye. Her body spasmed once and then went still.

A whoosh of air was the only warning I had before Curly Sue's friend tackled me to the ground. Her teeth snapped at my face, but I held her off with ease. Yes, they were fast, but they weren't any stronger than they'd been as humans.

"Peter, did you make these ladies?" I bit the words out, as I reached up and twisted the woman's neck with a sharp snap. Her tongue flopped out and she bit it in half, spewing blood all over my face. Some got into my mouth and I gagged.

"They taste like shit."

Peter laughed and pushed the last lady at me as he approached me from the other side. Tag-teaming me. "That they do. They aren't like us, Lea. They aren't real vampires. Undead, fast, stupid. Easy to dispose of."

"Not nice, Peter. What are you and Stravinsky up to?"

I growled, pushing the body off me; her boneless limbs flopped and her head hit the floor with a meaty thump. I had noticed that Rachel always managed to distract her marks by talking them down. I had nothing to lose by trying her methods.

"What are you doing teaming up with the Pol? You two hated each other, if I remember correctly." Standing, I sidled sideways, keeping the two of them in front of me. I managed to get one of the tables between us. "Can't be because you've had a change of heart, is it? Gone soft in your old age?"

Peter grinned, his fangs fully extended, yellowed with age. "Stravinsky is looking for a cure, Lea."

"Yeah, yeah, the humans and all their diseases."

Peter shook his head. "No. A cure for us. A way to be human again."

I'll admit, my jaw dropped. "That's not possible."

He put his hands on the table and leaned forward. "Are you sure?"

I heard the lie in his voice a split second too late. His hand was around my throat before I could get away from him. He dragged me across the table as I fought with everything I had. But matched as we were with speed and strength, he was still bigger.

"You were my best creation, Lea," he said softly as he drove his fingers deeper into my throat.

I ran my tongue over my lips, and his eyes followed, his hands easing up so I could speak. "And yet you'd kill me?"

Peter shrugged. "You have been a pain in my ass ever

since the day you were turned. Perhaps I should have just killed you then, but I wanted you as my own."

As he spoke, I slowly lifted my legs up, moving them incrementally so he wouldn't notice. "And now?"

He tipped his head to one side. "Now, I'd still like to fuck you, but—"

I kicked out with both feet, driving them into his gut and sending him flying away from me. The woman launched toward me, her teeth burying into my side. With a scream, I grabbed her hair and ripped her off me, wrenching her head so hard I nearly pulled it off. As it was, it hung lose by a few vertebrae when I let her go.

Peter laughed, shaking his head as I stood. "I really should have killed you."

I straightened up. "There are days I wish you had just slit my throat and been done with me. But here I am, and I am still a Cazador, Peter." I pulled a silver stake. "And that means you and I are on opposite sides."

He flexed his hands. "Time for one of us to die, I think. There can be no other way."

I flipped the stake into my right hand and pulled the second one from my other boot. "Come, then. Let us be done with this."

It felt like my first hunt again, the words so formal and familiar. I hadn't said anything like it in centuries.

With Peter, though, it felt right. He was my creator—there should be some formality before I killed him.

In a blur of movement, Peter rushed me. I stepped toward him, slashing upward, catching the side of his face. He let out a roar as he slammed his shoulder into my chest, sending me flying backward and into the far wall. I hit hard and slid down, but was up on my feet a split second later.

Peter was gone.

"What the fuck?"

He knew I was here. He was going to tell Stravinsky. Son of a bitch, Rachel and I were in deep shit.

A loud scream of pain snapped my head around. I *knew* that voice. I was running toward him before I thought better of it.

Under my breath I cursed him, and my need to protect him, even now. "Calvin, what the hell are you doing all the way down here?"

Chapter 36

RACHEL

The creature's razor-sharp teeth were dangerously close to my neck. I dropped to a squat, ripping out some of my hair the monster still had in his grip, and pulled the knife from my boot.

It took a step back, thrown off and bewildered.

I spun on my heels and rose, holding the blade at an angle. There used to be a person in that body. I had to try one last time to reach him. "I don't want to hurt you."

The creature studied me for a second with vacant

eyes. By the time he lunged, I knew this was just a shell. I wasn't killing a man. I was showing mercy to an empty soul. I jammed the blade deep into the creature's chest, between his ribs, jerking the weapon at an angle to make sure I reached his heart.

Surprise filled his eyes as he dropped to his knees and then fell face forward, his blood spilling onto the tile floor.

The screams of the people behind me formed a dull roar.

Get your shit together, Rachel.

I took a deep breath and spun around to face the melee. Rowland had a piece of metal and was beating the creatures off their intended victims.

One of the monsters had tackled a woman and was eating from her torso. I barely registered the dull look of death in her eyes as I leapt at his back, slashing his throat with my knife. The thing made a gurgling sound and collapsed on its victim as blood poured over my hand, making my hold on the knife slippery.

I got to my feet, resisting the urge to vomit.

Rowland and two other men had pummelled two creatures into submission, but they were still alive, albeit weak.

I stomped toward them. Leaning over the first one, I grabbed what was left of its hair and slit its throat with a cold calculation that shocked me. I made quick work of the second, then turned to look at Rowland.

"What are the damages here?" My voice shook, betraying my fear.

The men stared at me wide-eyed, no doubt shocked to see a blonde, blue-eyed woman do such a deadly deed.

Rowland looked around. "Looks like we have three dead and five wounded. About half of our number ran out of the room."

"Shit." I tried to focus. I had to think, trying to ignore the fact that I was covered in blood. If I let myself stop and think about what I'd just done, I'd probably fall to pieces. And I definitely didn't have time for that. "I don't think we have to worry about security finding out you all are free. They seem to be gone as far as I can tell. If they weren't, they'd already have swooped down on us." But staying here for any longer was not an option. I had to help them escape, and then I had to get all the information I had to the public.

I glanced up at Rowland. "Time to get everyone out of here."

He nodded. "Agreed."

I grabbed my walkie-talkie. "Lea. Things have turned to shit."

Talk about the understatement of the year.

Chapter 37

LEA

I hit the button on the walkie-talkie. "You're telling me. Calvin is here."

"I thought he was going to hang back."

"He was." I took a slow breath. "Meet me back at the hangar with the prisoners. If you aren't there in ten minutes, I'm coming to look for you." I turned a corner and slid to a stop, my finger slipping off the call button.

Calvin was on the floor, his back against the wall next to an air duct, a puddle of blood around him. He lifted a hand to me, and the corner of his lips raised for a split second. I ran to him, skidding to the floor on my knees in my eagerness to get to him.

"Lea, not how I wanted to end things."

"Hush." I searched his body, stopping when my hands found the wound under his shirt. His belly had been opened from hip to hip.

"You can't fix this," he said. "Victor did it."

Fix it... Calvin was wrong, I could fix this. "I can drink you down, Calvin. You could hunt with me for the rest of—"

"No. Go after Victor." His eyes drooped. "Go, Lea. And forgive me. I did...love you. I just couldn't admit it to you. Hell, not even to myself."

I leaned forward and kissed him as gently as I could. How long had I waited for those words? Too long, and now it was too late for anything but goodbye.

"There is nothing to forgive, my friend." His breathing was ragged as I backed away from him, the taste of his blood on my lips.

Emotions raging through me, I had to fight to center myself and find Victor's scent. There it was, under the smell of Calvin's blood and my own pain. Expensive cologne and a whisper of pine. With a snarl, I raced down the hall, hardly seeing the doors I passed. My entire being was focused on one thing.

Finding Victor and ripping his fucking head off.

The stairs were a gray blur as I raced down them, leaping down the final flight to land in front of a door. Distantly, I recognized it as the thirteenth floor. I kicked the door open and strode in, still following Victor's scent.

I was in a hallway that looked like an apartment building in New York.

And the smell of vampires was overwhelming. I booted the first door on my left and it clanged open.

The room featured hardwood floors and granite countertops, and was furnished in high-end materials—big-screen TV, leather couches, and china dishware. What few clothes were left flopped over the backs of the furniture were designer brands.

I pushed open a closet to see several orange jumpsuits hanging inside, Rikers Island stamped on them, along with the inmates' numbers.

This had to be where they'd been keeping all the vamps. Most likely they were pairing up a newbie with a mentor to try and train them a little.

Stepping out into the hall, I checked all the rooms. Victor would die soon enough, and Calvin would want me to make sure not to miss any other assholes.

I found someone in the last room.

Her headphones were on, and her fingers flew across a game controller. Her back was to the door, so she probably hadn't seen the blinking red light.

I tapped her on the shoulder. She jumped, then turned to look at me with a guilty look on her face. "Holy shit, you scared me."

I grabbed her shoulders with both hands. "They are evacuating the site. Do you know where they're going?"

Her jaw dropped. "Shit, for real?"

I nodded. "Where are they going?"

"Oh, man, there'll be a chopper up top, but you mean

after that?" She pushed past me and grabbed a designer bag, stuffing it with various items.

"Yes, after the chopper where will...we...go?"

She shrugged. "Some place in Iraq, I think. It was the original facility."

When she turned to face me, I drove the silver stake into her heart. "Thank you."

Her lips paled, moving soundlessly as she slumped to the floor and off the stake. Her body lit up with a burst of light, sending the grey ash of her remains floating into the air before settling on the hardwood floor.

I turned and headed to the door at the end of the hallway, catching another whiff of Victor. From Sean's memories, I knew it was the main laboratory where all the experimentation had been done. It was where Stravinsky spent the majority of his time.

I opened the door and crept inside. The scene was surreal, as if all the worst assholes I'd ever dealt with in my life had decided to form a brotherhood. Victor was speaking rapidly to Peter, and Stravinsky stood behind them.

"You don't get it," Victor said. "If Calvin is here, Lea is here."

"I know she's here, you whiny little shit," Peter snapped. "You killed her helper?"

Victor nodded, and I could almost feel the satisfaction roll off his smug-ass face. "I gutted him. It'll be a slow death."

Casually, as if swatting a fly, Peter backhanded Victor. "Fucking idiot. You want him to change? Then we'd have three Cazadors."

His words rocked me. So there *was* another hunter. But who?

Peter shook his head. "How the hell you came to be in charge..." From the way he trailed off, I knew my scent had reached him. He slowly turned to face me.

I pointed a finger at him. "You, I will deal with in a moment."

Without another word, I strode toward Victor. His eyes fluttered open and then widened at a rapid rate. "Lea, help me, none of this was my idea. None of this was my fault."

"Sure. Just like you helped Calvin." I grabbed him and lifted him up by his throat. With the other hand I sliced my stake across his belly. His whole body arched as he tried to scream around the pressure I was putting on his throat. I crushed his windpipe, then dropped him to the floor.

"Surely you aren't going to waste that blood?" Peter said, closing the distance between us.

I held up the stake, pointing it at Victor. "Not if he was the last human on earth would I put my fangs in him."

Peter, always the calm one, nodded. "True. Some just aren't made for this life."

He lashed out without warning, his fist connecting with my jaw, snapping the bone there. I fell backward, unable to stop myself as he followed me down, his mouth open wide. We slammed into the floor, him on top of me. "I'm sorry, Lea. But it is time to end this."

I squirmed under him, wrapping my legs around his waist and holding him tightly to me. "I agree."

Snapping my head forward, I smashed his nose with my forehead. He reared his head back, exposing his throat to me as blood rained down on both of us. I jabbed my head forward and bit into his neck, drinking him down in a matter of seconds.

I felt him sigh with what almost sounded like relief.

"Take my memories, I am done," he whispered against my skin. Peter's memories flickered through me, hundreds of years of them, stunning me with the magnitude of what I saw. I lay there under his body as I tried to get a handle on the flood of information. Of the flood of knowledge I could have never hoped to gain on my own. They blurred together; the distant past with the more recent. I struggled to breathe around the weight of them. Like an entire library had crashed down on me, every page demanding to be read at once.

Peter's final memory flitted to the forefront and I saw myself through his eyes. Pride. He was proud of me, how strong I was and how I'd honed my skills. Even though he knew it would be his death, he was happy he'd made me into a vampire.

A part of me understood...and a simple moment of peace flowed through me.

A pair of feet came into view, breaking the memories apart, and Stravinsky looked down at me. His pale green eyes were narrowed and partially hidden behind a pair of glasses. Glasses, what vampire wore glasses?

One trying to impress humans.

"Lovely to finally meet you, Lea, the infamous Cazador. But I must be going. I have things to do, and a world to change." He blew me a kiss and walked away as I heaved Peter's body off me. The door clicked shut as I stood. He'd had me dead to rights. Why hadn't he killed me?

But it only took a second for me to get my answer. As soon as I was standing, I could see that while Stravinsky was gone, two large wolves had taken his place. Wolves with hunched backs and glowing red eyes. I'd dealt with their kind once before, deep in the Ozarks.

"Why am I not surprised," I whispered as I backed away. Werewolves. What the hell else was hidden in this fucking place?

Chapter 38

RACHEL

If Calvin was here, it had to be as a trap for Lea. If I were smart, I'd take the evidence and run. The only reasons I'd come here in the first place were to get the evidence and avenge Derrick's death. But I couldn't ignore the fact that Lea was in a shit-ton of trouble.

"Get everyone out," I told Rowland, adjusting the strap across my chest. "I have to take care of something." I seriously hoped I wasn't making the wrong decision. Common sense told me the information in my bag was worth more than Lea's life, but I could never live with myself if I didn't help her.

Panic filled Rowland's eyes.

"Once everyone's out, call for help." I handed him my phone and gave him a tight smile. "You can give that back to me when I meet you outside."

He took it and nodded. "Thank you."

I gave his arm a shove. "Go."

The last she'd confirmed, Lea was on the tenth floor. I ran past the people from the cells, pausing to peek into the lab on the way. The two scientists were missing, and all the totes were gone. Besides what I had in my bag and on my phone, all the evidence had been erased.

The stairwell was noisy with the cries and shouts of the escaping people, and I was having major second thoughts about letting them loose. I should have waited for some kind of backup to help them escape, but there was no help for that now.

When I opened the door to the tenth floor, I heard the distant sound of shouts and banging. This was a terrible idea. How in the hell could *I* help a vampire? But I knew I had to try. She'd risked her life to save me. There was no way I could leave her in danger.

A heavy copper smell hung in the air as I turned the corner into the hall, and the hair on the back of my neck stood on end. But the hallway looked deserted other than a large puddle on the floor against the wall. It looked like something—or someone—had been sitting in the mess, but whoever it had been wasn't there now.

I gripped my knife tighter as I continued down the hall toward the stairwell that would take me to the thirteenth floor. I had no desire to end up in my own puddle of blood.

A woman in a lab coat ran around a corner ahead of me and stopped in her tracks. Taking a step backward, her eyes wide with fright, she asked, "Who are you?"

I knew I should be concerned that she might be a threat, but if she was, she had a career in Hollywood waiting for her. Her shaking voice practically emitted waves of fear. "I'm not here to hurt you. I'm only here to help."

"Nothing can help us now. The experiments are *all* loose."

"What experiments?" I asked, inching toward her. I had close, personal knowledge about the medical testing upstairs, but she held the key to what was going on down here.

She shook her head, her eyes wild. "You shouldn't be down here." She reached for a handle on the wall, but I rushed toward her and tackled her to the ground.

I suspected the handle was an alarm to alert security of intruders, and while we had to be long past that by now, there was no sense in letting them know exactly where I was. If there were even any security left.

The woman tried to buck me off, but I rolled her onto her stomach and pulled her arms behind her back at enough of an angle to keep her from squirming.

"Get off me!" she screamed.

"I need to ask you a few questions first."

"You stupid fool! There's no time for that. We need to get out of here."

"Then you better start giving me answers. I ran into

a group of men who looked mutated, but they were like mindless zombies. What happened to them?"

She released a bitter laugh. "You want me to explain decades of brilliant work to you in a matter of a minute. You wouldn't understand it if you tried."

I jerked on her arm, eliciting a shriek of pain. "Try me. *Dumb it down.*"

"Dr. Stravinsky is a genius," she sneered. "It's impossible."

Then I heard a familiar voice. "I'd start answering before she breaks your arm."

My head jerked up and I pushed out a breath in relief. Lea.

Chapter 39

LEA

I locked eyes with Rachel and gave her the slightest of nods, telling her I had her back. At least until the werewolves caught up with me. I'd managed to bar a set of double doors between us. My climb to the tenth floor had been filled with the chorus of their bodies hammering into the thick metal. A distant thud told me they hadn't given up.

"Take her with us," I said. "We have to keep moving." The only way I could see us getting out of here without risking a confrontation with the fucking werewolves would be to use the elevator shaft again. Even if it did mean facing the rat monsters climbing the walls. Those I could kill; I wasn't so sure I could destroy the mutts without a heavy dose of silver.

Rachel yanked the scientist, Adamson by her nametag, to her feet and dragged her behind us.

"Did you find Calvin?" Rachel caught up to me, her blonde hair sticking to the sweat on her face.

My jaw ticked as I fought the emotions welling up in me. "Yes, he's gone. Victor killed him."

"And you gutted the bastard for it?" She phrased it as if it wasn't really a question.

"Yes."

Adamson sucked in a breath. "Victor, he was our patron. How could you kill him in cold blood?"

I stopped in front of the elevator doors and grabbed the scientist by the arms. "Rachel, you want the answers to everything here?" Peter's memories were a start, but he'd been brought in late in the game, as someone to deal with me if I got too close. Stravinsky hadn't truly trusted him with information.

Rachel looked at me, understanding dawning in her eyes. "I can't believe I'm saying this. But...do it. She'll only slow us down."

Yanking Adamson to me, I bit down on her neck, draining her of her blood and her memories. The images flooded my brain, the testing, the trials, the decisions made by Stravinsky, everything they'd planned. And worse, all the people they'd hurt. From the innocent to the depraved, the missing inmates from Rikers Island... the numbers were staggering.

Thousands of lives lost and destroyed just so they could play God. Adamson let out a soft groan and I drew back from her, my voice cracking. "Rachel, it's so much worse than we thought."

The sound of a howl echoed along the hallway, and the unmistakable racket of sets of claws scrabbling against the concrete floors followed the eerie hunting call. The slathering werewolves stopped at the far end of the hall and stared us down. Without another thought, I threw the barely alive Adamson toward them. "That won't buy us a lot of time."

Slipping my knife from the sheath on my thigh, I jammed it between the doors and pried them open as the wet sounds of flesh being torn to shreds reached my ears.

"Hurry the fuck up, Lea!" Rachel yelled at me.

I slid my hands through the doors and pried them open. "In you go."

Rachel leapt right onto a cable, climbing it as if chased by the hounds of hell; which in a way she was. I glanced back at the werewolves as they lifted their muzzles to sniff at me. Their eyes blinked several times, flickering red like tiny demon lights.

I stepped through the door and started up the elevator shaft. Partway up the cables I grabbed Rachel and pulled her onto my back. "Sorry, but I'm faster."

"Show-off."

"Wannabe," I quipped, feeling the ridiculous urge to

laugh. Laugh in the middle of a crisis? What was wrong with me?

I swallowed the laughter as I climbed hand over hand, ignoring the clatter of the rat bastards above—they'd become a problem soon enough. "You shouldn't have come back for me."

"Had to," she said. "That's what friends do. They look out for each other."

I glanced over my shoulder at her as the scuttling above disappeared with a few sharp squeals. "That's not a good sign."

"That we're friends?" Rachel frowned at me.

"No, that the monsters above us just fucked off on their own."

We went still. There were no werewolves below us, and no rat bastards above. In the distance was the sound of a roaring windstorm, rushing toward us. But of course, that couldn't be, there was no such thing as an underground windstorm.

I swung us over to the door closest to us. Second level. It was going to have to do.

"What are you doing?" Rachel said. "This isn't the hangar."

"You hear that?" I kept swinging and then grabbed the edge of the door, jamming my knife in it as fast as I could. "They're going to burn this place to the ground with us in it."

"Holy fucking hell."

I wrenched the doors open and pushed her through

as flames lit up the top of the elevator shaft. "Couldn't have said it better myself."

Chapter 40

RACHEL

Lea shoved me through the opening, but the doors slipped shut behind me, closing before Lea could come through. My heart was beating so fast, I had make myself focus on the scene I'd just jumped into. Nothing could have prepared me for what I found.

"*Calvin?*"

He lay slumped on the floor, his back propped against the wall. His entire abdomen was wrapped in something that looked like an Ace bandage. IV tubing came out of his hand, leading to a bag of blood on his lap.

"Lea thinks you're dead." And if that was his blood back on the tenth floor, he certainly should have been. "How did you get *here*?"

"That sick bastard wants to make me into one of those monsters."

"Who?"

He grimace and covered his abdomen with his hand. "Stravinsky."

Shit.

He grabbed my hand with more strength than an old man who had nearly bled out should have possessed. "Don't let them do it."

"I won't."

His nails dug deeper, breaking skin, and his eyes were wild. "I want a vow."

What the fuck was up with these people and their vows? But Lea was still on the other side of the elevator and there was no way she'd let them do that to him. "I promise."

His eyes sank closed and I noticed how shallow his breath was. "Calvin, just hang on. Lea's coming."

"No time," he said in a soft whisper. "There's a paper in my pants pocket. The left one. Get it out."

His pants were drenched with blood, but I reached in and teased him. "Are you just an old pervert looking for a thrill?"

His eyes twinkled. "Oh, to be fifty years younger. I'd put the moves on you, girlie."

I grinned. "I bet you would, old man."

His voice softened. "Give it to Lea."

"Give it to her yourself."

The doors opened behind me and I jerked around to see Lea burst through the opening, her clothes singed. Her eyes widened. "Calvin." She dropped in a squat next to him.

His eyes had a vacant stare.

She grabbed his hand. "*Calvin.*"

It was clear he wasn't going to answer.

"He was alive just seconds ago. I'm sorry, Lea."

She looked up at me, her eyes cold. "How did he get here?"

"He wanted to…" I figured the rest was obvious. I handed the paper to her. "He said to give this to you."

She took the folded, bloody paper and stared at it for several seconds.

I could see it was a letter to her, and whatever he had said had temporarily stunned her. "Lea. We have to go. Do you want to take him with us?"

She didn't answer, only stared into Calvin's face.

I hadn't known her long, but I knew she wasn't behaving like herself. It was evident she loved him in some capacity. She was in shock.

"He probably came back to get you," I said, hoping it gave her comfort. "He would want you to get out and save yourself."

Her upper lip curled into a sneer. "No. He wouldn't."

Before I had a chance to ask for an explanation, a man in a lab coat ran out of a door down the hall. As soon as he saw us, his mouth dropped open and he turned and ran the other way.

Lea leapt over Calvin's body like a graceful panther. Lab Coat had only gotten a few feet before she knocked him to the ground, pinning him with a knee on his back.

"Who are you and what do you do here?" she snarled.

"Lancaster," he said in a whiny voice. "Dr. Lancaster. I work with Stravinsky."

I got up and moved close enough to hear her snarl.

"We have to get out of here," Lancaster wheezed. "They've initiated the Phoenix protocol."

It wasn't hard to figure out what that meant. Dammit.

Lea grabbed a handful of his lab coat in the center of his back and hauled him to his feet. "So?"

"We're all going to be incinerated if we don't get out of here. You'll never survive the burn and you'll never get out without me. We need to take the secret tunnel."

Lea cast a glance at me.

"Then you better start giving directions," I said. "Because it's starting to get a little toasty in here." I wasn't exaggerating. The temperature must have warmed at least ten degrees in the last five minutes.

Lancaster swallowed. "Down the hall. Then to the right."

But Lea remained in place, her gaze drifting back to Calvin. She didn't want to leave him.

"Lea. I can handle Lancaster if you want to get Calvin."

The lights overhead flickered three times before they blinked out. Seconds later, the eerie glow of the emergency lighting kicked in.

Lea was still for a moment, then gave a sharp shake

of her head. "No. We don't have time." Giving Lancaster a shove, she said, "Get moving."

As we started down the hall, I wondered if maybe we had a shot of escaping after all.

Chapter 41

LEA

Lancaster led the way, jogging ahead of us. He tugged at the edges of his lab coat over and over again—a nervous tic if I ever saw one. "This way. The tunnel leads to the first floor. From there, we should be able to get topside." He paused. "Are you one of Stravinsky's guards?"

Lancaster's words were nothing to me. I'd left Calvin behind. Not once, but twice. The fire would keep him from turning into a vampire, which was what he'd wanted. But I still felt like I'd let him down, that in the end I'd failed him and our friendship.

Rachel tapped my arm. "Lea, I got proof of what they were doing here. Samples, pictures, paperwork. We have everything we need to expose them."

Coming back to the present moment, I gave them both a noncommittal grunt and shoved Lancaster. "Keep moving."

He stumbled forward, his eyes wide as he stared back the way we'd come. "I don't think we're going to make it."

I glanced backward. "Fuck." The fire was licking along the walls behind us, spreading at a rate that was anything but natural. I grabbed Rachel with one hand and Lancaster with the other. Turning on the speed, I pulled them along like a boat towing water skiers.

"Left," Lancaster yelled as the oxygen disappeared around us. I didn't need it, but that was not true of Rachel. Her body began to slump as I rounded the corner. As I slid to a stop in front of a panel on the wall, I grabbed its edges and wrenched the whole thing off.

"My God, I had no idea how strong you vampires really were," Lancaster breathed as he passed out.

A rush of cool air swept through the tunnel, sucked into the hall by the fire. Rachel came around first. "What happened?"

"No oxygen." I helped her to her feet and pushed her ahead of me, then grabbed Lancaster and threw him over my shoulder. He let out a grunt and a fart as his stomach hit my shoulder.

Rachel laughed. "Glad you've got him and not me."

"Yeah, thanks." I gave her a bare smile as we jogged across two short flights with a landing in the middle. We found ourselves in front of another set of elevator doors.

The button beside them blinked green. Rachel looked at me, shrugged, and slammed the heel of her hand into the button. "Couldn't hurt to try—"

The doors slid open with a light bing, elevator music spilling out like some weird kind of time warp. As if the whole fucking building wasn't about to be dissolved in a baptism of fire.

Rachel stepped in first, and I followed, lowering Lancaster to the floor at our feet. "Mommy," he whimpered.

A laugh burst out of Rachel. "Talk about your manly man." She hit the only button on the elevator panel, a large, green *G*.

The doors slid shut and the volume of the music increased.

I frowned. "I know this song, but is this really playing right now?"

With a smile on her lips, Rachel started singing along with Gloria Gaynor. And I will admit, I joined in.

Grinning like a couple of shell-shocked fools, we sang at the top of our lungs, fist-pumping as the elevator climbed and the lyrics came to an end.

"Nice pipes," Rachel said as the elevator binged.

"Not bad yourself," I said, my hilarity dissipating as the doors slid open.

Morning sunshine spilled into the elevator and I couldn't help but take a step back as I raised my cowl.

"You going to be okay?" Rachel touched my shoulder as I bent to scoop up Lancaster.

"Might get a slight burn, but—"

I was rudely interrupted by the screech of a megaphone and then the deep bass of a man who thought he was in charge.

"COME OUT WITH YOUR HANDS IN THE AIR."

Rachel let out a sigh. "So much for thinking we were home safe."

"No such thing," I muttered. "Be ready; we're making a run for it."

She gave me a tight nod and I put Lancaster down, using his body to block the elevator doors open. Rachel stepped behind me and hopped up onto my back.

"I feel like this has been done before," she muttered.

"Yes, it has," I said. "But I don't fucking sparkle."

Chapter 42

RACHEL

I knew this had to be too easy. Ha. As if getting attacked by monsters and almost burned to a crisp could be called easy. But then I worried about all the people I'd helped escape. Had they made it out?

Lea took off, moving faster than ever as a round of gunshots filled the air. I tried not to tense, but I kept waiting to get hit by a flying bullet.

We made it all the way to the SUV. I slid off Lea's back and looked around.

"Where's Sean's body? We went right by the place where we left him."

Lea was perfectly still other than her gaze scanning the horizon. "Good question."

I heard a low growl and spun around, shocked to see Derrick. He was hunched over, a feral look in his eyes. And there was a perfectly round hole in his forehead. How could he be alive and mobile?

"Derrick."

Lea was ready to pounce, but I held up an arm to hold her back. "Wait."

"Rachel, that's not Derrick."

But it was. He'd done so much to help and protect me. I couldn't just leave him here like this.

I took a step forward and Lea released a low growl.

"*Mierda*, Rachel. It's not him."

Derrick watched us both with a wary look, still not saying anything.

"Derrick, come with me. I'll get you to the hospital." Maybe the bullet had hit the part of his brain that dealt with his language skills. I took several more steps toward him. Then he rushed me.

Lea tried to get to me first, but she wasn't going to make it. I ducked before he could reached me, then spun around behind him. I grabbed his arm and pulled it behind his back, but he wrenched it free. I took several steps back.

"Derrick, listen to me. I want to help you."

A slow grin spread across his face, but his eyes remained as vacant as a machine in motion. Lea was right. He really wasn't there.

"We don't have time for this." I knew she was right, but I didn't know how to handle the current situation. "We have to end this," she added quietly.

I gave her a quick glance of disbelief. She wanted to kill him. Was this an eye for an eye situation? She had lost Calvin so she wanted to dispose of Derrick? But I knew that wasn't the case. And I knew she was right, but dammit, I wasn't sure I could go through with it.

As if reading my mind, she said quietly, "I'll do it."

She wanted to spare me, and I was grateful for that, but I couldn't let her. I owed it to Derrick to handle it myself.

But first I had to keep from being attacked.

We circled each other like animals. Any trace of the man who used to be my best friend was gone, turned into something wild and animalistic.

Tears burned my eyes as I slowly slid my knife out of its sheath on my belt. "I did this to him," I whispered, willing my tears to dry. "I shouldn't have left him to question Caine. I could have saved him."

"Then you'd *both* be dead," Lea said.

"Better me than him."

"No. This is the way it should be. If he was the man he seemed to be, it's what he would have wanted."

But I didn't deserve this chance at life. He was a far better person than I could ever be.

"He wanted the truth exposed, Rachel. And now you have the chance to do that. You need to cast light on what they were doing and get it out to the world."

I knew she was right, but it didn't make it any easier. A new idea occurred to me. "Maybe we can take him with us. I think he's mid-transfer. Maybe we can stop it. Or study him and see how it works."

"You're only putting off the inevitable. Besides, he's already dead. You know that."

I shook my head, my anger surging. "No, you only told me he was dead. Maybe we can reverse this."

"No." Her answer was direct but not without sympathy. "Just end it now."

I choked back a sob and took a step to the side, then moved behind him and wrapped my left arm around his chest. With a quick move I plunged the blade into his heart.

Derrick slumped against me as his blood pumped onto my hand.

Lea grabbed my shoulder and jerked me back. Derrick's body hit the ground.

I turned to stare at her, every part of me numb.

She shoved me toward the car. "Let's go."

Lea drove, her cowl tucked low around her face, but she didn't seem to have a problem seeing. Feeling like I was going to be sick, I rolled down the passenger window and let the wind hit my face.

I hoped to God what was in my fucking bag was worth it. I hoped to God I'd made Derrick proud.

It was the only thing that kept me going.

Chapter 43

LEA

As soon as we could, we swapped the SUV out for a junker of a car we stole and hotwired from a quiet suburban cul-de-sac. The thing wasn't pretty, but it would do the job. Besides, nobody would be tracing us anytime soon. The bad guys had enough to do.

I talked as I drove, and Rachel held out a small microphone to record it. The memories of the female scientist Adamson were like a filmstrip rolling through my head. I peered through the dark sunglasses at the street names as I went. My cowl covered the majority of my face and I wore my long gloves so I could drive. It helped that the fall weather was dreary and overcast, keeping the day in a state of perpetual gloom.

"They have been planning this for years, ever since Victor's father let it slip that he a knew a vampire, that he was her patron."

Rachel sucked in a sharp breath. "You."

"Yes, me." I nodded, tightening my grip on the steering wheel. "With that information, and the fact that I was actively hunting the other vampires, the army used Victor's father as bait of sorts. The vamps needed a wealthy patron to keep the rest of the vamps safe from me. In exchange for a simple thing: access to their blood. He kept up the act as my dutiful patron to keep me at bay."

From the corner of my eye, I saw Rachel nodding. A small part of me was proud of her for how she'd handled Derrick's death. She was my friend, the first real friend I'd had in decades, and she'd done the right thing. Even though it had to have fucking torn her heart out.

"Access to their blood. You mean actively testing them."

"Yes. As soon as he caught wind of it, Stravinsky stepped into the ring. He got introductions to the right people, told them he was a doctor. He's no such fucking thing, but he is the oldest vamp alive that I know. And he's particularly good at manipulating people's minds. He told them he could cure all the human diseases given enough time." I drummed my fingers on the steering wheel as we pulled up to the sidewalk next to where Rachel's home should have been.

"I think perhaps we pissed off a few people," I said softly, as I peered out the windshield. Only a few timbers of the century-old building still stood, smoldering in the morning sun. The rest had been burned to the ground.

Rachel slammed the flats of her hands on the dash. "Where to now?"

"Let's see how good they are at tracking us." I cranked the wheel and headed for my safe house. It would give me time to spill the rest of the secrets I'd learned.

"So what was the point of all the testing, then? The real point?"

I cleared my throat. "While there was testing being done to cure the human diseases, and cures *were* found, they always ended...badly. Cure cancer, but turn into a monster. Cure diabetes, but create a hunger that was insatiable. So yes, they could cure everything, but at a cost. They used the Rikers Island inmates for a lot of the testing, but they used terminal patients who were civilians as well. And then there were the new creations. The head honchos in the army were brought in and shown the new creations along with the young vamps Stravinsky and Peter were making out of the inmates. They could be used, controlled. Sold. Made into soldiers. Soldiers already dead as far as the records were concerned. The next step was to ship them overseas for field tests."

I could see the conversation in my head, although Adamson hadn't known the name of the colonel who'd spoken with Stravinsky. Victor had been there too, offering his support and money as a backer. I picked through Peter's memories of the same time frame. He'd been breaking another batch of inmates out of Rikers Island while the main meeting had taken place.

"I have the evidence that will back that up, Lea. Pictures, the papers you found. It turns this story from conspiracy theory into fact. And I have a contact that can get me the coverage I need." The excitement in her voice was good; having a project to focus on would help her with her grief. I knew that better than anyone.

With Calvin gone, I needed to hunt. Needed to keep the end goal in mind and run from the grief of losing him as fast as I could.

Iraq and the vampires fleeing there waited for me.

I pulled over and a slow sigh escaped me. My hideout was in no better shape than Rachel's: burned to the ground.

"Fuck."

Rachel touched my hand and I glanced at her quickly. "What now?"

"I have one last place to try. It'll have all the money we need, and maybe some fun gadgets while we're at it."

Rachel laughed softly. "Fun gadgets?"

A smile quirked over my lips. "You'll see."

Victor's hideout wasn't that far, and we got there in no time. The underground parking lot was quiet, and the secret entranceway in the wall was no longer powered.

I pushed the door open and helped Rachel across the obstacle course.

"What is this place?" she whispered even as she

snooped through Victor's office off the side of the main room. The broken doors still hung at a bad angle. Nothing had been fixed. I was betting he had left in a hurry after our last tussle.

"This way." I crooked a finger at her and strode away from the office, toward Victor's bedroom. He'd shown it to me once, saying I was welcome anytime. I couldn't help the snort that escaped me.

The doors were double-wide and I pushed them open with a bang. Draped black silk was everywhere. The bed, the curtains, hanging from the walls. I shook my head. "He was an idiot."

Rachel held up a string of pearls and diamonds. "A wealthy idiot."

I nodded. "Take everything you can. I know places where we can turn the gems into cash."

What was amazing to me was that none of the employees had taken anything. I looked under the bed. "Bingo."

A large chest was tucked under the bed. I hooked my fingers through the handle and pulled it out. Snapping the lock, I opened it, and couldn't help but laugh. "Will you look at this? What did I say about goodies?"

My friend—damn, that sounded nice even in my own head—dropped to her knees beside me. "Goodies, indeed."

There were weapons of all sorts, but it was the tech stuff I was slathering over. Specialty items made specifically for Victor. Items that couldn't be found anywhere else, not even on the black market.

We closed the lid and I hefted the box onto my shoulder.

"Now, it's time to hunt."

CHAPTER 44

RACHEL

We were almost to the airport when I turned to face Lea. "Do you really have to go?"

She nodded. "Hunting is what I do. It's in my blood."

"But you're hunting the very thing you are. I know I vowed to help you until the vampires are all wiped out, but I agreed to it when I thought they were all like Caine. There have to be more like Louis."

"And what about the council? The ones who killed

innocent people just to lure me here so they could turn me in to the facility and run their fucking tests on me."

"I know." I sighed. "But just like there are good and bad people, there have to be good and bad vampires as well." I offered her a smile. "You're good."

She released a derisive laugh. "I am *not* good."

I watched her for a heartbeat. "Louis wasn't evil. You can admit that, can't you?"

She was silent for a few seconds, then nodded slightly. "I didn't want to kill him."

"I know. But maybe we should revise our vow. Your vow."

"I'll consider it."

It was a start.

She tapped the dashboard. "There's also the hint of another hunter. A Cazador like me. I can't let that go."

I nodded. It would be a boon for her to be able to rely on another person who shared her training.

"Is your report airing later tonight?" Lea asked.

"I'm heading for the station as soon as I drop you off. They're letting me do a live lead-in."

"You'll do great. Just watch your back."

"You watch yours. You don't have Calvin anymore to watch it for you. I don't like the thought of you being out there all alone. Call me when you know where you're staying."

Lea's eyes turned dark. "No one has worried about me for a very long time."

I lifted my eyebrows. "Well, get used to it. It's part of the territory with friends."

"Friends. I could get used to that."

"Good thing," I teased. "I think once you save someone's life, you're stuck with them forever."

The darkness returned to her eyes. "Forever is a very long time."

I thought of Derrick's promise to me. "Yes. It is."

I pulled up to the curb at JFK and Lea grabbed the door handle. "If you run into any trouble, call me on the burner."

We each had a burner phone, one that couldn't be tracked or traced. Just one of the many goodies we'd stolen from Victor's goodies.

"You do the same."

And then she was gone. I was never going to get a hug from her, but that was okay. She had other ways of showing me how much she cared.

Though Derrick was gone, I knew I wasn't alone.

Hours later, I sat in a leather director's chair while hair and makeup people powdered my face and fluffed my hair. Wardrobe had dressed me in a black turtleneck and dark jeans along with a tan jacket. They wanted me to have feminine appeal for the viewers, yet I had to convey strength and grit, or no one would believe I'd uncovered such a vast conspiracy.

"I'm Rachel Sambrook. For the last two years, Derrick Forrester, a fellow journalist, worked nonstop to discover the truth behind the U.S. government's experimentation on prisoners of war. What the two of us discovered went far deeper than either of us thought. Derrick died to expose the atrocities our government has committed, but I vowed to keep digging until I had uncovered the entire truth. Derrick's work was not in vain. What I'm about to report might seem unbelievable, but before I'm done, you'll question everything you know to be true."

No, Derrick hadn't died in vain. I suspected there was a whole lot more. I vowed to keep digging until it was all exposed to the light of day.

Or die trying.

AUTHORS NOTE

Thanks for reading "Silver Staked". We truly hope you enjoyed the first book in The Blood Borne Series. If you loved this book, one of the best things you can do is leave a review for it. This series is available on most major retailers or through our websites.

For more information on Shannon Mayer and purchase links to her other novels, please visit her website at www.shannonmayer.com.

For more information on Denise Grover Swank and purchase links to her other novels, please visit her website at www.denisegroverswank.com.

Enjoy!

Printed in Great Britain
by Amazon